SCAR TISSUE

A MR. FINN NOVEL

SHAMUS AWARD WINNING AUTHOR

TRACE CONGER

Scar Tissue

Cover design by James T. Egan of Bookfly Design

This book is dedicated to Dennis and Dottie Conger.
Thank you for your continued love and support.

It's also dedicated to Dave Conger.
Thanks for giving me so much material to work with.

"Rally round the family! With a pocket full of shells."
—*Bulls on Parade*, Rage Against the Machine

"Old man take a look at my life, I'm a lot like you."
—*Old Man*, Neil Young

"Death settles all obligations."
—Unknown

CHAPTER 1

Everyone pays for their mistakes. Some pay more than others. I'd learned over the years that blowback comes in all shapes and sizes, but it always comes. You can't hide from it. You can't outrun it. One day, you turn around to find it staring you in the face. Your next move defines who you are and who you'll become. There are right choices and there are wrong choices, and the line between them isn't always clear.

Blowback. It always comes.

Fat Sam stepped out of the home on Fort View Place in Mount Adams, a neighborhood on

Cincinnati's east side. He set his biggie-sized red-and-white cup on the front porch, pulled the door closed, slid a key into the deadbolt, and twisted his wrist. The metal bolt slid snugly into the strike plate.

He turned back toward the street and scrutinized the half dozen cars parked along the curb. Fat Sam's eyes assessed each vehicle, noting its license plate, whether the passenger seat was empty, or if it looked out of place in the familiar neighborhood. Satisfied, he bent over, grabbed his cup from the gray concrete porch, and then shuffled down the driveway toward his own vehicle.

To anybody on the street, Fat Sam would have been an imposing sight. He stood over six foot five, was as wide as a forklift, and might have weighed as much as one. He wore an oversized Memphis Grizzlies t-shirt, baggy jeans, and tan steel-toed work boots.

Sam arrived at the end of the short paver-stone driveway, a neatly manicured mosaic that was too narrow for his custom-built Ford Expedition. He slurped from his straw and inspected the street's vehicles again. Nodding to no one in particular, he clicked the key fob in his left hand, and the parking lights on the navy-blue SUV blinked as the doors unlocked. Sam crossed the street and opened the driver's door. He ducked his head and squeezed in behind the wheel, the SUV moaning as Sam settled into the seat. He wedged the monstrous drink container into the console's cup holder, fastened his seat belt, and fired up the engine.

He was about to shift into gear when he felt the muzzle of a gun pressed against the back of his head.

"You're Sam, correct?" said the voice from the back seat.

Fat Sam hesitated.

"Correct?"

"Yes."

"Good," said the voice. "I'm not here to kill you, Sam, but I damn sure will, unless you do exactly what I say. We good?"

Sam eased his head forward to relieve the muzzle's pressure. "We're good," he said.

"Peachy. Here are the rules. First, why don't you go ahead and move that rearview mirror so you're not tempted to get a look at me. Same with your side view."

Sam reached out and turned the rearview mirror upward, catching a glimpse of the green baseball cap behind him. Then he pressed the button on the driver's door. The whir of the mirror angling toward the pavement cut the silence inside the SUV.

"Second rule is you keep both hands on the wheel at all times."

Sam gripped the wheel at ten and two. "Okay," he said.

"Super. Now tell me about the contract on Finn Harding?"

"What contract?"

"I received a blast email last week from the Dark Brokerage, Bishop's little information-sharing service. It was an open contract on Finn Harding, whereabouts unknown. A twenty-five-thousand dollar bounty on his head. I assume it went out to your entire user database. That contract."

"Right." Sam rubbed his hands on the steering wheel. "Bishop set that up. An automatic protocol, a trigger in case something happened to him. All I was supposed to do was log into the website and hit send. When I found Bishop dead in the RV, that's what I did. I logged in and hit send. Just like he said to do. I didn't order anything."

Sam heard the man shift against the leather seat.

"So it was Bishop who had the brilliant idea to send every Dark Brokerage account holder after this Finn Harding character?"

"Right. Like I said, only if Bishop turned up dead. And he did."

"And Finn killed him?"

"I guess. I wasn't there. But, if it wasn't Finn, then it was someone working with him." Sam eyeballed his drink in the cupholder. A bead of condensation dribbled down the cup onto the console.

"How many people did it go to? The email? Did it go to everyone in your database or just a certain category?"

"Everyone, I guess. I don't know. I didn't manage the user list. Like I said, I just pressed send. Everything else was already set up."

"Why didn't you go after the contract yourself? You're local. Seems like you'd have an easy time finding Finn."

"I don't need that kind of heat on me. Plus, I'm a glorified admin, not a killer."

The man in the back seat was quiet.

"I can tell you that most of the people on that distribution list were hackers and information resellers," said Sam. "They're not killers either, but there might be a few who could pull it off. Assuming they can find Finn, which is probably a long shot. I'd wager he's long gone by now. There were two…" Fat Sam stopped.

"Go on," said the man in the back seat. "Two who?"

Fat Sam's shoulders slouched into his seat. He felt the muzzle bury deeper into the back of his head.

"I received an email yesterday, to our admin account. Two brothers. Last name's Nolan. They said they were close to finding him, but they didn't give any details. It could all be bullshit."

"Nolan? Brothers, you said?"

"Yes, but I don't know anything else about them. Don't even know their first names or where they are. Finn could be on the other side of the country by now."

The man in the back seat shifted again. "Sam, here's what I need you to do. Email that same distribution list and call off the hit. Tell everyone the contract has been closed and the twenty-five thousand has been claimed. Then reply to the Nolan brothers and tell them the same thing."

"Why? Then no one will be looking for..."

"Wrong. I'll be looking for him. And I'll get him. But you're going to call off the dogs so I can take care of Finn Harding my way. I don't need to worry about a bunch of hill jack amateurs fucking things up. I'll handle it the right way."

"But if more people look for him, there's a better chance of finding him."

"We're not painting a fence here. You've got too many cooks in the kitchen. I'd bet most of them have no idea what they're doing. That means they're more likely to do something stupid, which is either going to tip Finn off or get the police involved. If either of those two things happens, you can be sure Finn will disappear for good. We've only got one chance at this. And I'll do it the discreet way."

"And you won't have any competition for the bounty." Sam closed his eyes tight, regretting saying it before the last word crossed his lips.

"You're going to pay out anyway. Might as well pay someone who knows what the fuck he's doing."

Sam sensed a smile from the back seat.

"I'll wait while you send that mail," said the voice.

"I'll have to get my phone from my pocket. And I'll have to let go of the steering wheel."

"Fine, but do anything stupid, and I'll relocate your frontal lobe to that stop sign up the street."

Fat Sam arched his back and slowly reached into his front jeans pocket for his mobile phone. As he turned slightly to the right, he felt the muzzle slide across the back of his head. Once he slipped the phone from his pocket, he squared his shoulders against the seat and began typing, his fat thumbs tripping over themselves on the small screen. He replied to the Nolan email first. Then he sent a message to the original distribution list indicating the contract was closed. A moment after hitting send, Sam heard a muffled ding in the backseat. Whoever was behind him had just received his email.

"Okay, looks good," said the voice. "You'll have Finn Harding in a week."

"Assuming you can find him," said Sam. "What if he's already gone?"

"Doesn't matter where he is. I'll find him. Then I'll be in touch to get my money." The muzzle rattled against the headrest's steel rod as the man pulled it away. "You kept up your side of the bargain, and I'll keep mine. Put your forehead on the steering wheel and count down from sixty."

Sam struggled to place his forehead on the wheel. As he bent forward, his gut pressed against his insides, making his teeth clench. Fat Sam heard the rear door open. “Wait,” he said. “Who are you anyway?”

“You not knowing that is the only thing keeping you alive.”

The rear door closed, and Fat Sam sat alone in the SUV, grimacing and counting backward.

CHAPTER 2

BROOKE, my ex-wife, knocked on my apartment door at 11:00 am on Sunday morning. She was here to pick up our daughter Becca, who stayed with me most weekends. I twisted the deadbolt and opened the door. I'm not sure if Brooke intentionally dressed to get my attention, but regardless, she had it. She was the type of woman who looked good even when she wasn't trying to. Today it was a pale blue t-shirt with a brown leather jacket. Her long, tight jeans disappeared into light-brown knee-high boots. The gentle waves in her dark red hair told me she'd spent time on it.

Brooke walked in and dropped an oversized yellow purse onto my kitchen table.

“How was the weekend?” she said.

“Great. Pizza at Dewey’s on Friday night and then Disney on Ice yesterday.”

“Did she have a good time?”

“Of course, she had a good time,” I said. “It’s Disney on Ice. What kid doesn’t love that stuff? I have to give those characters credit. I’ve been on ice skates once in my life, and it’s tough as shit. I can’t imagine doing it while sweating my balls off inside a Goofy costume.”

“That’s something I’d pay to see.”

“Me on ice skates or in a Goofy costume?” I said.

“Both.”

Becca stepped out of the guest bedroom. She saw Brooke and raced to her side.

“Mommy!” she yelled, wrapping her skinny arms around her mother’s waist.

A cordless drill screamed from the guest bedroom. Brooke jerked her head toward the sound.

“It’s Albert,” I said. “He’s installing a bookshelf.”

Becca tugged on her mother's leather jacket. "I'm helping," she said.

"I'm sure it's wonderful," said Brooke. "Go pack up, sweetheart. We've got a few errands to run, and then later, we're having dinner with Daryl."

I waited for Becca to disappear into the guest room. "How is Dr. Dickhead anyway?"

"He's fine."

"You two still getting along?"

She twirled a lock of red hair between her fingers. "We're getting along just fine, thanks." Brooke looked around the condo as if ready to take roll. "How about your new little fling?" She peeked over my left shoulder. "She here?"

"You mean Jennifer? She doesn't visit while Becca is here."

"Right. Because then you'd have to explain to your daughter why you're diddling her school nurse."

"I guess I've got a thing for healthcare professionals."

“I’m a healthcare professional, Finn. She passes out bandages, checks for lice, and stops nosebleeds.”

“She probably sees it differently.”

Brooke shrugged her shoulders. “We should all have dinner sometime. The four of us. Like a double date.”

“No, thanks. The last thing I want to do is introduce my girlfriend to the guy who stole my wife.” I rubbed the finger where my wedding band used to be. “He might poach her away too.” I smiled. Brooke didn’t.

Brooke leaned to her left and stared through the open guest room door to check on Becca’s progress. A pounding hammer replaced the whirring drill.

Her eyes returned to mine. “I need to talk to you about something, but not in front of Becca.”

“What is it?”

“It’s about cheerleading,” Brooke’s voice was low. “Did Becca mention it?”

“Mention what?” I said.

"She wants to join the Catholic Academy's cheer squad, but the woman who runs the program won't let her."

"Why not?"

"Because she's a bitch, that's why."

"That's a bit snippy, even for you."

"She and I don't get along, and she's taking it out on Becca by not letting her join the squad."

I stepped into the kitchen and poured a cup of lukewarm coffee from the carafe. "I can't imagine you rubbing anyone the wrong way." I smiled again. Again, Brooke didn't.

"Trust me, that's exactly what it is. That bony bitch hates me, and she won't let Becca cheer with the other girls. It's not right to punish Becca like that. She really wants to do it."

"First, I didn't even know Catholic schools had cheerleading teams, and second, why does she want to be a cheerleader anyway? She's six years old."

"It's not a team, Finn. It's a squad. And she wants to do it because all her friends are doing it. She's too young to be pulled into the middle of Candy Cooper's petty bullshit." She leaned to her left again to make sure Becca wasn't in earshot. "So can you do something about it? Get her on the squad?"

I took a sip. "Wait, her name is Candy Cooper? That's horrible."

I didn't spend a lot of time at Becca's school—the Cincinnati Catholic Academy—so I never saw women like Candy in their natural habitat, but Jennifer had shared enough stories for me to know their type. Stay-at-home moms who always one-upped each other with a new luxury SUV, a shinier watch, or a bigger piece of jewelry. Don't get me wrong, I've got nothing against stay-at-home moms—or dads for that matter—but this was a peculiar breed. Always running committees, and apparently the cheerleading program, with an iron fist strong enough to make a dictator jealous.

These women never missed an opportunity to blabber on about their husband's job and spent most of their free time roaming the mall, sipping mimosas at the local salon, and talking shit about each other. And they were always looking to validate their significance beyond arm-charm status.

My guess was this Candy Cooper didn't like Brooke because Brooke didn't buy into her bullshit "I'm-better-than-you" society. Brooke was probably way hotter too.

"What in the hell am I supposed to do about it?" I said. "I don't have much pull with the Cheerleading Mom's Club."

"Hey," Albert's voice floated out of the guest room. "You guys talking about cheerleaders?"

"No, Dad," I yelled and turned back to Brooke.

"Maybe you could talk to her husband, Michael," said Brooke. "He's some big shot at the savings and loan on Harrison Avenue. Candy never shuts up about him."

"Savings and loan? I didn't know those were still around. Why don't people just use a bank?"

She shrugged.

"I'll see what I can do, but I can't promise anything. This really isn't my area of expertise."

"You'll figure something out," she said, finally breaking out a smile.

I took another sip of my coffee as Becca walked out of the guest room. She pulled her penguin suitcase, the one with the squeaker in the bill, behind her.

"I'm all packed up," said Becca.

She wheeled to a stop next to me, and I bent down to give her a squeeze.

"I hope you had a good time, sweetheart."

"I did. I always do. And I can't wait to come back next time."

I gave her a wink and then opened the door.

Becca turned to the guest room. "Bye, Grandpa," she yelled.

"Bye, kiddo!" Albert yelled back.

Brooke and I stared at each other the way we did every Sunday afternoon, unsure of the standard ex-spouse goodbye protocol. I grinned and wrapped my arms around her. Unlike Becca, with Brooke, I never knew how tight or how long to squeeze. She squeezed back, smiled, and walked out of my apartment with Becca wheeling her penguin suitcase behind her.

I closed the door and inhaled. Brooke's perfume lingered in the living room.

A moment later, my father emerged from the guest room with a cordless drill in one hand and a yellow Stanley level in the other.

"Seriously," he said. "Were you guys talking about cheerleaders?"

CHAPTER 3

THE MAN in the green baseball cap sat in a silver Cadillac Escalade, watching the entrance to the Shillito Lofts on West Seventh Street in downtown Cincinnati. He tapped his finger against the custom-modified Glock 17 nestled in a holster between the driver seat and the center console. The man watched as a tall redhead emerged from the apartment complex. She carried a yellow purse and held the hand of a young blonde girl who pulled a penguin-shaped suitcase across the sidewalk.

The man grabbed his cell phone from the dashboard and dialed. A moment later, a woman answered.

"How'd it go?" she said.

"Good, but there might be a small hitch. I need you to look through the Dark Brokerage's database and see if there's any information for someone with the last name N-O-L-A-N. There might be two listings. Brothers."

"Who are they?"

"Not sure, but according to an email they sent to Bishop's sidekick, they're close to finding our man Finn. They might be full of shit, and they might not. Get me their identities, and I'll find out how close they really are."

"Okay," she said. "Be careful."

"Always am." The man clicked off the phone and tossed it back onto the dashboard. He watched as the thin redhead buckled the young girl into the back of a green Range Rover and then pulled onto West Seventh Street.

CHAPTER 4

I MET Brooke McBride when we were both freshmen at Ohio University. She lived in the dorm room directly above me and frequently visited our floor. Brooke was dating some guy from her high school days, and I was too busy binge drinking and sleeping around to date one person exclusively, so we never progressed beyond the friend zone.

After our freshman year, we went our separate ways, and except for passing once or twice on the way to class, our paths rarely crossed.

That all changed in December of my senior year. It was a few weeks before Christmas, and I was spending the winter break on campus slinging coffee at The Percolator. A friend and I closed the coffee shop at 9:00 pm one Friday night and headed uptown to hit a few bars and make some poor decisions, our usual routine. I saw Brooke at the first bar we visited, and we struck up a conversation. We reminisced about our freshman days in Tiffin Hall, a co-ed dorm. About the strange RA who always blasted Metallica, and the time a campus cop caught us drinking rum-and-cokes in the dorm hallway at 3:00 am.

The conversation turned to our majors and what we had planned after graduation. She'd arrived at college with dreams of being a doctor but realized at some point her brain wasn't cut out for it. Then she changed course and focused on hospital administration, then medical research. She knew she wasn't going to change the world, but she thought she might be present when someone else did. I talked about my interest in criminology and sociology and everything that made the criminal mind tick.

We'd talked so long that I hadn't noticed that the friend I'd arrived with had already left and that the bar staff was wiping down the tables and flipping the chairs. We slipped on our jackets and stepped out into the bitter Athens, Ohio night. I don't think I actually invited her to my apartment, but I started walking that way, and she came with, huddled close for warmth.

It was somewhere during that walk home that something happened. Maybe it was the amber hue of the street lamps lighting our way, or maybe it was the flurries falling to the deserted cobblestone street, but sometime during that walk, I realized that for the first time, I thought I'd found someone I cared about more than myself. We went back to my apartment on Mill Street and spent the night together. She was a permanent fixture in my head and my bed until graduation five months later.

After graduation, we moved to Cincinnati and got married. She nabbed a nursing position at a prestigious hospital. The medical research thing never panned out, but she took the nursing job as a temporary gig until she figured how to parlay her nursing degree into a career. I'd abandoned the idea of being a criminologist, because I didn't want to go to grad school and end up stuck in an office, analyzing individuals who led more exciting lives than I did. While I was figuring out my own career, I answered an ad from a law firm looking for an investigator. Part of my college coursework had included spending time with police officers, studying criminals, and learning my way around police and legal databases. I thought I could take on investigative work while I figured out my next step. I hit it off with the partners at the law firm, and they liked me enough to cover the costs of my PI education and license certification.

A year after taking the gig, I was a full-fledged private investigator. Brooke wasn't thrilled. She saw me doing something more lucrative, not to mention safer. She pressed me to leave the law firm and open my own private investigation agency. It sounded like a great idea, but the more I thought about it, the more I realized I'd get caught up in the business side of things; hiring and firing, looking for new business, and the high cost of liability insurance. I realized that I'd be off the street —more of an administrator than an investigator. I forgot the idea as quickly as I could.

Our downhill slide started one afternoon when Brooke found the .45 in my messenger bag and nearly stroked out. I told her it was for protection, and that I'd probably never have to use it, but all she saw was her husband carrying a firearm and the potential risk it signaled.

I never knew if it was more about the perceived danger of the job, my inadequate career goals, or the lousy salary—it was probably an even split between the three—but we started to fight more often. What started as once a week ended up as a daily event.

Of course, the best thing about fighting was the make-up sex. That was the one part of our relationship that didn't suffer, and I'm not sure which argument did it, but one of them produced Becca, the most beautiful thing I'd ever seen. Brooke delivered our daughter at the same hospital where she worked.

For the next four years, we tried to keep things together, but it unraveled a little every day until there wasn't enough of a relationship to salvage. It was like being on a roller coaster and knowing there wasn't anything you could do to get off. I knew we were doomed when our conversations began to focus on how great things used to be. We always looked back because neither of us could see anything ahead of us. Toward the end, we were just going through the motions, pretending we were a happy family.

Brooke was the hottest woman I'd ever been with, and she turned a lot of heads. I loved that when we were in college, but I loathed it when she went to work at the hospital. I knew she'd be walking the halls surrounded by guys in white coats who made quadruple my annual salary. And I knew every one of the med-heads on her floor was ready to pounce on her, give her a luxury car, a vacation home, and a reason to never work again. After being married for seven and a half years, I discovered I was right.

It was a Tuesday night when she came home from work and said she was leaving me. "Drifted apart" was the phrase she used, and she was spot-on as usual.

Two weeks later, she took Becca and moved in with an anesthesiologist she'd met at work. He promised her all the things I couldn't. His name was Dr. Daryl Jennings.

I preferred to call him Dr. Dickhead.

CHAPTER 5

On Sunday afternoon, the cell phone buzzed on the dashboard of the silver Escalade. The man in the green baseball cap clicked on the speaker without taking his eyes off the main entrance of the Shillito Lofts apartment complex.

"I've got the information you wanted for the Nolan brothers," said the woman on the other end of the line.

The man grabbed a small notepad and clicked open a pen. "Go ahead."

"It took some time to access what's left of the Dark Brokerage's servers."

"Is the website still down?"

"Yes, it is."

"And the Nolans?"

"You were right," said the woman. "Two of them. James and Charlie. They've got two vehicles registered to separate addresses in Kentucky." The man in the cap scribbled in the notepad. "The first is a Ford F-350 pickup. Color black. That's registered to James Nolan. The second is a Yukon Denali registered to Charlie Nolan. Color red. I pulled their information from the licensing bureau. I'm emailing the addresses, license info, and license photos to your phone."

"Thanks. I'll pull it up."

"Listen, these guys look like bad news," said the woman. "They've got some colorful records and a few open warrants. I'm sending info on all of it. Be careful, they're not lightweights."

"They never are."

THE MAN IN THE CAP EASED BACK INTO HIS SEAT, sipped his gas-station coffee, and reviewed the Nolans' information on his phone. He'd been parked at the Shillito Lofts complex for six hours before spotting the red Yukon Denali in his rearview mirror. It stood out among all the black and gray sedans and mid-sized SUVs he'd seen pass by.

The man in the cap grabbed his phone and clicked open Charlie Nolan's DMV file. He glanced at the license photo, and a man with a wide face and shaggy blond hair stared back at him. Charlie's license indicated he was six-two and two-hundred-and-thirty pounds.

He caught the Denali's Kentucky plate as it slowed, rolled past the front of the apartment complex, and then turned right onto Race Street. The man in the cap slipped the Glock from its holster, quickly screwed on the suppressor, tucked it under his jacket, and watched his rearview mirror. A moment later, the Denali appeared again. This time it turned into the apartment complex parking lot.

The man in the cap stuffed two rolled up industrial-sized garbage bags down the back of his pants, jumped from the vehicle and walked toward the Denali, his right hand tucked inside his jacket. Before the driver had time to exit his vehicle, the man in the cap stepped to the Denali's passenger door and knocked on the window.

"Do you know how to get to 71 from here?" he said, his voice low. He studied the driver's confused look and waited for the blond man behind the wheel to roll down the passenger window.

The driver lowered the window. "What?" he said.

"I said, do you know how to get to 71 from here?" The man in the cap glanced around the parking lot. "My cell died, and I need to get back on the highway."

The driver shook his head. "No, sorry, buddy."

His jaw hadn't closed before the man in the cap pulled the Glock from inside his jacket and fired two quick rounds into the blond man's head. The first shot ricocheted off the man's cheekbone and struck the driver's headrest. The second shot exploded through the back of Charlie Nolan's skull, painting the window with red and gray chunks. Bullet number two also cracked the drivers-side window, but it didn't shatter. The man in the cap raced around the car, opened the driver's door, released the seatbelt, and kicked Nolan to the passenger side. He yanked the bags from his waistband, laid them out across the driver's seat, climbed into the SUV, and closed the door.

He checked the ignition. No key. He ducked beneath the dashboard and scoured the vehicle's floor. Finding the key, he pushed it into the ignition and turned the engine. As he lowered the cracked driver's window, parts of Charlie Nolan's brain dropped off and fell onto the edge of the driver's seat.

The man in the cap pulled the Denali onto Race Street and then caught Fifth Street to I-71. As he drove down the highway, he glanced at the map on his cell phone, searching for a large parking lot. Six miles later, he found one.

He pulled into the Rookwood Commons' parking lot and took a spot at the rear of the lot away from the other vehicles.

The man leaned over toward the passenger side and searched Nolan's jacket pockets for a cell phone but didn't find it. He ducked his head under the dashboard again, but still nothing. Then he clicked open the glovebox. There it was. He turned on the phone and searched through the text message history until he found several messages from James Nolan. He turned to his own phone and punched in the addresses for James and Charlie Nolan that he found in their BMV files. The satellite view revealed that James lived on a cul-de-sac in a Florence, Kentucky neighborhood. Charlie lived in a rural part of Jonesville, Kentucky, 40 miles away from his brother. According to the satellite image, Charlie's home was isolated and surrounded by trees on three sides.

The man in the cap placed his cell phone inside his jacket pocket and returned to the text message screen on Charlie's phone. He pulled up the last text exchange with James Nolan. The last message appeared to be sent just after he arrived at the Shillito Lofts, probably moments before he took two to the head.

It read **Just arrived. Will call after it's done**.

Okay read the response.

The man in the cap typed on the screen.

Done. Need help getting rid of the package. Meet me at my place in one hour.

Seconds later, James Nolan replied, **Will be there.**

The man in the cap wiped his prints from Charlie's phone and tossed it onto the passenger floor mat. He typed Charlie's address into his own phone's GPS app, slammed the Denali into drive, and followed the monotone voice as it guided him through the twists and turns of Kentucky's back roads to Charlie's home at 4408 Gooseneck Road in Jonesville. As he drove through the sleepy town, he noted the sign for the bus station in Dry Ridge, Kentucky, six miles from his final destination.

THE MAN IN THE CAP ARRIVED AT THE HOME ON Gooseneck Road and parked the Denali in the dirt driveway. He turned to the passenger seat. The absence of a wedding ring on the dead man's left hand indicated he likely lived alone, but the man stepped out of the SUV to confirm his suspicion. He quickly walked the perimeter of the home, noting the steep ravine beyond the back yard. He peered through the windows but saw no one.

When a knock on the front door returned no answer, he walked back to the driveway, crouched down in front of the SUV, and waited, the Glock gripped tightly in his hand.

The black F-350 pickup truck arrived ten minutes later. The man listened as the truck's door opened and closed and the soft thud of boots approached.

The man pulled the green cap low over his face and rose to his feet in front of the Denali. "James Nolan?" he said, mentally comparing the man in front of him to the photo in his DMV file.

James Nolan turned and ran back toward the pickup truck as the man in the cap raised his weapon and fired. The shot clipped James' shoulder but did little to slow him down. The second round pinged off the drivers-side mirror.

In one fluid motion, James reached the rear of the pickup, grabbed a 12-gauge pump-action shotgun from the back, turned, and fired. The shot exploded through the rear of the Denali, shattering the rear window and forcing the man in the cap to take cover behind the front of the SUV.

"Where's my brother?" shouted James as he racked another shell into the shotgun's chamber from behind the tailgate.

"He's dead," said the man in the cap. "Same as you're gonna be."

James stepped out to the side of the pickup truck and fired another blast, which blew the Denali's passenger mirror off the side of the vehicle. "I can do this all day, you piece of shit."

"Me too."

"I'm gonna blow your dick off either way, but it'd be nice to know why you're here," said James.

"Finn Harding."

"You competing for my contract?"

"Ain't your contract, dipshit. It's open to anyone who wants it."

"Well, step on up, then." James fired a third shot, which tore through the Denali and shattered the front windshield, sending shards of glass raining down onto the green baseball cap.

The man in the cap lay on his stomach, brushed the glass off, and watched from underneath the SUV as James retreated back behind the pickup and racked the shotgun again. The man in the cap aimed the Glock at James' lower left shin and fired. The shot splintered James' tibia, dropping him to the dirt ground behind the pickup.

James fired a blind shot from the ground, but the blast missed the Denali and instead found the front of the house. As James struggled to re-grip the shotgun from the recoil, the man in the cap sprang across the hood and onto the pickup's roof where he fired another two rounds into James' head and neck.

The man in the cap jumped to the ground and secured the Glock back inside his jacket. James coughed once, gurgled on the blood in his throat, slapped the dirt with his hand, and then fell quiet.

The man in the cap opened the Denali's liftgate. He slipped off his jacket and shirt, dragged James' body across the ground, and heaved him into the back of the SUV. He redressed, drove the Denali to the back of the property, wiped the inside for prints, and pushed it down the ravine.

A few minutes later, the black pickup truck followed down the hill.

The man in the cap wiped the sweat from his forehead, checked his watch, and walked toward the bus station in Dry Ridge.

CHAPTER 6

Brooke Harding flicked on the single-cup coffee brewer on the granite countertop in her kitchen and smiled at the thought of Becca playing in her room upstairs. She poured a cup of filtered water into the machine's reservoir, popped in the pre-packaged plastic container, and pressed the "brew" button. She stepped back and watched the array of colored lights blink on the front of the machine. It looked like a time machine about to take off for another era. After a few seconds, the machine gurgled, siphoned the water up from the reservoir, and spit out a stream of coffee into the cup below.

A shuffling sound came from the living room. The whirring of the coffee machine drowned out most of the commotion, but Brooke assumed it was Becca. Perhaps she had abandoned her bedroom for the play kitchen in the corner of the living room.

Becca loved to pretend she was cooking dinner in her red-and-white plastic kitchen, complete with cooking utensils and miniature pots and pans. She would display her plastic cuisine on the carpet for a mother-daughter picnic. If Daryl was lucky enough to return from the hospital in time, Becca would set a place for him too. If everyone was still hungry after their imaginary dinner, Becca would pass out slices of plastic chocolate cake and card-board cookies. If they were lucky, tea and coffee followed.

Brooke grabbed her steaming mug from the coffee machine and rounded the corner, eager to see what kind of feast Becca had cooked up. As she turned into the living room, a fist collided with her jaw, knocking her into the side of the doorway and onto the floor. Her coffee mug shattered on the white ceramic tile. The punch didn't quite knock her unconscious, but the kick to the head that followed did.

BROOKE OPENED HER EYES. SHE WAS SLUMPED TO her side on the couch. A man in a black leather motorcycle jacket, t-shirt, and ripped jeans sat on the coffee table in front of her. There was a Union Jack patch on his right shoulder, and he wore thick-soled black boots.

"What's your name?" he said. He wasn't British, as the jacket patch had suggested.

"Brooke." She pushed against the couch's armrest to right herself, then wiped a stream of blood from her lower lip with her hand. Her head felt like a throbbing cotton ball, as if someone had somehow jammed a pillow between her ears. Pain and numbness battled for supremacy on the side of her face. She ran her hand across her head checking for blood from the boot stomp, but she didn't find any.

The man sitting on the coffee table handed her a tissue. "For the lip," he said. She blotted her lip and checked the tissue. A crimson streak stared back.

"Brooke, I'm looking for Dr. Daryl Jennings. He lives here, right?"

Brooke was about to answer when she heard her daughter singing in the upstairs hall. The gentle melody grew louder as Becca approached the top of the steps. The man in the motorcycle jacket slipped a knife from inside his boot and shook his head from side to side, silently telling Brooke not to call for her daughter.

"Don't hurt her," Brooke whispered.

"That all depends on you," he said. The man nodded his head, and for the first time, Brooke realized there was a second man standing behind her. This other man, who was much larger than the man on the coffee table, lurched across the hardwood floor and took the steps three at a time. Brooke listened as her daughter screamed once and then fell silent. A moment later, the man carried Becca down the steps, a beefy hand covering her mouth. Becca kicked her feet from side to side, knocking the man into the banister as he stomped back toward the living room.

The big man pushed Becca onto the cushion next to her mother. Brooke turned to hug her daughter, and their tears merged and trickled onto the couch.

"Is there anyone else in the house?" said the man in the leather jacket.

"No," said Brooke, wiping her daughter's eyes.

"Are you sure?"

"I'm sure."

"Good, then we can begin." He nodded again, and the second man returned to his post behind the couch.

"I expect this to go very smoothly," said the man in the leather jacket. "Tell me what I want to know, and everyone goes on about their day like we were never here." He leaned forward and whispered into Brooke's ear so only she could hear. "If you don't tell me what I want to know, I'll open your daughter's throat, and you can watch her bleed out right here."

Brooke nodded as he returned to the coffee table. She wiped her eyes with the palm of her left hand, her right wrapped tight around Becca.

"So, back to Dr. Daryl Jennings. This is his house, correct?"

"Yes," said Brooke, wiping away more tears.

"Mommy, I'm scared," said Becca burying her face in her mother's side.

"It'll be okay, sweetie. No one is going to hurt you."

"Where is he?" said the man.

"He's still at work. At the hospital." She wiped her face again. "Sometimes he's there late. I don't know when he'll be home." She paused. "Why are you looking for him? What do you want?"

"For the past several months, he's been delivering something very valuable to me. Then all of a sudden, those deliveries stopped. I've left several messages with him, inquiring why this has happened, but he must not want to return my calls. So, now I'm here to follow up in person."

"I don't know what you're talking about. What deliveries?"

"That's between him and me. When do you expect him home?"

Brooke wiped Becca's face with her sleeve. "I don't know. He was at the clinic this morning and he was supposed to be in surgery this afternoon, but that can take a long time. Sometimes he sleeps at the hospital."

The man in the leather jacket sat silent for a moment. Thinking. Then he stood up and checked his watch. "Well, we don't plan to wait that long, so here's what you can do. You tell him to call Adler when he gets home. He knows how to reach me. And you tell him he needs to turn the valve back on. Otherwise, things are going to get messy around here." He slipped the serrated blade back into his boot, reached out and ran his index finger across Becca's chin. Brooke clenched her tight in her arms. "We clear?"

"Yes," said Brooke.

"Good," he nodded to the man behind the couch. "Tell him to turn the valve back on, Brooke. And remember, you and me can have another chat like this anytime I want. 5711 Tangerine Court is pretty easy to remember." He ran the same index finger down the side of Brooke's face and brushed a lock of red hair behind her ear. "And you're pretty easy to remember, too."

Brooke jerked her head to the side, still gripping Becca in her arms.

"Mommy," wailed Becca.

"We'll let ourselves out." The two men walked toward the front door. "Oh, and if you've got a brain in that pretty little head of yours, you won't be calling the police. If you do, bad things are gonna happen. Real bad things."

Brooke nodded as Adler and the big man walked out of the house and closed the door. Brooke rushed the door and locked the deadbolt. She ran into the den and picked up the phone from the desk, her finger hovering over the keypad. Then she stopped, set the phone back down on the desk, returned to the couch, wrapped her arms around Becca, and cried.

CHAPTER 7

AT 11:47 THAT NIGHT, Dr. Daryl Jennings' black Mercedes pulled into the driveway. He grabbed his leather bag from the passenger seat and headed toward the front door. It was locked. He fumbled with his key ring to find the right key, unlocked the door, and stepped in. The house was dark. Daryl scanned the living room and then stepped back outside to confirm that he had indeed walked past Brooke's Range Rover in the driveway. The green SUV sat in its usual spot. He turned back to the front door and stepped inside the house. He flicked on the front porch lights and did the same for the chandelier above the foyer.

Daryl was walking toward the den to set his bag on his desk when he saw Brooke sitting in the high-backed leather desk chair. His eyes met hers in the dimly-lit room, and for the first time, he noticed how she was sitting. Her knees were pulled up to her chest, her lean fingers interlocked in front of her shins.

"What's wrong, honey?" he said, taking off his coat. "Why are all the lights off?" Daryl scratched his head. "Right, I was supposed to take you and Becca out for dinner. I'm sorry, I got slotted into an emergency surgery and forgot all about it."

Brooke sat motionless in the chair. "Who's Adler?" she said. Her eyes locked on his face.

"What?"

"Adler." She wiped her eyes with a fist. "Who's Adler?"

Daryl's shoulders slouched, and he dropped his coat to the floor. "What do you mean?"

Brooke released her arms and let her feet slide onto the floor beneath the desk chair. "The man who broke into our fucking house tonight, Daryl." She rubbed her lip. "He said his name was Adler and that he knew you. He said you owed him something. Who is he? Do you owe him money? Is that why he came here?"

"I don't know what you're talking about…"

"Becca was here," Brooke interrupted. "That piece of shit threatened to slit my daughter's throat right in front of me, so don't for a second tell me you don't know what the fuck is going on." She stood up, walked toward Daryl, and threw a right jab that connected just below his sternum. He staggered backward. "I'll call the police, Daryl. I'll call the police, take my daughter out of this house, and never come back!"

Daryl didn't respond.

"Is it money? Do you owe him money? Talk to me, goddammit!" She cocked her arm back again.

Daryl raised his hands. "Okay, just stop," he said. "I don't owe him money."

"Then what does he want? Why did he come here? He said something about turning a valve on. And that you've been delivering something to him. What did he mean?"

Daryl closed his eyes and exhaled. He opened his mouth to speak but caught his words. He took a deep breath and began again. "He came to see me at the clinic a few months ago. Somehow, he knew that I had privileges at Christ Hospital and that I could get access to certain narcotics. He threatened me, Brooke. Said he wanted me to get him fentanyl. Apparently, that's valuable on the street. Said if I didn't get it for him, he'd mess things up for me."

"So, you're selling drugs for him?"

"I wasn't selling drugs. I was just getting one thing for him."

Brooke bent toward the floor and placed both hands on her knees. "I think I'm going to be sick," she said.

"I thought I could do it a few times, and he'd go away. He could make his money, and we'd be done with it. And that's what I did. After a while I stopped. I cut him off and told him that the hospital was getting suspicious and that I couldn't get it for him anymore. I figured that would be the end of it. I didn't think he'd come here. You have to believe me, Brooke."

"I'm calling the police." Brooke spun toward the desk, but Daryl jumped in front of her and grabbed her outstretched arm.

"Damn it, Brooke," he said. "If you call the police, you're going to cause even more trouble. I could lose my license."

Brooke pulled her arm away. "What do you expect me to do? Just pretend nothing happened? You didn't see his face, Daryl. You didn't see how he looked at me. At Becca."

"I think he's just trying to intimidate us," said Daryl.

"You're fucking right he's intimidating us. He threatened to kill us. All of us."

"Look, once he realizes I can't get the fentanyl any longer, he'll move onto someone else, some other doctor, and this'll be over."

Brooke stepped closer to the desk.

"You weren't here, Daryl. You didn't see the way he looked at me. I don't think he's going away."

"Let me handle it." Daryl placed his hands on Brooke's shoulders. "I'll take care of it. Just let me talk to him. He'll realize he's barking up the wrong tree and he'll move on. I can reason with him."

"He didn't look like someone you reason with."

"We don't need to involve the police. That'll only make things worse."

Brooke stepped backward out of his grasp and eyeballed the phone on the desk. "Fine," she said. "But I'm not staying here waiting for this guy to come back. Becca and I will be somewhere else until you fix whatever you got us into."

"What are you talking about? Where are you going to go?"

Brooke thought for a moment. "I'm taking her to my sister's house first thing in the morning."

"All right." Daryl turned and looked at the stairs. "Is Becca asleep? I'll go say goodnight."

"She's asleep, but she's probably going to have nightmares for the rest of her life."

Daryl turned back to Brooke and wrapped his arms around her. "Everything is going to be fine. I promise." He released his grasp and headed up the stairs to Becca's bedroom. On his way up the steps, he thought he heard Brooke pick up the phone on the desk.

CHAPTER 8

I LIKE READING AT NIGHT. It calms my mind and lets me focus on something other than life. It also puts me into sleep mode. It was 12:05 am, and I was three chapters deep into Lee Child's *The Killing Floor* when my cell phone rang. I don't like late-night calls. They never offer good news. No one calls at midnight to tell you they got engaged or that you got the job. Nighttime is reserved for the shit life throws at you. Like dying smoke detector batteries and bad news.

I grabbed my cell from the nightstand. Brooke's image smiled back.

"You're up late," I said, answering the phone.

"I need to talk to you," said Brooke.

"Mission accomplished. What's going on?"

"It's Daryl."

"Did he get hit by a bus?" Maybe good news did come at night after all.

"No, but he's in trouble."

"What he do? Overdose a patient?"

"No." She paused. "It's bad, Finn. He got into something. Over his head."

"All right, what is it?"

Brooke was silent. She was either composing her thoughts or second-guessing herself for bringing me in. "Out with it," I prodded.

"He stole some narcotics and passed them off to some dealer who's selling them on the streets."

"Shit," I said. "This a one-time thing or something more?"

"He's been doing it for a few months."

Daryl appeared to be a squeaky-clean guy. The guy who always did the right thing. The level-headed, make-the-best-decision guy. That's what

Brooke liked about him, and it's what I hated about him. I guess everyone had secrets.

"How did you find out about it?" I said.

She paused again.

"How did you find out?" I repeated.

"Daryl realized he'd made a mistake and stopped supplying the dealer."

"I assume that didn't go over very well," I said.

"No. The dealer came by our house this afternoon looking for Daryl, pushed me around a bit, and scared the shit out of Becca."

"Back up," I said. "He came to your house? Did he hurt you? Or Becca?"

She was silent again.

"Did he hurt you, Brooke?" It rose inside me—that feeling of blind rage, where you want to put your hand through a wall, or through someone's head, without giving a shit about the consequences.

"He pushed me around and split my lip, but I'm fine. More emotionally scarred than anything else."

"What about Becca?"

"She's fine. Just scared."

"Then she's not fine," I said, already searching for my keys. "I'm coming over there."

"No, Finn. That's not going to help."

"I don't care if it isn't going to help. I want to see my daughter. And make sure you're okay."

"I said I'm fine. And Becca's asleep. Coming over isn't going to help anything."

My grip tightened around my cell phone, and I waited for the device to shatter in my hand. I could feel my pulse jump, the anxiety building. I moved the phone to my other ear and paced the perimeter of my bed.

"Daryl is going to hit the fucking roof when he finds out I told you about this," she continued. "But I didn't know what else to do. Daryl is in way over his head, and I can't go to the police."

"The fuck you can't go to the police. You should have called them before calling me."

"This guy. Adler. He told me there'd be consequences if I did."

"There are consequences for everything, Brooke. That doesn't mean you shouldn't do it. Call the police. If you don't, I will."

"I'm hoping we can settle this without the police. Right now, the hospital doesn't know about the drugs. If I go to the police, it'll all come out, and Daryl will…" She stopped.

"Why are you protecting him?" I tried to be sensitive to Brooke's situation. On the one hand, Dr. Dickhead was in deep shit, and as far as I was concerned, the deeper, the better. Like him or not, he was a fixture in Brooke and Becca's lives, but taking any blowback from his bullshit wasn't an option.

"I'm asking for your help, Finn."

"Of course, I'll help you. Right after I split your boyfriend in two for bringing his shit home." I thought I felt the phone buckle in my fist. "The first thing you need to do is get out of that house.

I'm coming over and bringing you and Becca back here. It's not safe there."

"No. This Adler…he's not coming back tonight. I'm taking Becca to school tomorrow morning and then we'll stay at my sister's place. I've already cleared it with her. We'll be fine tonight."

"Is Daryl at the hospital or the clinic tomorrow?"

"The clinic." She rattled some paper. "He's supposed to be there by nine."

"I'll call him, and we'll get started fixing his fuck-up," I said. "I seem to remember you telling me a few weeks ago that you picked Daryl over me because he was the safer choice. Never got into trouble. Always came home at night. Seems like…"

"I'm asking for your help, Finn," she interrupted. "Don't throw this back in my face."

She was right, and I regretted the comment.

"I'm sorry," I said. "Everyone fucks up from time to time. I'll fix this. I promise."

"This is a pretty big fuck-up, Finn. And I'm not used to having to deal with the big ones."

"That's all I deal with," I said. "I don't want you or Becca back in that house until this is done. You sure your sister is okay having you two stay there?"

"I told her Daryl and I had a fight, and we needed some time apart. She's only a few miles from Becca's school, and she's got plenty of room. She won't ask too many questions either."

"Okay," I said. "Get out of the house first thing tomorrow. And call me if you need anything."

I clicked the phone off and slipped it into my pocket. I'd envisioned punching my fist through Daryl's smug face more times than I can count, but this was the closest I'd come to following through on it. I threw on a jacket, grabbed Lee Child's novel from my bed, and headed for the door. I'd be parked on Brooke's street within thirty minutes.

What would Jack Reacher do? I thought on my way to my car. After pummeling Daryl into small bits, Reacher would find the dealer and toss him through a window. Probably break all his ribs with his toothbrush first. As much as that sounded like a fine scenario, I'm no Jack Reacher. He's six foot five and two hundred fifty pounds. I'm six-foot-one and one-ninety. He's got short blond hair. I've got longer brown hair. He's barrel-chested and broad-shouldered. I'm no statue, but I'm solid where I need to be.

But Reacher wouldn't work in this situation. This was going to require more finesse than bashing a few heads. Dealers are connected, and whatever Daryl was into, it didn't end with whoever he was supplying. There was someone up the chain, and I was going to find out who.

Over the past several years, I'd made a solid business out of fixing people's fuck-ups, but I never thought I'd be working for my ex-wife.

IT'S HARD TO TAIL A CAR AFTER MIDNIGHT. THERE aren't enough vehicles on the road to blend in, and you stick out like a dick in a salad bar. After two right turns it was obvious the silver Escalade in my rearview mirror was following me, but it wasn't obvious why. I buried the speedometer, took two quick rights and then a left, and lost him in the parking garage on Third Street.

Ten minutes later, I pulled into Brooke's neighborhood and camped out in my car a few doors down from her place. I split my time between staring at her driveway, my Lee Child novel, and my rear-view mirror. The novel was the only one that provided any excitement.

CHAPTER 9

I WAS BACK at my place by 6:00 am. I'm no criminologist, but I knew enough about the criminal mind to know they don't get out of bed before 8:00 am, so whoever Adler was, he wasn't going to be a threat this early. Brooke and Becca would be safely out of the house in the next few hours, and I could relax enough to grab a shower, brew a pot of coffee, and dig up some breakfast.

There are few things in this world that I loathe. Plumbing and talking to Dr. Daryl Jennings are at the top of that list. As much as I normally hated talking to him, I looked forward to hearing his voice this morning. I polished off my everything bagel and checked Albert's room. He was already gone, but he was nice enough to leave a note on the kitchen counter.

"Finn, meeting a friend for breakfast. Please drop off my dry cleaning on your way out this morning. It's in the bag next to the front door. I'd take it, but I'm heading the other direction. Thanks."

Everyone has quirks. The list of my father's quirks ran into double digits. One of his most irritating traits was his insistence on sending all of his laundry to the dry cleaner. For some reason, he had an aversion to washing machines. It usually didn't bother me since Albert handled the laundry delivery and pick-up himself, but today he decided to bestow that honor to his youngest son.

I shook my head at the powder-blue duffle bag with the drawstring next to the front door and scrolled through the contact list on my cell phone. My thumb hovered over the entry for "Dr. Dickhead." I inhaled and dialed. He answered on the fourth ring.

"Finn, what can I do for you? It's been a busy morning." I was surprised he had me in his directory.

"Good morning to you, too," I said smiling. "I need to speak to you in person. Meet me at Winan's Coffee on the corner of Eighth and Walnut in a half-hour."

"I'm a bit busy at the moment. Some of us have real jobs and can't just drop everything for java."

"How about I rephrase it then? Meet me for coffee in thirty minutes, or I call Christ Hospital and tell them about your new career as a drug dealer."

He was silent for a moment.

"Brooke told you?"

"She told me," I said, my grip tightened around my coffee mug. "She also told me that your pusher roughed her up and fucked with my daughter, and that doesn't sit right with me. So I'll say it again. Winan's Coffee. Thirty minutes." I hung up the phone.

I was on my way out the door when I received a text message from Cricket, one of my Cincinnati contacts.

Finn, I've got the information you asked for. Will drop it off at the coffee shop. - C

I HANDLED MOST OF MY BUSINESS MEETINGS AT Winan's Coffee. A few bucks for a cup of coffee and a few more for a tip was much cheaper than renting office space. Plus, they had good coffee. The coffee shop was small, but not small enough that other customers would listen in on my conversation. And they had fantastic banana nut muffins on Mondays.

I stepped into Winan's at 9:30 am, grabbed a cup of Highlander Grogg and a muffin, and took a seat at my usual table near the front of the shop. By now, the morning crowd had disappeared into their cubicle farms, but it would pick up again for lunch around noon.

There were two other people in the place. I'd seen them at least once a week for the past year. He always arrived first, and she stepped in about fifteen minutes later. If I had to bet on it, I'd wager they were having an affair. Both wore wedding bands, but they talked low and always seemed a little uncomfortable, looking over their shoulders like they weren't supposed to be there. I'd love to know their story, but until someone paid me to get it, I'd have to wait.

The couple left as Daryl entered. Dr. Daryl Jennings was about my age. He was shorter than average, with thinning black hair. I knew he dyed it from the gray roots struggling to free themselves from his scalp. It crushed my ego that Brooke picked him over me. I might not compete with him on the financial or professional level, but I was confident I had him beat in the looks department.

Daryl came through the door with his white lab coat flowing behind him like a superhero's cape. He waved off the coffee jock's advances and settled into the seat across from me.

"I can't just leave the clinic like that," he said, leaning close. "I've got people waiting to see me. Shit, Finn, I have appointments scheduled all day. Do you know how difficult it is to reschedule with patients?"

"Do you know how difficult it is not to leap across this table and rip the fucking skin off your face?" I took a sip and watched the lines in his face deepen. "Your pusher, what's his name?"

He took a breath. "Adler. Adler…Browning, I believe."

"How did you get wrapped up with him? From the beginning."

"He came into my clinic a few months ago. Said he was having shoulder pain that started after playing with his kids. We did an X-ray, and it showed inflammation in the AC joint. I gave him a cortisone shot, referred him to an orthopedic surgeon, and sent him on his way. I left at the end of the day and found him standing next to my car in the lot. He showed me a gun in his waistband, told me to get in the car, and then he got into the passenger seat. He told me he needed fentanyl. Told me I have to get it for him. Said his other supplier is out of the country, and he needed several vials."

"What's fentanyl? And pretend like I don't have a medical degree."

"It's a very potent pain medication, but it's also an anesthetic. We generally use it after surgery."

I watched as a tall, thin man in a faded jean jacket and graying hair came into the coffee shop with an orange folder tucked under his right arm.

“Fentanyl, is that a pill?” I said.

“No. We use it the hospital as a solution, but you can get it by prescription in a pain patch.”

“And he’s selling it on the street? An anesthetic doesn’t seem like your usual street drug.”

“It’s not,” he said. “I didn’t know it at the time, but apparently some dealers use it to cut heroin.”

I took another sip of my coffee and watched as the man with the orange folder grabbed his cup from the coffee jock and sat down a few tables away from me.

“So then what happened?” I said.

“I told him he’s got the wrong guy, that I couldn’t get it for him, and that I’d call the police if he ever came to the clinic again.” Daryl checked his watch and then looked back up at me. “Then he slammed my face into the steering wheel. I’m surprised he didn’t break my nose. He told me that he worked for some powerful people and would fuck up my life if I didn’t help him.”

“Why didn’t you go to the police?”

"I tried to forget the whole thing. I honestly thought he would just go away."

"Just go away? Come on, Doc, you're a smart guy. Things like this don't just go away."

"A few years ago, someone else in my practice had something similar happen to him. Someone came in and threatened him for meds. My colleague ignored it, and that guy went away. I figured if Adler thought I'd hold out, then he'd go on to someone else too."

"I assume he didn't go away?"

"The next morning, I came out of my house to go to the clinic, and I saw Adler standing on the other side of the street. He came over to the driveway and said he'd seen my wife and daughter, and that if I didn't want something bad to happen to them, I'd better deliver the vials. He said he'd hurt them, Finn." Daryl tapped two fingers on the table and then scratched the side of his face. "I had no reason not to believe him."

"So, you got him the vials?"

"Yes, he met me in the parking lot every Wednesday, and I gave them to him."

Daryl seemed like an honest guy. It's one of the reasons why Brooke was with him. She needed stability, something I couldn't provide, but Daryl could. That inclination to do the right thing was probably why Adler picked him. I guessed that Adler used that first shoulder appointment as a way to feel Daryl out. To find leverage and see if he was someone Adler could snare. Daryl said Adler mentioned he'd hurt his shoulder playing with his kids. That comment probably led Adler to ask whether Daryl had kids, which introduced Becca into the equation. And there's your leverage. People will do anything to protect their kids, even if they aren't their biological children. I know. I've done it. I put two bodies on the bottom of a lake in Maine for the same reason.

"How in the hell did you get fentanyl out of the hospital?" I said. "Don't they monitor that?"

"They do, but it wasn't that difficult. Fentanyl is ordered pretty frequently. Let's say it's a five CC order for a patient. I draw five CCs, squirt four CCs into an empty vial in my pocket, and replace the four I took with saline. The patient still gets his five CC cocktail, but he's getting one CC of fentanyl and four CCs saline. At the end of my shift, I walk out of the hospital with a vial or two of fentanyl. It all checks out in the system because the barcode scans are accurate. The patient still gets his five CCs. He's just not getting five CCs of pain meds."

The thin man a few tables over spun the orange folder on the tabletop and sipped his coffee. He looked at me with a grin.

"But if the patient is only getting twenty percent of the dosage, he'd still complain of pain," I said. "Wouldn't that raise some eyebrows?"

"Not really. Some people don't respond as well to fentanyl as other patients do. Especially those who are heavy drinkers. Every patient has a different tolerance. We'd just switch to another drug if they complain. No one would ever question it."

"So, you've been delivering the fentanyl to Adler, and then what, you have a change of heart?"

"Adler initially said he only needed me to get it a few times. Something about his other supplier being out of the country for a few weeks, but then it became obvious there was no other supplier. He was leaning on me for all of it. And he kept wanting more. It wasn't sustainable. I told him that the hospital was looking into some thefts, and they were clamping down on monitoring and I couldn't get it for him anymore. I thought he'd just move on to someone else. I thought that's how this stuff worked."

"So you cut him off?"

"Yes," said Daryl. "He called a few times, but I never called him back. Like I said, I was hoping he'd just move onto someone else."

"That's when he came to the house?" I said.

Daryl looked at his watch again. "Look, Finn, I'm sorry Brooke brought you into this, but I can handle it. I'm just going to tell Adler that I can't be his source, that the hospital is looking into inventory discrepancies, and I can't get it anymore…"

"He won't care," I interrupted. "He's not concerned about how you get it, only that you keep the pipeline open. He's locked you in, and he'll apply more pressure until you find another way to get it. Eventually, you'll do something stupid and get caught. That's when he'll find another source. That's how these guys work."

Daryl scratched the back of his left hand. "Then I'll go to the police."

"Not smart," I said. "You'll lose everything, and worse, you'll put the heat on Adler. He might retaliate by going after Brooke or Becca. You don't have a lot of plays here."

"Then what am I supposed to do?"

"I can help you," I said.

"How can you possibly help me, Finn? You couldn't even keep your PI license."

"I lost my license because I'm good at making people like Adler go away. As much as I'd like to see you go down for this, I won't put Brooke and Becca in harm's way like you did."

"That's not fair. I didn't know all this would happen."

"Regardless, I'll get him off you."

"You can help me?"

"Yep."

"And what do you want from me? You want me out of the picture?"

Nothing would make me happier than kicking Daryl out of Brooke and Becca's lives, but now wasn't the time for that.

"Believe it or not, Daryl, I'm not as big an asshole as you think I am." He was quiet. "I'll make this go away, and all it'll cost you is your word that you won't do something stupid like this again."

He thought for a moment. "Okay," he said. "What are you going to do?"

"Don't worry about how the sausage gets made. I'll take care of everything, but I do need you to call Adler."

He slid his chair back a few inches. "And say what?"

"Tell him to meet you here tomorrow at 9:00 am."

"I can't be here tomorrow morning," he said. "I've got patients."

"You won't be here. I will." I downed the rest of my Highlander Grogg. "Now, make the call and get back to your clinic."

Daryl called Adler and set up the meeting. I could hear Adler's voice through the receiver. He sounded excited, happy that Daryl was back on the leash, but he'd lose that high tomorrow by 9:05 am.

"You sure this is going to work?" said Daryl.

"Nope. But I guarantee it'll be better than your plan."

Daryl stood up and for the first time in his life, shook my hand. He thanked me and walked out the door.

After Daryl was out of the coffee shop, the man in the jean jacket approached and dropped the orange folder on the table in front of me.

"Here you go, Finn," he said. "We're even."

I opened the folder and checked the contents. "Thanks, Cricket."

He nodded, tossed his paper cup into the garbage can, and walked out the door.

I knew Daryl had a hard time processing his current situation. He'd been uneasy in the chair the entire time he recounted the story with Adler. Scratching his face and hands. Checking his watch. He wanted to get out of that coffee shop, away from me, and away from his current reality as quickly as possible. I bet he's as calm as still water when he's calculating how to mix a cocktail that won't kill a patient on the operating table. But that's a different kind of pressure.

The pressure that Adler applied was the type that robs you of sleep, makes your palms sweat like you're at a middle school dance, or squeezes your insides tight enough to kill your appetite and make you want to vomit at the same time. I didn't know what kind of guy Adler was. He might be some low-level pussy who gets off by jacking anesthesiologists, or he could be a lot worse. I hoped to find out before I met him face to face in the morning, but there was something else I needed to do first.

Brooke and Becca were getting the real shit-brown end of the stick with this whole thing. Daryl deserved his part since he willingly helped Adler, even if he did it to protect Brooke and

Becca. Regardless of his motives, he's a big boy, and he made his own bed. Brooke and Becca didn't make shit, and now they were paying for it. I thought it was time they got some good news for once, so I headed over to Cincinnati Savings and Loan.

CHAPTER 10

Ollie Stoner walked through the double-swing gates in front of the Downeast Correctional Facility in Machiasport, Maine. His prison-issued white t-shirt reached to his knees. Ollie waved to the idling pickup parked at the sign that read *INMATE DISCHARGE*. He waited for two guards to close and lock the gate before he kicked it with his worn leather boot.

"It's a federal offense to vandalize prison property, Ollie," said one of the guards.

"We might have to throw you back in," said the other.

Ollie wrapped two aging fists around the gate. "You two guys, you know what you can do? You can go fuck off. That's what." Ollie tugged on the t-shirt. "You coulda least given me a shirt that fits. I could trip over this thing. Then I'll sue ya to pay for my medical expenses."

"Blame your kin, Ollie," said the guard. "They were supposed to drop something off for you to wear home. Can't send you home in your blues."

The old man turned and started toward the idling vehicle.

"See you soon, Ollie," said one of the guards.

"Not likely," said Ollie without turning around.

A middle-aged man in jeans and a button-up flannel shirt jumped out of the pickup, ran around the front of the vehicle, and opened the passenger door. "Hey Pop," he said as Ollie climbed in and closed the passenger door.

The man returned to the wheel. "Where do you want to go?"

Ollie rolled down the window, threw up his middle finger to the guards, and then turned to his son. "Take me to the yard."

An hour later, the pickup rolled into the Stoner Salvage junkyard off Route 191 in Meddybemps, Maine. Stoner Salvage had been in operation since the 1940s. It sat on 61 acres about five miles west of Meddybemps Lake. The junkyard was a mosaic of rusted vehicles, scattered tires, and mounds of used items that had reached the end of their lives. Sun-bleached oil drums, faded shipping containers, and the green grass that sometimes crawled its way up through the scrap piles provided the only patches of color in an otherwise brown and gray landscape.

Ollie climbed out of the pickup and pointed at the main office, a building flanked by two rusted-out railway boxcars.

"Go call your brother and tell him to get his ass over here," he said. "I'll meet you back here in a bit."

"Where you goin'?"

Ollie looked across the mountains of scrap that reached into the Maine sky. "I've got to make a withdrawal. Now git."

He watched his son walk into the office, then he turned and jogged deeper into the junkyard. He passed rows of abandoned automobiles and piles of wooden beams and pallets. He turned left and continued past heaps of tangled bed frames, mildewed mattresses, and broken furniture parts. Ollie stopped next to a roached-out Buick, which hadn't moved in half a century.

He looked around to see if anyone had followed him, then he grabbed the handle and opened the car door with a metal-on-metal screech. Ollie looked around again, then ducked his head inside the vehicle and leaned into the back seat. A moment later, he emerged with empty hands and an empty stare. He brushed the dirt and gravel from the vehicle's hood and then heaved himself up, placing his leather boots on the crooked bumper. Ollie Stoner looked up at the sky and then buried his face in his hands.

By the time he returned to the office, William and Peter, his twin boys, were waiting for him.

"Good to see you again, Pop," said Peter stepping toward Ollie with his arms out.

Ollie pushed him backward and grabbed a box cutter from the desk. He pushed the black button forward and the dull blade emerged from inside the handle.

“Either you two been messin’ with that old Buick in the yard? The one my daddy put there?”

“No way,” said William. “You told us to leave that one alone. Why?”

“Because there was $20,000 in two satchels in the back seat that ain’t there no more. I’d like to find out where they gone to.”

“No idea,” said William. “You think someone took it?”

“Got a good idea Albert Harding and Mitch Skinner are involved.”

“How’s that?” said Peter.

“Because they’re the only two dumb enough to steal from me.”

William walked up next to Peter and leaned up against a metal four-drawer file cabinet.

“So, what do we do now?” said William.

Ollie crossed his arms. “We start killin’ people.”

CHAPTER 11

It was nearly 10:15 when I stepped into the Cincinnati Savings and Loan on Harrison Avenue. The duffle bag in my hand was bulky enough for the silver-haired security guard in black wingtips to notice. Besides the guard and me, there were three people waiting in line for a chance at one of two tellers. Two more customers filled out deposit or withdrawal slips at a counter against the left wall. Silver-beaded chains ensured they wouldn't be pocketing the pens. I was still surveying the room when a brunette in a navy blue skirt and jacket and black high heeled shoes that looked too small for her feet approached me from her office along the right wall.

"Hi. I'm Stephanie. Can I help you with something?"

"I'm here to see Michael Cooper," I said.

"Do you have an appointment with Mr. Cooper?"

"No. I'm more of a walk-in kind of guy. I want to talk to him about opening a savings account."

"Well, Mr. Cooper is the branch president and doesn't really handle that kind of thing, but I can get you set up." She motioned to her office. "If you can follow me, I'd be happy to help."

"No offense, Stephanie, but I really need to see Mr. Cooper."

She took a step back and then shifted in her tight heels.

"Well, Mr. Cooper sees customers by appointment only. But like I said, I'd be happy to help."

"Stephanie," I jostled the bag in my hand. "I've got a hundred thousand dollars in this bag, and I'm ready to hand it to you guys to do whatever it is a savings and loan does with it. I'd normally just go to a bank like everyone else on the planet, but my ex-wife is insistent that I conduct my business here. Now, I'd like to open a savings account and deposit all this cash with you this morning, but only if I speak with Mr. Cooper."

She looked at the duffle bag, the security guard, and then back at me.

"Why don't you have a seat there," she pointed to the five red, thin-cushioned chairs along the wall next to the front door. "I'll be back in a moment."

She disappeared down the hallway beyond her office and returned a minute later.

"Why don't you follow me, Mr.?"

"Finn."

"Right this way, Mr. Finn."

Stephanie led me down the hallway to an office. Michael Cooper's brass nameplate was bolted to the open door. She ushered me in and introduced me to Cooper before walking out and closing the door behind her.

Cooper was on the heavy side, probably the result of sitting behind this same desk day-in and day-out for the past twenty years. He wore a navy blue suit that was a close match to the outfit Stephanie wore. His neck bulged around his white shirt collar, indicating either his red tie was too tight, or his dress shirt was too small. I'd bet half of Albert's retirement fund on the latter.

"Have a seat, Mr. Finn," said Cooper, shaking my hand and eyeballing the duffle.

I dropped the bag in front of the chair, took a seat, and crossed my legs.

"Stephanie says you want to talk about opening a savings account with us?" Cooper grabbed a form from his file cabinet, placed it on his desk, and clicked open a silver pen. There was something engraved on the side, but I couldn't make it out.

"Actually, I want to talk about cheerleading," I said.

Cooper glanced up from his form. "I'm not sure I follow."

"My daughter Becca wants to join your wife's cheerleading team…squad. At Cincinnati Catholic Academy. And apparently your wife doesn't like my ex-wife, and because of that, she isn't allowing Becca to join up. If it were up to me, I'd like to see her get involved with gymnastics or swimming. Something that could actually help her develop a real skill. As far as I'm concerned, all you do in cheerleading is memorize chants and shake your ass. Totally inappropriate for a six-year-old girl, but if that's what she wants, so be it."

Cooper glanced back at the duffle. "I thought you were here to open an account with us."

"I want to settle the cheerleading thing first," I said.

Cooper grinned and clicked the top of the pen, sending the tip back inside the silver cylinder. "Look, if you want to open an account, I'd be happy to help you, but I'm not talking to my wife about your kid. You can reach out to her yourself if you've got a problem. I don't have time to worry about cheerleading. I've got a bank to run."

"Technically, it's not a bank," I said.

Cooper smirked but didn't reply.

"Look," I said. "I know you're a big deal in town, and you've probably got lots to do, but if you could just call your wife and tell her to reconsider putting Becca on the squad, that would be great."

Cooper stood up. “Listen, buddy. I don’t care how much you want to deposit, I’m not having this conversation. If you have a problem with my wife or cheerleading or whatever, I suggest you take it up with her. You’ve already wasted enough of my time. Don’t make me call security.”

I looked over at the door. “You mean that old guy up front? You ask him to run back here, and he’ll stroke out before he makes it halfway down the hall.”

Cooper reached for the phone on his desk.

“All right,” I said. “Just one last thing.”

I unzipped the duffle, grabbed the orange file folder Cricket had given me, and slid it across his desk.

“What’s this?” said Cooper.

“Have a look. But sit down first.”

Cooper took his hand off the desk phone, opened the folder, and flipped through the pages. He was looking at a dozen naked photos of a middle-aged brunette named Connie Butler. Connie, while quite flexible as was evident in the photos, was not his wife. Cooper leaned back in his chair.

"I like the one where she's getting into the shower," I said.

"Where did you get these?"

"I got them from someone who owed me a favor. He got them from your cell phone. From your text log, to be more specific. And from your little chats with Miss Butler, it's obvious there's more to your relationship than just a few tit pics."

"How…"

"My friend also looked into Miss Butler," I continued. "Turns out she isn't a miss. And she's also on the Cincinnati Catholic Academy's board. Isn't that something?"

"How did he get them?"

"That's not important, Cooper. What is important is that my daughter wants to be a cheerleader."

"You're blackmailing me for a spot on the cheerleading team?"

"Cheerleading squad. And yes, I am."

Cooper shifted in his seat, paused for a moment, and then leaned a thick elbow on the top of his desk. He wiped his forehead.

"Look, Mr. Finn," he said. "You might not be aware that I'm friends with the chief of police. I don't think he'll take kindly to someone trying to blackmail one of his close friends. I make one call to him, and your life gets a whole lot harder." He placed his hand back on the receiver.

"That right? Well, I'll bet that if I send these pics to your wife, she'll make your life a fuckload worse than the chief of police can make mine." Cooper didn't respond. "And I'm willing to make that bet. Are you?"

Cooper thought for a moment. Then he slid his hand away from the phone, placed the photos back into the orange folder, and slipped it into his desk drawer.

"What's your daughter's name again?"

"Becca," I said.

"And how do you suggest I convince my wife to sign her up?"

"Don't care. I'm sure you'll figure something out. Maybe you can get the chief of police to help." I paused. "Did you notice the photos are date-stamped? Going back two years? That's a long time to be tagging the co-chair of the school board."

"I get it."

"Great," I said. "My ex-wife's number is in the folder. She gets a call within forty-eight hours telling her where to buy pom-poms, or you start Googling divorce attorneys."

"And you destroy all the copies?"

"That's right," I said.

"Okay. I'll figure something out."

I stood up, slipped a business card from the brass holder on Cooper's desk, grabbed the duffle, and headed for the door.

"Wait. What about the deposit?" Cooper's eyes were fixed on the duffle.

"I'm not opening an account today."

"Then what's in the bag?"

I jostled the duffle in my hand. "My father's laundry."

CHAPTER 12

THAT NIGHT, I sat in bed, my laptop warming my thighs. I wanted to learn everything I could about Adler Browning before meeting him in the morning. I started with the criminal record databases to see if I could build a profile, but I was having difficulty focusing on Adler with the shower running in the bathroom adjacent to my bedroom.

Jennifer Reynolds was the school nurse at my daughter's Catholic school, but there was nothing Catholic about her. We met a few weeks ago when Becca got sick and purged her breakfast onto her classroom floor. Jennifer called me to pick her up, and the rest is history. She only stayed over a few nights a week, and she was very enthusiastic when she was here. I hoped I'd find what I was looking for on Adler before she got out of the shower because I knew I wouldn't get much done afterward.

After hitting the usual databases, I hadn't found dick. I had uncovered several people named Adler, but no one with the last name "Browning."

It was possible Browning was just a name Adler tossed Daryl to throw him off. I narrowed my hot zone to a three-hundred mile radius of Cincinnati. The closest Adler was a thirty-two-year-old who did a short stint for a string of burglaries in Sioux City, Iowa a year ago. It could be my guy, but it wasn't a slam dunk.

Aside from the guy in Iowa, I found no criminal records for anyone in the area named Adler. No local Adlers with open warrants, no court records, and no mention in the local papers. Nobody—and that was bad news.

Almost every pusher has some shit on their record, but not this guy. He was as clean as a nun in a washing machine. That wasn't good, because it meant that he'd never been caught. From the way he threatened Daryl and Brooke, it sounded like he'd played the hardass before. He had some level of comfort with intimidating people.

Problem is, when you act this way for long, you get careless, and the law catches up with you. And that lands your name in a database. In my business, you don't worry much about the low-level criminals with records. They get caught because they're stupid. You worry about the ones who have never been caught, the ones with no records. They are either smart or protected, and I didn't know which category Adler fell into.

I started to think that Adler wasn't some low-level pusher like Daryl led on. Or if he was low level, he was in a solid organization, and that could be bad for Daryl. And me.

The shower cut off, and a few minutes later, Jennifer stepped out of the bathroom wearing a gray Army t-shirt and nothing else. For some reason, I was more focused on where she got the shirt than how good she looked in it. Neither of us had served our country, and I wanted to think she'd picked it up at some retail clothing store instead of lifting it from some past soldier boyfriend.

She set a glass of ice water on the nightstand and climbed into bed.

"What are you working on?"

"Just some research."

"What kind of research?" She seemed interested.

"You're a nurse. Know anything about fentanyl?"

"Sure, we used it in the hospital all the time?"

"You worked in a hospital?"

She ran a hand down my thigh. "I wasn't always a school nurse, Finn."

"So, what do you know about it?"

"It's a painkiller. Pretty common stuff."

"Ever hear about it being sold on the street?"

"Sure. We had to watch a slew of videos on drug abuse at the hospital. I remember something about drug dealers mixing it with heroin. To make it more powerful."

"How powerful is it?" I said.

She sipped her ice water and rolled over to my shoulder. "It's potent shit. Something like a hundred times stronger than morphine." Her hand was on the move. It was cold from the ice water, and her touch sent shivers up my thigh. "I remember hearing a story about an old guy who picked up a few fentanyl pain patches at a pharmacy. He stuck them in his back pocket and drove home. Apparently, his heated car seat activated the patches, and he absorbed several packs worth right into his ass cheek. He died before making it home."

"Sounds like something Albert would do," I said. "Would it be hard to get? From the hospital?"

"Why? Are you thinking about changing careers?"

"No. It's relevant to a case I'm working."

"I'd think so, especially in a hospital. All that stuff is locked away. Most everything is monitored with barcodes these days. Nurses have to scan everything they give to patients, so there's a clear record of where everything goes. I'd think it would be hard to sneak anything out of a hospital. Maybe if they were switching labels, but that's pretty tough to do."

"Ever hear of an anesthesiologist pocketing the stuff?" I said. "To smuggle it out?"

"Not really." Her fingertips lingered on my thigh. "I knew some doctors who slipped a few meds for their personal use. For stress, I guess, but nothing like fentanyl. I can't imagine anyone stupid enough to try to lift that from a hospital."

I can.

"Now I've got a question for you," she said as she peeled off the Army T-shirt and tossed it on the floor. "How is it you're more interested in learning about pain meds than having fun with me?"

She was right. Dr. Dickhead had fucked up my life enough already. I didn't need him in my bedroom too.

"I'm sorry," I said. "Just prepping for a meeting tomorrow."

She rolled over and took another drink of water. "Going to be long?"

I closed the laptop and tossed it to the foot of the bed. "I'll be as long as I can be in a few seconds."

She smiled, slipped a few ice cubes into her mouth, and disappeared under the sheets.

CHAPTER 13

My emotions were usually in check. My brain knows when it's time to throw a punch and when it's time to talk my ass out of a bad situation. But, I'd never been tested like this. Rounding the corner of Eighth and Walnut, I was about to come face to face with the man who knocked Brooke around and threatened to murder my daughter. That's not something anyone can dismiss. I was going to have to straddle the fine line between reasoning with Adler and ripping his throat out.

There were only six people in Winan's Coffee when I walked in, and it was easy to spot Adler and his sidekick. They glanced at me when I entered, but returned to their conversation once they saw I wasn't Daryl. I stepped to the counter, ordered a large Yirgacheffe coffee, and looked them over while I waited.

One of the men was about six-foot-two. He looked Italian, maybe mid-thirties. He was slim and trim, had short and styled black hair, and he hadn't shaved in a few days. He wore a black leather motorcycle jacket, a cafe-racer style with no collar. His jacket had a Union Jack patch on the right shoulder and a faded patch just above his left breast, but I couldn't make out what it said. The unzipped jacket revealed a black t-shirt with a motorcycle club logo, maybe a racing event or something, it was hard to tell given his seated position. He wore faded jeans and thick-soled black boots. I thought I saw a bulge in his jeans near the top of his right boot. Probably a knife.

The guy next to him was taller by about six inches. He looked older, but harder, like he could do some damage. He was bald with a graying mustache and goatee and wore wrap-around sunglasses. He sat with his hands on the table. There were two large silver rings on his right hand, the kind of bling they give you when you win something. From the size of his hands, he could easily shatter a bone with one punch, but the rings were an added bonus. They could hit as hard as brass knuckles, but wouldn't draw as much attention.

I paid the coffee jock and took a seat at their table.

"That seat's reserved," said the man in the sunglasses.

"I know," I said. "You're saving it for me." I looked at both men. "Which one of you is Adler?" By the way, the man in the sunglasses looked at the Italian, I knew who was who.

"Why do you want to know?" said Adler.

"I just want to make sure I kill the right person." The man in the sunglasses leaned back in his seat, but Adler didn't flinch.

"Look, friend," said Adler. "I don't know who you are or why you're here, but we've got big-boy business, and you're wasting our time. So why don't you just get up and walk back out that door before you get hurt."

"Your business is with me. I'm pinch-hitting for Dr. Jennings. And we've got a lot to discuss."

The man in the sunglasses shifted again.

"I don't think so," said Adler pointing to the door. "Run along and get the doctor so the men can talk."

"He's not coming," I said. I watched Adler's hands as he moved them across the table. I wondered which one he used to hit Brooke. "I'm Dr. Jennings' new partner." I took a sip of my coffee and crossed my legs. "I'm handling the business side of things now. He has a knack for falling into the deep end. I'm a much better swimmer, and I'm right at home with you two."

"I guess we know why you're here," said Adler. "So why don't you tell us who the fuck you are."

"I'm the guy who delivers bad news. You can call me Mr. Finn."

Adler leaned back in his chair. "I don't like bad news." He pointed to the man in the sunglasses. "And neither does he."

"I don't give a shit what you like." I could feel it rising up inside me again—the same feeling I had when Brooke told me what happened the other night. All I wanted to do was kick Adler's chair out from under him, knock him to the ground, slip that knife out of his leather boot, and plunge it into his chest.

I exhaled, took another sip, and waited for my heart rate to slow. "Dr. Jennings is out of the narcotic supply business."

Adler placed his elbows on the table. "Your doctor friend might think he's out of the business, but he isn't. He's currently my main supply line, and I can't have him bitching out. I'm low on product as it is, and low ain't good."

"Then you're going to have to find another fentanyl supplier," I said.

"Fentanyl doesn't grow on trees, so unless you're also in the fentanyl business, your friend and I still have a supply conflict."

"He's not my friend." The light from the decorative lamp hanging from the ceiling shimmered off the big man's two fat silver rings.

"Don't care if he's your friend or your Goddamn fuck buddy. Fact is, he's late with his supply, and you don't seem to be fixing that, so why the fuck are we here?"

"We're here because you're going to cut him loose. If you don't, we're going to have problems," I took another sip of coffee. "You and me."

"Is that right?" said Adler, lowering his voice. "Lucky for me, I'm quite the problem solver. My last supplier pulled this same shit. Tried to walk away. I beat him to death with a shovel, cut him into little chunks, and fed him to a racehorse in Indiana. I'm not the kind of person you want to have problems with, Mr. Finn."

"You might be able to intimidate women and little girls, but I don't scare that easily," I said. "I deal with people like you all the time, and I've gotten pretty good at it." I leaned in. "The way I see it, you've got two options. You can keep going round and round with Dr. Jennings and me. You can keep muscling him, and I can start causing real problems for your organization. But while all that's happening, your supply dwindles, and eventually, you run out. Then you're fucked. Option two is you leave Dr. Jennings and his family alone and move on. Go find yourself another supplier and go back to business as usual. Either way, Dr. Jennings is out. His hospital is investigating the thefts, and he can no longer secure the product.

You're tapping a dry well with him. If I were you, I'd go with option two. You get to stay in business, and I don't have to put a bullet through your forehead."

The bigger man to my right slipped the sunglasses from his face. He pulled a plastic case from an inside jacket pocket, tucked the glasses inside, and set the case on the table.

"What is it you do exactly, Mr. Finn?" he said. "Besides threaten people?"

"I'm an investigator of sorts. I locate people who think they've disappeared. And when I find them, they don't get found again. So, I'll tell you both one last time. Dr. Jennings is out. His family is out. Back off, or I start thinking of nasty things to do to you."

The man to my right folded his hands and placed them on the table next to his plastic sunglasses case. "Maybe now we can all put away our dicks and get down to business." I realized Adler wasn't the man I should be talking to. "What kind of investigator are you? What type of people do you locate?"

For the first time, both men seemed interested in what I had to say. "I find the people others can't. Or won't."

"So, it's safe to say that your cases require a bit more discretion than finding the usual skip or runaway?"

"You could say that," I said. "You got a name?"

"Darby. But you should be more concerned about how we solve this little impasse of ours. I understand your commitment to your friend…"

"He's not my friend," I interrupted.

"Regardless, fentanyl isn't that easy to come by, and your solution to just find another supplier is going to take some time. However, I also understand that if Dr. Jennings really is having security issues at the hospital, that puts us all under a microscope we'd rather not be under." He knocked his folded hands on the tabletop. "But I think I might have a solution that will make us all happy."

"What's that?" I said.

"Excuse me for one moment." Darby stood up. "I'm going to step outside and make a phone call.

That call will determine what we do next, and whether or not you and Dr. Jennings continue to breathe."

He pulled a phone out of his front jeans pocket and stepped outside. I turned back toward Adler.

"You went to Dr. Jennings' house the other day, and you met Brooke."

"The redhead. She's a nice piece of ass. How you know her?"

I didn't answer.

"You got a thing for her? You pissed at me for knocking her around?" Adler studied my face. "Or maybe you're more pissed about the little girl." I shifted in my seat, but immediately realized that had been a mistake. The gears turned inside Adler's square head. "Maybe you're closer to the good doctor and his family than you're letting on."

"My relationship doesn't matter. What matters is, you crossed the line."

"It's my job to cross lines, asshole. Just business. I'm a fucking drug dealer. If I had better interpersonal skills, I'd be working in HR somewhere."

"Business or not, that'll come up again."

He pulled his seat forward and leaned across the table.

"I look forward to it. You can sit there and talk tough all you want, but your bones'll break just like everyone else's."

"There are two things in this world I won't hesitate a second to kill for, and you've already met both of them."

"Good to know," said Adler. He turned and looked out the front window to see the big man still talking on the phone. "Depending on how that call goes, I might be paying your two girls another visit. I won't be as nice as I was the first time."

"Keep talking. You're just giving me more reasons to kill you."

"You have no idea what you're getting yourself into," said Adler. "No idea."

I'd been so focused on Adler that I didn't notice Darby had finished his phone call until he rejoined us at the table.

"You're in luck, Mr. Finn." He looked at Adler and then back at me. "My boss is interested in your services. He's offering a deal. You find someone for us, and we find another fentanyl supplier." He paused. "It's a one-time offer, and I need to know right now. You in or out?"

I'm normally a confident guy, but this had me rattled. I had no idea what I was agreeing to, and it was becoming more obvious that this wasn't a two-man operation. My plan had been to convince these two to cut Daryl loose and move on to another mark. To make them realize that the longer they leaned on Daryl, the more money they'd lose on the street. I'd thought they'd see it was more profitable to cut ties and move on. That was my first mistake. I hoped I wouldn't make a second.

"What's the job?" I said.

"Not here," said Darby. "You can discuss it in person with my boss."

"And who's that?"

"Mason Holbrook."

I didn't know Mason Holbrook, but I did know that I was getting deeper into this than I wanted to go. Had it just been Daryl, I would have thrown him to the wolves from the start, but now that Brooke and Becca were involved, I had to go along for the ride and head deeper down the rabbit hole. Time to meet Holbrook.

"Okay, I'm in. When can I meet him?"

"He's in Tennessee for two more days. Adler'll pick you up here at one o'clock on Friday and take you to him."

"I'll be here," I said.

"Friday. One o'clock. If you don't show, Adler kills Dr. Jennings and then comes looking for you."

Both men stood up and headed for the door.

"Adler," I said. "We'll continue our other conversation later."

"Can't wait."

I reached for my coffee cup, and realized for the first time that my hands were shaking. I took a sip and watched them disappear into the parking lot. I didn't like agreeing to things before I had all the facts. That had gotten me in trouble before, but there wasn't much I could do. I didn't know dick about this job and I had no idea who Holbrook was, but then again, I wasn't an authority on every criminal in the area. Lucky for me, I knew someone who was. It was time to put my three-day wait to good use. In Detroit.

CHAPTER 14

Constable Alex Hafner, the only law enforcement officer in Meddybemps, Maine, climbed out of his cruiser with a shotgun in one hand and a take-out sack from Palmer's Restaurant in the other. He opened the office door to find his secretary, Adrienne Braxton, sitting at her desk reading a Jonathan Valin novel.

"Morning babe," said Hafner eyeing the deep neckline of her faded red t-shirt.

"I think it's officially afternoon now," she said.

Hafner propped his shotgun against the wall, stepped behind Adrienne, and wrapped his free arm around her chest. He kissed the back of her neck. "I've got some time before I have to go see

Tom Harper about his missing boat trailer. Want to step inside my office and take a memo?"

Adrienne smiled, leapt from her chair, and followed him into his office. Adrienne giggled as she climbed underneath the desk and unzipped his pants.

A few minutes later, Ollie Stoner walked into the constable's office carrying a shotgun. Two men, each carrying a baseball bat, followed him into the room.

"Afternoon Constable," said Ollie, raising the shotgun into the air and resting it against his right shoulder.

"Ollie!"

"Where's that secretary of yours?" said Ollie. "The one with the nice tits?"

Hafner shifted in his seat, placed his hands on the armrest, and slid his chair closer to the desk. "Ran out to get lunch. Just missed her."

"That right?"

"Yeah. She always takes lunch around now. Probably headed to Palmer's."

"Good, then you and I got a chance to talk." He swung the shotgun forward and back again like a pendulum. "You must have pussy on the brain, Constable. Can't think of any other reason you'd leave your shotgun against the wall out there. Pussy makes a man dumb."

Hafner pointed to the shotgun. "Why don't you just set that down, Ollie? You don't need to be throwin' that around up in here."

"I think I'll keep it for now." Hafner shifted in his seat again. "You remember my boys?" Ollie pointed the shotgun from one to the other.

"Yeah. I remember them."

"We thought we'd come down here and have a little chat."

Hafner looked at the brothers and then back at Ollie. His right shoulder dropped as he slightly arched sideways.

Ollie leveled the shotgun at his chest. "I wouldn't go reaching for that service revolver. I might not be the best shot in town, but I can damn well guarantee I can hit you from this distance drunk and with my eyes closed."

Hafner sat up in his chair again.

“I don’t get why you didn’t back me, Constable. We had an understanding. You and me. Then that fucking game warden picked me up and hauled me away. They gave me thirty months in Machiasport for some stupid shit about a stolen boat.”

“Sorry, Ollie. There wasn’t anything I could do about that. Look, I had no problem looking the other way with what you had going on, but what was I supposed to do when that warden came in? Nothing. There’s nothing I could do.”

“I guess I can see your pickle.” Ollie bounced the shotgun’s barrel on his shoulder. “Problem is it was all bullshit, cuz I never touched that boat. Had nothing to do with it. I reckon it was Mitch Skinner and Albert Harding set me up. You know ‘em?”

“Yeah. Everyone knows ‘em.”

“I think they wanted to get rid of me. Both of ‘em. They cooked this whole thing up, but they weren’t satisfied with throwing me in the pen. Decided to steal from me too.”

“I don’t know anything about that, Ollie.”

"Yeah, I bet you don't." Ollie looked around the office and then approached the window that looked into the parking lot. "Guess I'll be payin' Mitch a visit. See who knew what. He still living on Lombard?"

"I think so," said Hafner. "Haven't seen Albert in some time, though. He was a summer fella if I remember."

"That's right," said Ollie. "I guess I'll have to wait for him. Gonna git to the bottom of this shit."

The man to Ollie's right adjusted his grip on the wooden bat as if he was about to take a pitch.

"When's that secretary coming back from lunch, Constable?"

"Leave her out of this. She's got nothing to do with it."

Ollie surveyed the parking lot through the window and then turned his ear toward the desk as if something caught his attention. He walked around to join his sons at the front of the desk. "That skinny bitch drives a Dodge, right? Just like the one parked in the lot." Ollie lowered the shotgun to the desk. "Guess I was right, boys. Pussy does make a man dumb." He gripped the shotgun pump with his left hand, racked it, and fired. The blast tore through the top of Hafner's desk at a downward angle spraying blood and wood shards across the constable's khaki shirt, gold badge, and the window behind him.

Hafner screamed and pushed his chair away from the desk. He stood up, but the bats connected and dropped him to the floor. Ollie's boys didn't stop swinging until they could see his brain through his cracked skull.

Two minutes later, Ollie Stoner and his blood-soaked boys walked from the constable's office into the lobby. Ollie wiped the shotgun's pump and stock with a handkerchief and tossed it behind Adrianne's desk. The three men were through the door when Ollie stopped, returned to the desk, picked up the Jonathan Valin novel, and rejoined his boys in the parking lot.

CHAPTER 15

I PULLED into the parking lot next to DTC Woodworking in downtown Detroit and parked next to a box truck that had the shop's logo and a few inches of road dust on the side. There were two dead trees looming over the parking lot and a gray Jeep Grand Cherokee parked next to the entrance.

DTC Woodworking was a legitimate operation, but it was also a front for Micah Dunbar's criminal activities. Dunbar was one of the cornerstones of the Detroit mob. He wasn't at the top of the food chain, but he was close. His network was entrenched deep throughout Michigan and bled into both Ohio and Indiana. I wasn't sure how deep it was, but as far as criminals go, he was the biggest one I knew, both figuratively and literally. The guy was bigger than most NFL linemen and was the type of person who didn't look over his shoulder in the most violent parts of town. He was always the baddest guy in the room.

As a PI, I could easily run the usual profile information on Holbrook. Who he worked with, how much time he'd served, how much he paid to the IRS, his spouses, kids, and bank accounts, but that wasn't what I wanted. I needed to know what I was walking into with Holbrook. How did he run his operation? Did he run a crew or an entire organization? What was he involved with? Anything that could help me prepare for my face-to-face with him in three days. Getting that type of information wasn't the same as running the typical background check on a babysitter, and I couldn't find what I was looking for in an online database. I needed an expert.

Dunbar could fill in the blanks, but getting him to talk wasn't going to be easy, given the last time I saw him, I leveled a .45 at his face and threatened to bury his entire crew. That's not something you easily forget, but Dunbar had no reason to come gunning for me since I had information on his

Cincinnati activities tucked away in a safe deposit box. I'd informed him the last time we butted heads that if any of his men moved on me, one of my associates would turn over everything I had on him to the FBI. It was safer for Dunbar to forget about me, but now I was about to ask him a personal favor, that might make him reevaluate our truce.

I walked through the front door and stepped into a medium-sized showroom packed with Shaker furniture, mirror frames, chests-of-drawers, tables, chairs, and desks. If I didn't know better, I'd swear I was in Amish country.

There was a black man with three fingers on his right hand, talking to an elderly couple who were looking over a four-drawer coffee table. I recognized him from the last time I saw Dunbar. From the way Three Fingers looked at me, he recognized me too.

I strolled over to the rear wall and stared at a row of wall clocks when a shadow appeared on the wall in front of me. I turned around and was face to face with Dunbar's armpit.

"Something I can help you find?" he said.

"I'm here to talk about a job."

"You might be interested in a Shaker nightstand or a blanket chest..."

"No, I'm here for some information," I said.

"Or maybe I can show you a steamer trunk or a craftsman-style barrister bookcase?"

"You're not hearing me, Dunbar. I'm here to talk about a job."

Dunbar crouched so we were eye to eye. "It's not my hearing that's fucked up. It's my vision. I must be hallucinating because I can't believe you're actually standing here in my shop. I told you three weeks ago that if I ever saw you again we'd have problems. And now here you are, Mr. Finn."

I took a step back and felt my shoulders press against one of the clocks on the wall. "I need to talk to you about someone named Mason Holbrook. He's a heroin dealer in Cincinnati. You know him?"

"Mason Holbrook?" Dunbar turned and looked toward the double swinging doors at the back of the room. "This is the showroom. Not a good place to talk." Dunbar motioned to Three Fingers who had finished with the elderly couple. "Davy Bill, why you don't take our friend here back to the workshop so we can talk?"

I looked around Dunbar's massive left shoulder at the twin metal doors. "No, thanks. We both know if I walk through those doors, I'm not walking back out."

"That might be true." Dunbar smiled. "Bottom line is you shouldn't have come here. It's best if you just leave now and go fuck yourself. You made a long drive for nothing." He turned and headed back toward the double doors.

"Come on, Dunbar. I just want to know who he is." Dunbar didn't stop. "There might be something in it for you."

Dunbar turned. He closed the twenty or so feet between us in three strides.

"There's nothing in it for me," he said. "You don't know what the fuck you've gotten yourself into." Dunbar stepped forward, bumping into my chest and sending me back a few feet. "I don't like you, Mr. Finn, and normally I wouldn't tell you shit, but I'm going to make an exception today because I want you to clearly understand who you're up against. Mason Holbrook isn't a heroin dealer. He runs one of the biggest criminal operations in the Midwest. Runs it from some horse farm near Indianapolis. If you're mixed up with him, you're in way over your head, and there's no way in hell I'm gettin' caught up in it."

"What do you mean, 'biggest criminal operation?' What's he into?"

"He's into everything a guy like him should be into. Heroin is a small piece of it, but it gets way bigger. Got some roughneck, named…" Dunbar thought for a moment. "Named Adler. He's bad news. Likes shovels. Why are you involved with him anyway?"

"It's not by choice. A friend…" I stopped myself. "Someone I know got roped into supplying fentanyl to Holbrook, and now my associate wants out. I've got a meeting with him in three days to discuss an exit strategy."

"Why is it that things have a way of escalating once you get involved?" I could feel Dunbar's breath on my face. "If I were you, I'd cut ties with your associate and disappear. Holbrook isn't someone you want to do business with." Dunbar turned back toward the double doors. "Stick to working with the dime-store criminals you're used to, and stay away from the big fish, or you might get eaten." He pushed open the double metal doors so hard they ricocheted off the walls on the other side and swung back open into the showroom.

Before stepping inside DTC Woodworking, I had no idea what I was up against with Holbrook. I still didn't have a lot to go on, but Dunbar had confirmed I'd stepped deeper into things than I wanted to. Dunbar was one of the few people who scared me, and I didn't like the idea of dealing with anyone who scared him.

I'd made that second mistake after all. It was a long drive home.

CHAPTER 16

I ARRIVED at Winan's coffee on Friday, a half-hour before Adler was to pick me up. I grabbed a large Highlander Grogg, took a seat at the front of the shop, and cracked open my Lee Child novel. My eyes shifted from the page to the street, and I saw a red minivan pull to a stop outside the coffee shop. I didn't pay it much attention at first, because the last thing I expected Adler to drive was a minivan, red or otherwise. But after a moment I looked up again to find Adler standing beside the vehicle, waving me out. Darby was nowhere to be found.

Nothing about this situation made me feel warm and fuzzy. I didn't make a habit of getting into vehicles with strange men, and I avoided minivans as much as possible, but this was the only opportunity I had to get Daryl out of his current situation and put all this behind us.

I walked out of the coffee shop. Adler slid open the side door. As I ducked my head to climb in, he grabbed my arm, threw me up against the passenger door, and patted me down.

"I'd hoped you bailed on us," he said. "Would have loved to hunt you down." He finished his pat-down and pushed me into the back of the minivan. "Course, I might still get my chance." He slid the door closed, returned to the driver's seat, and we pulled away from the curb.

Faith plays a large part in this job. Not faith in God, but faith that every criminal you work with won't plug you in the face Pulp Fiction style. From what Dunbar told me, these were bad people, but bad people want things too, and some things they can't get for themselves. That's why I knew Adler wasn't going to kill me. At least not yet. Mason Holbrook wanted something, and he was smart enough to recognize I could help him get it. If Dunbar was right, and Holbrook did run his operation from Indianapolis, I'd know what Holbrook was after in about two hours.

After a moment of silence, it was obvious that Adler wasn't the chatty type, so I flipped open my novel to pass the time. Every few minutes, I glanced up to check the road signs. Adler turned onto I-75, and then miles later, he picked up I-74. Indianapolis it was.

TWO-PLUS HOURS LATER, WE PULLED ONTO A freshly paved two-lane road. Sensing we were close to our destination, I closed the book and took in the scenery. There wasn't much. Mostly trees and more trees. We drove by a dilapidated graying barn that could have passed for a tobacco shack had it not been for the tractor and harvester poking out the front. Another quarter mile and we took a left onto a single-lane road. We passed a white sign with "Triple Bend Farm" embossed in gold lettering, and I saw a large white house and several barns on a hill maybe a half-mile out. The road gently curved around a bend, and if the sign was accurate, we'd see two more.

Adler stopped in front of a massive white colonial house. It had four columns, two wide bay windows, perfectly manicured landscaping, and looked like something out of a Hallmark television special.

Darby met the minivan in front of the house. He opened the sliding door and waved me out. Before I could stand up straight, an older man thrust a wrinkled hand in front of me.

"Mason Holbrook," he said. "Happy to meet you."

Holbrook was trim, in his late fifties or maybe early sixties. He wore a neatly-pressed short-sleeved white button-up collared shirt. The kind my grandfather always wore. The outline of two thick Velcro straps across his midsection were visible through his shirt, a telltale sign of a bullet-proof vest. His shirt was buttoned at the neck, and he wore a black leather bolo tie with a red gem at the top. A belt with the largest brass buckle I'd ever seen, probably some sort of rodeo prize, held up his ragged blue jeans. His short gray hair poked out from beneath a sun-faded cowboy hat, and a black watch adorned his right wrist. He looked more like a farmer than a drug kingpin.

I shook his hand.

"Comfortable ride?" he said.

I looked over my shoulder at the minivan. "I usually don't ride in that much style."

Holbrook grinned from ear to ear. "Ain't that right? I'm more at home in a pickup myself, but this one's pretty roomy."

He turned to Adler. "Any weapons?"

Adler shook his head.

"Good." He turned back to me. "Can't be too careful these days."

I nodded to his flak jacket. "I see that."

Holbrook smiled again. "Crazies everywhere."

"Ain't that the truth," I said. "Just the other day, some dipshit threatened to cut my daughter's throat. What's the world coming to?"

"Sorry about that." He put his hand on my shoulder, and I noticed the digital watch on his wrist wasn't the typical timepiece. It had a digital face that counted backward, like one of those Budweiser clocks you see in bars counting down to St. Patrick's Day or Cinco de Mayo.

"I'm sure you're eager to get into it," he said. "Let's take a little walk."

We walked away from the massive house toward a white barn. Adler and Darby followed us like two dogs looking for scraps. Adler kept his right hand behind his back. He looked eager to put me down at the first opportunity.

"You've got a nice piece of property here," I said.

"Three hundred acres. Been here for about thirty years."

I looked at the imposing barns. "You board horses?"

"We do a lot more than board 'em. I've got a thoroughbred breeding and a training operation too. We've trained two Preakness winners and one that finished second at the Derby."

We approached the open end of a large white barn with green trim.

"Aren't you in the wrong state?" I said. "I thought they only raised racehorses in Kentucky."

A cartoonish laugh came from Holbrook's mouth. "Kentucky has birthed the most winners, but they come from all over. Far away as California and Florida."

Holbrook led me into the barn. It had mahogany walls, and the place was cleaner than most of the homes I'd been in. The barn housed ten stalls per side, each with a sliding wooden door with brass bars. The top of the doors could be folded down to allow a horse to stick its head out of the stall. A lead rope, riding blanket, and brass nameplate hung from each door. The dozen ceiling fans spinning overhead emitted a low hum. Holbrook pointed down the right side of the barn.

"Most of these are yearlings here," he said. "They'll be ready to race next year." He pointed to the two front stalls. "Boy, these two here are gonna be something special. Both are competitive as hell. You get 'em out on the track, and they run like there's nothing they'd rather do. Real special."

He put his hands on his hips, and I could see the pride in his smile. "They're gorgeous animals," he said. "Especially when they're at full stride. Beautiful creatures." He turned back to me and slapped me on the shoulder again. "So, tell me about your friend, Dr. Jennings."

"He's not really my friend." The strong scent of hay wafted through the barn propelled by the fans above. “He’s more of a…” I struggled for the words. “We’re kind of like two convicts shackled together. Neither of us asked for the other, but sometimes life just shits on you.”

“I’m surprised you’re putting your neck on the line to get Dr. Jennings out of his current obligation. You not being so keen on ‘em.”

I looked over my shoulder to check if Adler and Darby were still behind us. They were.

“I’d hardly call it an obligation.”

Holbrook shrugged his shoulders. “Call it whatever you like, but the fact is, he’s supplying me with fentanyl, and it’s easier to continue getting it from him than to find someone else.”

“As I understand it, Christ Hospital is investigating the thefts. With the heat, he doesn’t think he can get it anymore.”

“That’s what he says. I’d wager he’d say anything he could to get me out of his life.”

“What do you want with it anyway? The fentanyl.”

“Ever do heroin?”

“No,” I said. “I’m fine with caffeine.”

Holbrook laughed. “Me too. Heroin is a sonofabitch, but just like any other high, it gets stale after a while. Users want the next big thing. The next great high. Cuttin’ fentanyl into the mix gives it that extra boost.”

Holbrook placed a bony finger on the mahogany wall and dragged it in an up-and-down motion as if admiring the wood’s rich color and smooth texture.

“I’ve heard people can die from it. Wouldn’t that hurt your business?”

“Heck, my boy. People can drown brushing their teeth.” Holbrook looked up. I followed his gaze to a man in blue scrubs standing at the other open end of the barn. Holbrook slipped his glasses out of his shirt pocket and jockeyed them onto his face. Then he waved, slipped his glasses back into his pocket, and motioned me to follow him. “You know what’s funny? The more people who die from my product, the hotter it gets. Buyers know it’s high-quality shit. Demand is through the roof, and I can’t keep up with it, which is why your pal is such an important asset to me. I used to get fentanyl from Columbia, but that place is wilder than a mustang now. Can't get much of anything outta there, so we have to secure it domestically. Which, again, is why Dr. Jennings' services are in high demand."

We reached the end of the barn, where the man in scrubs waited for us. "Excuse me for a moment, my boy," said Holbrook. He walked over to the man. "Is it positive?"

"It is, Mr. Holbrook." The man handed Holbrook a red file folder. "I'm sorry."

"Well, we did what we could, Doc. I'll take care of it from here." The man in scrubs nodded, turned, and walked toward a heavy-duty pickup parked outside the barn. Holbrook looked at the file folder and shook his head.

"Darn it," he whispered.

"Everything okay?" I said.

"Just some bad news from my vet." He waved me forward. "Come on. We got a lot to discuss."

We exited the mahogany barn and started toward a second barn, a smaller one, about fifty yards from the first.

"Excuse me for asking," I said. "You've got a legitimate business here with the horses. Why the heroin?"

"Because this business is damn expensive. I've got twenty-two full-time staff at this place. That includes breeders, trainers, veterinarians, even dieticians. And not a one of 'em is making minimum wage."

Dunbar seemed to think Holbrook was one of the biggest criminals in the Midwest. I had a hard time believing that because this guy seemed as ruthless as a retired schoolteacher. I didn't know what happened behind the scenes, but it was time to find out.

"I think we've danced around it enough," I said. "Let's talk about why I'm here."

"Right, enough with the small talk. I need you to find someone for me. And Darby says that's what you do. That right?"

"That's right."

"Are you good at it? At finding people."

"I like to think so."

Holbrook stopped, pulled a handkerchief from his pants pocket, tipped his cowboy hat, and wiped his forehead. "I hope so, Mr. Finn. I truly hope so."

"Who are you looking for?"

"It's my banker," he said. "He disappeared with quite a bit of my money. I want you to find him and bring my money back."

"How much money?"

"Five million dollars," said Holbrook wiping his forehead again.

"I assume we're not talking about your everyday bank teller."

"Got that right. I'm sure you can understand why someone like me doesn't patronize the local bank. I use a private banker who specializes in serving people like me. No reporting, no questions, and immediate access to cash."

Holbrook tucked the handkerchief back into his pocket as we arrived at the smaller barn. He bent down, pulled a key ring from his other pants pocket, and unlocked the fist-sized padlock on the barn door. He swung open the metal bracket, stepped back, and heaved the wooden doors open. He led me inside, Adler and Darby following close behind.

This barn was much smaller than the first. It was about fifty feet long, and unlike the first structure, this one had a low-beamed ceiling. There were four stalls on each side of the barn, and stacks of hay bales lined the walls, reaching to the ceiling. All of the stalls stood vacant except for the first one. There, a young horse stood in the corner. Its brass nameplate read Penny's Flame.

"This private banker of yours," I said. "He got a name?"

"No."

I felt the prickly hay particles penetrate my nasal passages as I breathed, and fought back a cough. "How do you work with him?" I said.

"It's completely anonymous. I call a phone number, and he picks up my deposit. When I need it back, I call him, and he brings it back. He keeps a small percentage of each deposit for himself."

Holbrook unlocked a latch on the side of the stable door and lowered the top half. The horse sniffed the air and approached us. Holbrook grabbed a long carrot out of a brown plastic bin next to the stall. He held it out, and the horse stuck his head out of the stall door and gnawed at the carrot.

“This banker, where does he keep the money?” I said.

“Don’t know. I don’t know who he is or where he keeps it. That’s kind of his business model.”

I had Holbrook pegged as an intelligent man. Until now. “That doesn’t seem like a very good strategy,” I said. “Trusting someone you don’t know with that kind of cash. You might want to look into something a bit safer. Maybe a savings and loan.”

Holbrook smiled. “I know you probably think I’m a fool, trusting my money to a ghost, but this has been the model for more than two decades. The entire relationship is based on mutual trust, and for the last twenty years, we’ve never had a problem.” He wiped his forehead with the back of his free hand. “The banker is more secure than any financial institution, Mr. Finn, and his very presence assures my cash is safe.”

"What's the benefit of working with him? To me, it seems riskier than other alternatives."

"Not really. The banker operates under three guidelines. My money stays in cash, it changes locations at least once a day, and it's available within a half-hour anytime, day or night. Plus, the banker's got a reputation for eliminating threats. Last year, I heard that one of his customers tried to shake him down. The banker skinned him alive and nailed him to the side of his house. The neighborhood kids found him on their way to the bus stop in the morning. His reputation alone is enough to keep most vultures away. You tell me an alternative that's as secure or accessible."

I couldn't. In theory, the plan seemed solid, but it relied completely on trust. I hate dealing with banks. Sometimes I have to wait for checks to clear before I can get to my money, but I know that when I do come calling, it'll be there. I don't really care if a bank reports my deposits to the IRS, but I'm not sitting on 5 million either. Nor are criminals actively scheming to liquidate my bank account, which I imagined was a real and constant threat to someone like Holbrook.

The grimace on my face must have told Holbrook that I wasn't sold on the banker's method.

"I'm not stupid if that's what you think," he said. "But a guy like me doesn't have a lot of options. I have to use higher-risk methods."

"How did you find out he was missing?"

"I called him to make a withdrawal, and he never showed up. That's never happened before. Until then, he was like clockwork."

"When was this?" I said.

"A week ago."

"I'll need that phone number. The one you call for deposits and withdrawals. Maybe I can trace him that way."

"Not likely," he said. "The number always changed. It was one of the banker's security precautions. He would mail me a postcard with a new phone number every few weeks."

Holbrook handed me the red folder he'd received from the man in scrubs as Penny's Flame finished the carrot. Holbrook grasped the horse's bridle with his left hand and gently rubbed its face between its forehead and muzzle with his right.

"Any theories on what might have happened?" I said.

"The banker has been a trusted partner for years, so I know he didn't turn and run. I think someone got to him. Some of my associates used him, but it's impossible to know who else he worked for. It could be anyone. My gut is that one of them was able to track the banker down. They got to him and took the bank for themselves. That's all I can think of."

"That seems likely," I said. "Especially if he appears every time you call him to pick up a deposit. What's to stop someone from calling him with a pickup, only to jump him when he arrives? Seems pretty simple."

He stroked the horse again, this time behind its ear. "Not really. I don't think he made the pickups himself. It was a younger guy. I don't know much about the banker, but I know he was older. Like I said, I've used him for twenty-some years. The most recent guy who did the pickups looked younger than thirty."

"Maybe it was the courier."

"Could be. I don't know what happened to the money once it left here. That was all confidential. I only know that he moved it from place to place to keep it safe. He was very thorough with his process, so I can only imagine he'd be just as thorough with his employees."

"You seem to know a lot about this guy," I said. "Except for the important details."

"I looked into you, Mr. Finn, and I know you're capable. And if you come through, maybe I could keep you around. Use you again."

"I've heard that before," I said. "So to sum up, you're asking me to retrieve your five million dollars from a man with no identity, no known location, and with no way of contacting him?"

"I'm not asking." Holbrook smiled again. "Get my money back, and we sever all ties with Dr. Jennings."

"And the fee for recovering your money?"

"Your fee is Dr. Jennings' freedom, and that's all. However, if you find the banker's money and whoever got to him, I'd assume you could drum up some additional business from his client list. I imagine he stole from all of us, and if I'm looking for him, all his other clients are too."

Holbrook withdrew a folding knife from his back right pocket and opened the blade. In one quick motion, he stepped to the side and drew it across the horse's throat. The horse staggered, but Holbrook held tight to the bridle, holding it at an angle so the blood sprayed down across the stall door and onto the ground below but missed Holbrook and me. He knew what he was doing. The blood flow slowed to a trickle. The horse made a gurgling sound, and Holbrook released the bridle. The horse collapsed onto the stall floor, kicked its legs a few times, and stopped moving.

He held out the knife like a discarded tissue, and Darby jumped forward and grabbed it.

Holbrook snapped the red folder from my hand and tapped it with his finger. "Vet's report," he said. "Equine anemia. Highly infectious. Couldn't risk it spreading."

"What is this place?" I looked around again.

"Quarantine," said Holbrook. "It's where animals come to die." He turned to his men and placed his hand on my shoulder for a third time. "Good news. Mr. Finn here is going to prove you fellas wrong by finding my money." He turned to me. "They don't think you can do it, but I have faith in you, my boy."

WE RETURNED TO HOLBROOK'S HOUSE. ADLER slid open the minivan's door, and I climbed into the back. He slipped into the driver's seat while Darby fumbled through his pocket and pulled out a cell phone. He held it up and snapped my picture. "In case we have to identify you later," he said.

"This is all I've got to get you started," said Holbrook. He snapped his fingers, and Darby handed me four postcards. "These are the postcards the banker sent every time he changed his phone number. Not sure if they'll help or not." Holbrook smiled at Adler, who smirked in the driver's seat like a chauffeur about to cart around a gaggle of drunk college girls. "Good luck, my boy. I'm sure you'll come through for Dr. Jennings and me.

"What's with the watch," I said pointing to his wrist. "I noticed it runs backward."

"You're an observant one. Just a reminder that we all run out of time."

Darby jerked on the sliding door, but I stopped it with my foot.

"I'll find your banker friend, and I'll get your money, Mr. Holbrook. And then we're going to have a chat about what your man Adler did to the woman and girl at Dr. Jennings' home."

"I'm sure we will, son," he said.

I moved my foot, and Darby slammed the door closed.

CHAPTER 17

ADLER WAS as talkative on the way back to Cincinnati as he had been on the way to Indianapolis, so I took the time to gather my thoughts on the banker.

The idea of a criminal banker who stockpiled money for the mob was an interesting concept. Most people still believe that criminals simply throw their money into a Swiss bank account and call it a day, but that's Hollywood, not reality. Swiss banks are obligated to turn over details of suspicious accounts—those linked to anyone involved in illegal activity—if asked. There's a lot of paperwork and legal jockeying involved, but the bottom line is that foreign accounts aren't the safe haven they once were. Rely on a foreign bank to hide your cash, and you're going to have a short career as a criminal.

This wasn't going to be an easy case, but given what Holbrook shared, I had three theories.

One: the banker got popped by the authorities and was sitting in a cell somewhere. Maybe he got picked up for something related to his cash inventory, or maybe he had an open warrant and got nailed at a traffic stop. Maybe he'd been under investigation and his time was up. If he was picked up, there'd be a record somewhere, and I had enough law enforcement contacts to find out if anyone fitting his business model was under investigation at the state or federal level. This would be easy to run down. The others, not so much.

Two: Maybe the banker decided it was time to stop working with people like Holbrook, and he took the money and disappeared. Let's say he had five clients, each with five million in the bank. That's a lot of incentive to make a run for it. Holbrook said he had history with this guy, but you get enough money on the table, and history doesn't mean much. I didn't like Option Two, because the banker would be long gone, out of the country gone, and things get complicated on foreign soil.

Three: Someone got to the banker, killed him, and took the bank. Regardless of what reputation this guy had, just like history, reputation loses weight as more money builds up on the table. People do crazy shit for a few thousand dollars, let alone several million. That made the most sense, but it also raised additional questions.

Holbrook mentioned a courier, but I had no idea how deep the banker's organization went. The more people working for him, the more likely it was an inside job. If you've got the stomach and the skills, it's easy to pillage criminals because they can't run to the authorities. They can, however, handle things on their own, but if you're smart, it's easy to slip away. For anyone willing to take the risk, someone like the banker would be a huge mark.

Of course, there were a host of other possibilities. Maybe he choked to death on a muffin or got hit by a city bus. Maybe he was rotting away in a house somewhere with a bag of Holbrook's money in his closet.

The other thought I couldn't shake was the shithole in the front seat. I had a nagging suspicion that Adler was going to be on my ass at every step of the investigation. It was obvious Holbrook wanted to find the banker and retrieve his cash as soon as possible, and he'd tap Adler to push me if I slowed down. Today, I was a valued asset, but there was a fine line between a valued asset and a loose end. At some point, I would cross that line. But I'd have to deal with that later.

THE RED MINIVAN STOPPED IN FRONT OF WINAN'S Coffee. Adler turned and handed me a card with a telephone number.

"Call with updates," he said.

I stepped out.

"And tell Brooke I said hello."

I turned, but Adler had already pulled away from the curb. It was almost six o'clock. Brooke would drop off Becca at my place in an hour as usual. The banker would have to wait.

CHAPTER 18

I WALKED through my front door to find Albert on the couch reading the newspaper.

“Where you been?” he said.

“Indianapolis.”

“Now, why in the hell would you be in Indianapolis?”

“Business,” I said.

“What kind of business? You didn’t mention anything to me. What’s in Indianapolis?”

“Seems Daryl got himself into some trouble.”

"Brooke's Daryl? Good for him," he said, turning a page. "Maybe now Brooke'll cut him loose, and we can get you two back together."

"It's not that simple. He got wrapped up with the wrong people. They paid Brooke a visit looking for him. And who said anything about wanting to get back together?"

Albert tossed the newspaper to the side and stood up. "What the hell are you talking about? Paid her a visit?"

"She's okay. They just scared the shit out of her. Becca too."

"What's Daryl into?"

"Got roped into securing narcotics for some heavy hitters. It went south."

"So what?" he said. "Why do you give a shit what happens to that asshole? They just improved your situation."

"Not at Brooke and Becca's expense."

Albert's jaw clenched. "What happened to Becca?"

"Nothing I can't handle," I said.

"Spill it, Finn." He tapped his index finger on my sternum, like some high school bully. "This is family you're talking about."

"Daryl was supplying fentanyl. He was stealing it from the hospital where he works, but he got cold feet. Now his handlers in Indianapolis want to re-open the pipeline, and they're using Brooke and Becca as leverage."

"And what are you going to do about it?"

"They're looking for someone. Someone who disappeared with their bankroll."

"And you're going to help them find him?"

"Yeah," I said. "I find him, and they release Daryl from his contract."

"I still don't understand why you just don't throw Daryl to the wolves. He got himself into this mess, so why should you bail him out?"

I looked down and shook my head. "Like him or not—"

"I don't," Albert interrupted.

"Regardless, he's still a huge part of Brooke's life. Becca's too. So that means I'm getting him out of trouble."

"I don't like it, Finn. I've got a bad feeling about it."

"That makes two of us."

BROOKE KNOCKED ON THE FRONT DOOR AT 7:00 pm sharp. I opened the door and watched as Becca wheeled her penguin suitcase into my apartment. "Hi, Daddy," she said as she wrapped her arms around my waist.

"Hello, sweetheart." I took the suitcase. "Dad, why don't you show Becca your bookshelves?"

Albert motioned Becca over to the guest bedroom. "Come on, sweetheart," he said. "You're going to love this."

After Becca and Albert disappeared, I stepped out onto the breezeway with Brooke. "How's the head?"

"Fine. Nothing forty ibuprofen couldn't cure."

"How are you holding up at your sister's place?"

"We're good," she said. "What did you learn from Daryl?"

"I learned he makes poor decisions. I can't believe he's responsible for people's lives. He can't even take care of his own."

"How bad is it?"

"It's not good."

"Can you get him out of it?"

"I think so, but I have to give Daryl credit. When he steps into something, he steps in deep."

"What does that mean?" she said.

"It means he crawled into bed with some pretty bad people."

"That doesn't make me feel any better, Finn."

"Don't worry about it," I said. "This guy who's been working Daryl… He's looking for someone, and I told him I'd find him. If I do, he cuts Daryl loose."

"And if you don't?"

"I don't want to think about that. And neither should you." I heard Albert and Becca walk back into the living room. "Go home and get some sleep. Don't give it a second thought. I'll take care of it."

She hugged me longer than usual. "Thank you. Have fun with Becca." She turned and walked toward the steps.

"Always do," I said.

MY WEEKLY DINNER WITH BECCA AND MY FATHER was a welcome distraction from what awaited me on Monday. The three of us arrived at Dewey's Pizza on Montgomery Road at 7:30 pm. Dewey's had become our weekly Friday night tradition. Same night, same pepperoni pizza. My father and I always downed a few beers while Becca went for a lemonade.

Normally, I wasn't much for routines. If you do what I do for a living and you fall into a routine, bad things happen. It's why I take different routes to and from my apartment every day and run errands at irregular hours. You never know who might be keeping eyeballs on you, but it's better to be paranoid and safe than be predictable and dead.

I suspended that philosophy every Friday for Becca. She relied on routine. Almost every hour of her school day was structured, and I'd learned over the years that she thrived in an environment that favored consistency. I did what I could to foster that need for routine, even if it meant looking over my shoulder every ten minutes while I shoved pizza down my throat. It was a small price to pay to watch my daughter smile while sword-fighting my father with a garlic breadstick.

"So how's Aunt Allison?" I said.

"She's good. She's really nice. And likes to bake cupcakes."

"I remember she always loved the kitchen," I said. I rarely used my daughter as an informant, but I couldn't resist digging up some intel. "Has Daryl been by?" I bit into a slice of pizza and then recoiled as it singed the top of my mouth. "To see you and your mom?"

"No. She's not talking to Daryl. She said they had a fight. That's why we're staying with Aunt Allison."

"Right," I said, eyeing my father.

Becca blew on her pizza slice and took a small bite out of the end. “Aunt Allison doesn’t like Daryl either. She uses a lot of sandpaper words when she talks about him.”

“Does your aunt use a lot of those words when she talks about me?”

“No,” said Becca. “She uses some. But more when she talks about Daryl.” She took another bite. “Mom says I shouldn’t use sandpaper words.”

“That’s right,” I said. “You shouldn’t.”

“Why not?” said Albert. He winked at Becca. “They’re the best kind of words.” He raised a finger to signal the waitress for the check. “Tell me about cheerleading, kiddo. How’s that going?”

“It’s fun. We’re still having practice. We haven’t had our first game yet. Mom wrote it on the calendar.” She turned to me. “Are you coming to the basketball game?”

“I wouldn’t miss it,” I said. “Do you know all your cheers?”

“Still learning ‘em. I’ll know ‘em by the game.”

"I didn't know they fielded a basketball team for second graders," said Albert. "Probably not many dunks."

"It's non-competitive," I said. "They go at a slower pace, and they don't keep score."

"Don't keep score? How do they know who wins?"

"That's why it's called non-competitive."

"Sounds like a waste of time to me. Not to keep score." Albert pointed his slice at me. "You've seen the cheerleading outfits? They're not inappropriate, are they?"

"Haven't seen 'em, but it's a Catholic school. How bad could they be? They're probably wearing turtlenecks and parkas."

"Good," said my father. "Because if they're wearing anything short, I'll have some sandpaper words for the administration."

The waitress brought the check in a black leather case. Albert paid in cash as I polished off the last slice of pizza. We left Dewey's and hit the ice cream parlor across the street. Two hours later, I tucked Becca into bed in our guest room. I turned in a few hours after.

On Saturday, Becca and I went to the zoo and then spent a few hours at an outdoor playground downtown. Albert made some kind of chicken dish for dinner, and we made it halfway through a Harry Potter movie before Becca fell asleep in my arms on the couch. I dropped her off at Aunt Allison's house early on Sunday morning so she and Brooke could make the 9:00 am church service.

Then I got back to work.

CHAPTER 19

From his Escalade, the man in the green cap opened a bottle of apple juice and tore open the pre-made turkey sandwich he'd grabbed from the gas station down the street. His eyes moved from the sandwich to the cell phone on his dashboard to the Shillito Lofts apartment complex a hundred yards in front of him.

He watched as a Lincoln Navigator pulled into the lot. The driver stepped out of the vehicle, looked over his shoulder to survey the lot, and climbed the steps to the fourth-floor unit.

After dropping off Becca at her aunt's house, I returned to my apartment to the smell of sizzling bacon and the sight of Albert manning the stove in his bathrobe. He squinted and looked at me over his thin bony nose. "So spill it," he said.

"Spill what?"

"Daryl's situation." He slipped two eggs from a skillet onto a plate. "I've been biting my tongue all weekend. What's going on?"

"Daryl's handlers agreed to cut him loose if I find someone for them."

"Who do you have to find?"

"They've been using a private banker. Seems he up and left town with their cash. They want me to find him and bring back their money."

Albert used a fork to lift six strips of bacon out of the skillet, blotted them with a paper towel, and placed them next to the eggs. "How hard will he be to find?"

"It's not going to be easy. They didn't give me much to go on. No name, no description, and no address. Just a disconnected phone number."

"Not much to work with."

"Thanks, Dad. I know." I looked at the plate. "Are you going to eat all of that?"

"It's not for you," he said, placing the plate on the table. "I've been thinking. Maybe you could use some help with this. Make sure it gets done right and quick. I don't like the idea of my granddaughter hanging in the balance."

"No, thanks, I don't want to get you wrapped up in this, too. I can handle it."

"Christ, I wasn't going to help you, but I know someone who can."

I ran through the mental Rolodex of Albert's known associates. The only one dumb enough to get roped into something like this was Mitch Skinner, but he was pushing seventy and lived twelve hundred miles away in the backwoods of Maine.

"No offense, Dad, but I think this is a bit higher than Mitch Skinner's pay grade."

"Hell, no. I wouldn't drag Mitch into this. He'd get us all killed. I've got someone else in mind." He poured a cup of coffee and set it down next to the plate.

"I said, no, thanks. I've got it under control."

"Don't sound like it."

"I've got it covered," I said.

Albert pointed to his breakfast. "Don't touch that. I'll be right back." He slipped the wireless phone from its cradle on the end table, walked into his bedroom, and closed the door. I walked into the kitchen and grabbed a coffee mug from the cabinet.

THE MAN IN THE GREEN CAP POLISHED OFF HIS turkey sandwich, crushed the plastic wrapper in his hand, and plunged it into the empty apple juice bottle. He sat back in the driver's seat and watched as someone on the fourth floor raised a window shade. He pulled his hat down over his eyes and watched the apartment breezeway until the buzzing cell phone on the console shattered his concentration.

My father had only been in his bedroom for a few minutes when he returned to the kitchen and poured a second cup of coffee.

"I said I could handle it, dad. I don't need you bringing in some ringer to mess things up."

He blew across the top of the mug and took a sip. "This guy can help you. He's really good."

"Who did you call?"

There was a knock at the door.

I looked at Albert, who took another sip of his coffee. "You better get that," he said.

I walked toward the front door, slipped the .45 from my messenger bag on the kitchen table, and held it tight behind my back. I stood on the left side of the doorframe and torqued my body so I could look through the peephole while staying away from the center of the door. I squinted and peered through the tiny lens.

On the other side, partially distorted from the concave lens and obscured by a green baseball cap, my brother Connor stared back at me.

CHAPTER 20

CONNOR WAS five years older than me. When I was in the seventh grade, he graduated high school and then left for the Army the next day. He did his basic and AIT in Missouri, then he went onto Airborne School and completed Ranger School at Fort Benning, Georgia. I lost the thread from there.

Aside from returning home for my mother's funeral five years ago, I hadn't seen him since. Albert provided sporadic updates on Connor over the years, and the last I remembered, he was living somewhere near Boston.

"You've got to be shitting me," I said to my father as I dropped the weapon back inside my messenger bag and then opened the door.

"Hello, Finn," said Connor. He winked and then slipped off his green baseball cap and handed it to me as he stepped over the threshold. He looked at Albert, who still stood in the kitchen, sipping his coffee. "Dad."

My father smiled and nodded as if he'd just seen Connor yesterday.

"What the shit?" I said, tossing the cap onto the dining room table.

He slapped me on the shoulder. "It's been a while."

"Five years," I said. "What are you doing here?"

"Had a problem in town and needed to take care of it. Thought I'd swing by and see you two."

"Just in time," said Albert. "Finn's got himself in a bit of a pickle." He pointed to the kitchen table. "Connor, I made breakfast."

I looked at my father and contemplated for a moment crushing his skull with the still steaming skillet on the stovetop.

"That so?" said Connor "Spill it."

"I'm not in a pickle," I said.

"Then what is it? Maybe I can help you out."

"Look, Connor, no offense, but this is something I need to handle myself." I turned back to Albert. "I'm not swapping out brake pads here."

"You don't think I'm qualified to help?" said Connor.

"I don't know a goddamn thing about you."

"What do you want to know?" he said.

"You can start by telling me why you're really here."

"I had business in Cincinnati," he paused. "Defense and security consulting."

"Elaborate," I said.

He paused as if thinking about how much he really wanted to tell me. "Okay, if you really want to know, I had to mop up a little fallout thanks to someone putting a few slugs into Charles Bishop."

Charles Bishop was a black-market information broker who hired me for my last case. He paid me to find someone who was blackmailing him, and after I did, he set me up and handed me to his competition, who tied me to a chair and tried to suffocate me with a nasty mix of ammonia and plant fungicide. A business associate of mine plugged Bishop in his RV before skipping town. When Bishop first hired me he mentioned getting my contact information from an associate in Boston. At the time, I had no reason to think it was my brother who set our relationship in motion. Now it was clear.

"That was you?" I said. "You sent Bishop to me?"

He nodded. "I've been keeping tabs on you and Dad for a while. I followed your career as a PI. Heard you lost your license, got divorced, and then went off the grid. Also heard you started working underground after losing the PI gig. I run in some of the same circles. Heard about the Bishop job, figured you could use the cash, and thought I'd throw you a bone."

“That bone tried to kill me,” I said.

“I’m sincerely sorry about that. I’d worked with Bishop on and off for a few years, and I thought he was solid. I didn’t know things would turn out the way they did. Figured I could hook you two up, and it would be a long-term thing. Stability doesn’t come around too often in our business.”

“And what kind of business are you in, Connor? I thought you were an Army Ranger.”

“I am, but I’ve got a side business that introduces people like you to people like Bishop. The Army helped me establish a lot of relationships with people who have a variety of skill sets.” Connor’s phone buzzed. He slipped it from his pocket and looked at the screen. “I help people make connections with others who can help them do whatever it is they need to do.”

“You’re some type of criminal recruiter?” I said.

“Are you a criminal, Finn?”

“I don’t classify myself as such.”

“Neither do I. But sometimes things need to get done, and sometimes I help figure out who’s going to do it.” He studied my face. “Finn, I really am sorry about Bishop. I had no idea things would turn out that way. I hope you at least made some cash before the shit hit the fan."

"I broke even," I said.

"Sorry it didn't go better." Connor checked his phone again. "So, I honored my side of the bargain. Told you why I'm here. Now it's your turn. Tell me what you got cooking? I'd really like to help."

Even though I hadn't seen Connor in five years, I could see in his eyes that he was sincere. Holbrook wasn't someone I was used to dealing with, and the idea of having to find the banker with nothing to go on and my ex-wife and daughter in the balance made my stomach do summersaults. I wasn't sure if I could pull this off alone, and if I had to have someone in my corner, Connor seemed as good as anyone. He also said he made some connections in the Army, and sometimes connections are what make or break a case.

"What do you know about finding people who don't exist?" I said.

"More than you might think."

Connor's phone buzzed again. He checked the screen and shook his head. "I've got to take care of something that can't wait. I'll be back first thing tomorrow, and we can get started finding your man. You can fill me in then."

"You just got here," I said.

"I know." He held up his phone. "Blowback. It can't wait. You've got my word. Starting tomorrow, I'm all yours. No distractions until we take care of this." Connor reached out and shook my hand. "It really is good to see you again, little brother." He waved to Albert, who nodded back.

"You too," I said, watching Connor grab his cap and walk out of the apartment.

"Guess you can have it," said Albert.

"Have what?"

"The breakfast."

CHAPTER 21

Over the years, I'd found a slew of people. They ranged from bail jumpers to insurance scammers to hackers and career criminals. Most, if not all, of these people thought they'd covered their tracks, but none of them did. Finding someone is easy when you know where to look, and thanks to the Internet, most databases are available online, which means you can find almost anyone in a day or two without leaving the comfort of the couch. And they've got databases for everything. Motor vehicle registration, criminal records, marriage licenses, fishing licenses, credit bureaus, social security databases. The options are endless, and no matter how much a skip tries to hide one area of their identity, they always forget something simple, and that's how I nail them.

The secret is in the profile. A profile is a data sheet, complete with all the details of someone's life. Birthdate, social security number, spouse's name, previous addresses, current or past employers. All of these components are like breadcrumbs. Everyone leaves breadcrumbs, and once I find one, I'll find another, and then another, until they lead me right to your door. No one can disappear completely, no one I've been hired to find anyway. All it takes is time, patience, and knowing which rock to look under.

My last case—finding a no-name hacker who was blackmailing my client, Bishop—was my hardest to date, but thanks to a lucky break, I cracked that case in a few days. It all came down to an Internet forum post from nearly a decade ago. That's what gave up my mark. A simple post to an IT forum. An afterthought to him, and a nail in his coffin for me.

But in all of my past cases, I had something to work with. A name, an email address, a past, a place to start. This case was different. The banker's entire business model rested on his ability to remain anonymous. I was fascinated by the story Holbrook told me, but what enthralled me the most was the dichotomy of the relationship, one built on trust and anonymity, two things that usually don't play nice with one another. But this was a symbiotic relationship. Both the banker and his clients coexisted in the belly of the same criminal ecosystem.

The criminal organizations the banker worked with needed a secure channel where they could deposit and withdraw cash. Traditional banks were out. But, any of these clients, if they knew the banker's identity, could make a play for his cash, removing him and possibly their own competition from the gene pool. Everyone had something big to lose. For the banker, it was his life, and for his clients, it was their bankroll. As long as everyone stayed in line, they all flourished under the model, but if anyone broke the unspoken commitment to live and let live, everyone would wither away. And that's what was happening. Either one of the banker's clients discovered his identity and location, buried him under a few feet of concrete, and took the bankroll, or the banker finally decided to make a run with the cash. Neither scenario comforted me.

Connor returned to our apartment at 8:00 am the next morning. I'd been awake for two hours and was already on my second pot of coffee. Albert still snored from the comfort of his bedroom as Connor and I dove into the case.

"Where do you want to start?" said Connor slipping off his beige jacket and laying it over a chair.

"How about we start with you telling me where you've been for the last five years and why I haven't heard from you since Mom's funeral?"

"This again? I told you why I was here. About Bishop."

"You told me why you're here, but not where you've been."

"Finn, look, by the end of the case, you'll know everything there is to know about me, but I'd rather get started on finding your friend. The past five years can wait."

I stared at Connor, and he stared back. I was hesitant to bring him in on the banker, but I needed the help, and he was all I had at the moment. I was also eager to get started, and since his past didn't have a direct impact on the banker's whereabouts, it could wait.

"Before this is over, I want the whole story," I said.

"And you'll get it. You've got my word."

I grabbed my messenger bag and set on the kitchen chair. "Let's go over what we know," I said. "Holbrook told me that he and the banker had three guidelines. The money was in cash, the banker moved the cash at least once per day, and the cash had to be accessible within thirty minutes." I pulled a 1983 State Farm road atlas, which was the size of a placemat, from my bag and plunked it onto the table. Connor's wide eyes told me it had been a while since he'd seen one.

"Looks like the one dad used to keep in the back of that light-blue station wagon," he said. "The one we always took on vacations as kids."

"Where do you think I got this one?" I thumbed through the pages. "I've had it stashed in the back of my closet for years. I'm assuming the cities haven't moved since '83."

I opened the atlas to the Indiana section. The first page showed the entire Hoosier State with its network of red and blue highways and interstates that resembled the human circulatory system. The second page was divided into two sections. The top half of the page was a map of Indianapolis and the surrounding area. The bottom of the page was divided between similar maps of Fort Wayne and Evansville.

I grabbed a pen and marked the location of Greenwood, Indiana, the location of Holbrook's farm, which was about fifteen miles south of Indianapolis. Then I swiped a five-dollar bill from my wallet, laid it on the map's bar scale, and ticked off the thirty-mile mark. I placed the corner of the bill on the black dot indicating the city of Greenwood and used the mark I'd made to transfer a thirty-mile radius around the city.

"There's our target area," I said. "If the banker can deliver Holbrook's cash within thirty minutes, he has to be operating somewhere within the circle."

"If he hasn't fled," said Connor. "If he's on the run, the radius isn't going to mean much."

"It's been a week, so if he's still alive, you're right, he's probably long gone." I tapped the pen inside the circle. "But his identity is still somewhere in this circle. Once we can identify him, we can start to track him."

Connor and I had been so focused on the map in front of us that we hadn't seen Albert emerge from his bedroom. It wasn't until he clanked the coffee pot against a ceramic mug that I realized he'd joined us.

"Look at you two," said Albert. "Back together again." He took a seat, stared at the map as if he recognized it, and took a sip. "So, what-a-we got?"

"So far, we got a circle on a shitty atlas," said Connor.

"And a phone number," I said. "But it's not going to give us much."

Usually, a phone number was gold. I could toss it into a reverse lookup database and find a name or go through the phone company and get a billing address, but Holbrook said the number changed every few weeks, which meant the banker was using a burner phone. Burner phones are a bitch to track, because they're cheap, disposable, pre-paid phones with dedicated numbers. I can still run the number through a reverse look-up system, but the best I could do is get a carrier, not an individual name, and even then, the carrier name might not be accurate.

"Is he using a burner?" said Connor.

I nodded. "According to Holbrook, the banker was buying and tossing phones every few weeks to stay hidden."

"Thanks to crappy TV crime dramas, everyone thinks burners are untraceable," said Connor. "But that's not true."

I nodded again. "Of course, without a subpoena or a contact at the NSA, we're not going to get far."

"You could canvas the local phone stores and see if they recognize anyone who's buying a new phone every few weeks. Pretty odd behavior." Connor thought for a moment. "But there's got to be more than a hundred mobile phone retailers in Indy and he's probably going out of town to buy them. Or he's getting them online."

"What else you got?" said Albert.

I pulled the four postcards that Holbrook gave me from my bag and tossed them onto the kitchen table. "After the banker switches phone numbers, he passes the new number to Holbrook using postcards."

Connor flipped through the postcards. "They're all postmarked in Indy, so your radius fits." He studied the postcards again. "I've got contacts at a few wireless carriers, so I might be able to get someone to triangulate the numbers. It's not a slam dunk, but it's a start."

My father stood up and slapped Connor and me on our shoulders.

"Glad to see the Bandit and the Snowman back together again," he said, and walked toward his bedroom.

"How quickly do you need this done?" said Connor.

"The quicker, the better," I said.

"Let me see what I can dig up through my network. Give me twenty-four hours, and I'll let you know what I find."

Connor stood up to leave.

“Where you going? Thought we were in this together?”

“We are,” said Connor slipping on his jacket. “But let’s not waste our time until we’ve got a clear trail to walk down. Twenty-four hours isn’t going to kill you.” He opened the door and stepped out, then turned back, the crisp morning air blowing into the living room from the breezeway. “Why are you looking for this guy, anyway?”

I explained the details.

“Why doesn’t this Daryl gent find your banker himself? It’s his mess.”

“Daryl couldn’t find his dick in the shower with GPS and a magnifying glass. I’m doing this more for Brooke and Becca than anything else. I don’t like Daryl, but I can’t let him go down like this.”

“You’re a bigger man than me. I’m not sure I could bring myself to help someone who’s banging my wife.”

“Ex-wife.”

He started to close the door.

"These aren't small-time stick-up kids," I said. "They're dangerous people, Connor."

"I'd hope so. Wouldn't want to drive all the way from Beantown for something you could handle yourself." He winked and closed the door behind him.

I didn't like sitting around and doing nothing, but Connor was right; there was no reason to spin our wheels until we had something definite on the burner phone. It's like being lost in the woods. Better to orient yourself and find your bearings before starting your hike out. Otherwise, you start off in the wrong direction and end up deeper in the woods, worse off than when you started. The banker's phone numbers were the only lead I had, so if it meant waiting twenty-four hours for my next breadcrumb, so be it.

CHAPTER 22

THE BLACK PICKUP truck eased into the parking lot of Palmer's Restaurant and Grocery on Route 191 in Meddybemps, Maine. The gravel popped under the truck's weight. William parked the truck in front of the store. Peter had jumped out of the bed and opened the restaurant's front door before William killed the engine. Ollie stepped out of the passenger side, and all three men walked into the building.

"How do you know he'll be here?" said Peter.

"Old shit is always here," said Ollie tucking the revolver into his waistband under his shirt.

Meddybemps, Maine had two watering holes. One was the 6,700-acre lake, and the other was

Palmer's Restaurant and Grocery. Part sundry and part bar, Palmer's was the place to find townies trading tales of fishing, logging, and anything else that passed the time, all under the watchful eye of Jack Palmer, the owner, cook, bartender, waiter, and grocery clerk.

Ollie and his boys dismissed the grocery side of the building and stepped into the restaurant side. They walked past the several booths, past the long pine bar, and approached the man playing pool in the red-and-black flannel shirt and worn jeans.

"Thought I'd find you here," said Ollie.

"Hello, Ollie," said Mitch Skinner wrapping both hands around his pool cue. "Figure you ain't here to play pool."

"Got that right. You and me got some things to work out, Mitch." Ollie scanned the room. "I don't guess Albert Harding's with you?"

"Nope. Long gone. Hasn't been back this way in three years or so."

"I should 'a guessed that piece 'a shit would have turned tail and run. Course, now you're probably wishin' you'd done the same."

"I'm not much for running," said Mitch. "Too old for that shit."

Peter and William flanked Mitch from the side, trapping him between two pool tables.

Jack Palmer, a lanky man in his late fifties, emerged from a side storage room carrying a box of hamburger buns. He stopped, arched his head forward and looked at Ollie through crooked glasses.

"Been a while since I seen you in here, Ollie," said Jack.

"Yep. Been about three years, Jack." Ollie nodded at Mitch. "Thanks to this piece 'a shit here."

"Can I get you and your boys something to eat?" Jack walked passed Ollie and set the cardboard box on the bar. "Got a fresh shipment of clams. Fry 'em up real good for ya."

"No, thanks. We're not here to eat. Just came in to see Mitch about something."

"All right. Let me know if you change your mind." Jack picked up the box and moved it to the floor behind the bar.

Ollie leaned over the pool table, grabbed the white cue ball, and slammed it into the corner pocket. "Game's over, Mitch. Time for you to come with us."

Peter and William each grabbed hold of Mitch's arms and pulled him out from behind the pool table. Mitch reached for the table, but William slammed a fist into his side, then kicked his legs out from under him, while Peter dragged him toward the front of the restaurant.

"Let's go have a talk about a boat," said Ollie. "And your house on Lombard."

"I got nothing to say to you, Ollie." Mitch struggled against the four arms that pulled him across the floor. "And you're not getting the house."

"What you did ain't right, Mitch. Three fucking years. A guy my age can't part with that kind of time."

"Maybe not," said a voice. "But I can't let you take him out of here like this."

Ollie turned to find Jack Palmer standing behind the bar, his right eye sighting down the barrel of a rifle.

“This don’t concern you, Jack,” said Ollie.

“You come in here and try to drag a man out of my bar? You’re damn right it concerns me.”

“You need to think about what you’re doing here,” said Ollie. “You want to risk your neck for this asshole?”

“Some men are worth standing up for,” said Jack. “I don’t know what score you got to settle, but he ain’t going out like this.”

Ollie slipped his right hand behind his back.

“Don’t do it, Ollie. I seen that piece stuffed in your pants. Now put those hands out front, or I’ll put two in you.”

“You think you can hit us with a rifle this close?” said William.

“Seen him take out a black bear from closer than this,” said Mitch finding his footing.

“I ain’t foolin’, Ollie.” Jack nodded toward the wall behind them. “I need to replace that paneling anyway. Don’t matter to me if there’s blood on it.”

“All right,” said Ollie raising his hands in front of him. “We’re goin’, Jack.”

Mitch yanked his arms out of the brothers' grip and stepped back toward the bar. He tucked his shirt back into his jeans as Ollie, William, and Peter stepped out into the parking lot.

"Thanks my friend," said Mitch. "I owe you one."

"You owe me a shit-ton more than that," said Jack stepping to the window to watch the pickup pull out of the lot. He set the rifle back behind the bar. "You better handle your shit, Mitch. I can't stand up to Ollie forever. And he'll be back."

"I'd wager you're right." Mitch thought for a moment. "Can I borrow that phone of yours?"

Jack ducked down, pulled a black rotary telephone from underneath the bar, and handed it to Mitch.

Mitch snatched his wallet from his rear pocket, opened it, and searched through the contents. He slipped a torn piece of paper from behind a credit card, lifted the receiver, and dialed.

TWELVE-HUNDRED MILES AWAY, ALBERT HARDING answered the phone in his apartment.

"Albert? This is Mitch Skinner. We need to talk."

"Goddammit." Albert shook his head. "What part of 'don't call me again' didn't you understand?"

"Remember that thing we had a few years ago? Well, it's back. And it's really pissed off." Mitch paused. "How quickly can you get your old ass up here?"

Albert drew in a deep breath. "I'm going to need some time."

"Some time? Figured you might want to move a little faster than that."

"Trains only run up there about once or twice a week. Keep your head down, and I'll get there when I can."

"Fine," said Mitch. "You might want to bring that son of yours. The younger one. We're gonna need all the help we can get. Plus, he owes me for gettin' him outta some trouble."

"I'll be there, but my boy's wrapped up in his own problems. We're gonna have to settle this one ourselves. Be ready to pick me up at the train station in Portland. I'll call you with the arrival information once I buy the ticket."

CHAPTER 23

THE NEXT MORNING, I was two cups into my daily coffee regimen when Connor knocked on the door. He stepped in and handed me his jacket and a green file folder.

"You're going to owe me, little brother."

"How's that?" I tossed the jacket onto the back of a chair and opened the folder. Inside were four sheets of paper stapled together. They showed a map of Indianapolis with various points plotted across it. Each point had a number, which corresponded with a chart at the bottom of the page that included times in fifteen-minute increments. Each page showed data for a different day.

"Turns out your boy's burner phone is registered with Verizon. I had them run all the numbers, but they only had data for the last one." He tapped the stack with his finger. "That's a triangulation report for the phone's activity."

Most mobile devices have a GPS-enabled chip, which makes it easy for users to get location-specific information like weather and driving directions. These chips also mean mobile phone companies and law enforcement agencies can pinpoint a device's exact location within a couple of feet. There are a ton of criminals rotting away in prison because they were too stupid to leave their cell phones at home when they murdered someone. It's hard for a suspect to talk their way out of a long prison sentence when a technology expert can place their cell phone at the crime scene within the time-of-death window.

Burner phones don't have GPS capability. That's one of the reasons why they're so popular with people like the banker. Determining the device's exact location is impossible, which comes in handy when you don't want to be found. But, while it's impossible to locate the phone via GPS, it *is* possible to triangulate the device's approximate location by identifying which towers it's communicating with and then measuring the signal strength and time lag between the device and the towers.

Triangulation is helpful, but far from exact. The accuracy of the location depends on how many cell towers are near the device. One cell tower and you don't get much, but I got lucky with the banker. The report Connor pulled triangulated his position off three towers to within three-quarters of a square mile. That's still far from perfect, but by comparing his cell phone's approximate location with the time of the triangulation, we could identify the general location where the banker spent his time.

"You wanna share how you got this?" I said, flipping through the stapled pages.

"I've got a few contacts in Boston who have ins with the carriers. Not that difficult to find someone making 30K a year who's willing to run a report for a nice quarterly bonus. It's not exact, but it'll get us started."

"What do I owe you? For the quarterly bonus?"

"Nothing," said Connor. "Consider it reparations for the Bishop job."

"This is a huge help." I went back to the atlas weighing down the kitchen table, flipped it open to the Indianapolis page, and compared it with the report. "Let's find this bastard."

For the next several minutes, I transferred the location markers from the triangulation map Connor provided to my atlas. I used the time stamps on the grid and the banker's approximate cell phone location to plot his route on my map of Indianapolis. It was like playing dot to dot, and when I finished, I had a snapshot of where the banker was every fifteen minutes over a four-day period two weeks ago. After I was finished plotting, I slid the atlas over to Connor.

"Well, look at that," he said, tracing my blue ink lines with his finger. "He's circling Indianapolis on I-465."

I tapped the atlas. "He also spending time on I-65, I-74, and I-70, but it looks like most his day is on 465."

Connor reviewed the triangulation report and then turned back to the atlas. "It's the same route, every day. Almost down to the minute."

Most people travel the same routes every day, usually around the same time. They go to an office and stay there, then they go home. Starts and stops. If someone could ping my cell phone they'd find me at my apartment, Winan's Coffee, and a few points in between. Our routines don't change that much, except for maybe on the weekends. The difference with the banker is that he appeared to be in constant motion. And the only people who travel like that are long-haul truck drivers and marathon runners. Normal people have a destination, the banker didn't. The report showed him traveling aimlessly around the city in the same pattern.

Connor traced the route again. "How much did you say the banker was transporting?"

"Five million," I said. "And that's just Holbrook's money. Holbrook isn't the banker's only client, so God knows how much cash he's carting round. Could be five times that."

"How many clients are we talking about?"

“No way of knowing. If Holbrook knew, he didn’t tell me.”

“His behavior makes sense,” said Connor. “It’s hard to knock over a bank when it’s traveling down the highway at 70 miles per hour.”

“It’s a solid deterrent. We have the route, maybe we start with the vehicle. Find the banker that way.”

Connor studied the map again. “You ever seen five million dollars?”

“No. You?”

“Once or twice. It’s a lot of cash, and it’s not easy to transport. And again, we should assume the banker is hauling more than just your client’s share.”

I knew where he was going. “If you were carting around that kind of cash, what type of vehicle would you use?”

“It’s got to be big enough to haul the payload, but small enough to maneuver around the city. And it has to be something that wouldn’t draw a lot of attention.”

"He'd need a CDL to drive a big rig, so that's probably out," I said. "Not to mention, it would be a bitch on gas."

"No way he could get that cash in an SUV. If it were me, I'd use a box truck."

"That's assuming we're talking about one vehicle," I said. "He could be using two or three smaller vehicles to move the money. Then he could use an SUV."

"Maybe, but then he'd need multiple drivers, and from what we know about this guy so far, he's careful. And that means he's probably a loner. Multiple drivers means more people who know what's going on. The banker is doing everything he can to protect his identity. Burner phones, switching his numbers every other week. Moving from place to place. He's probably working alone."

"There is a courier," I said.

"We're probably still looking for one set of wheels." Connor went to the kitchen and poured a cup of coffee. "What about his starting and ending point? He's got to live somewhere."

I traced the banker's route with the pen. "After circling I-465 three times, he exits onto I-31 south." I cross-referenced the time with the triangulation report. "Looks like he pulls onto I-31 around 12:45 pm. Then he travels south on I-31 to Franklin, Indiana, and then he cuts over Route 44 to Shelbyville." I checked the triangulation report again. "He arrives in Shelbyville around 1:45 pm." I wrote it on the map.

"Then where?"

"He takes 74 back to 465 for two more laps," I said, confirming with the triangulation report. "He exits on 37 south, and we lose the signal around Waverly, Indiana about 4:30 pm."

"Fewer cell towers," said Connor. "His base of operations is probably somewhere around there. Otherwise, his signal would bounce off more cell towers, and he'd appear on the radar again as he got closer to a larger city."

I thought for a moment. "The easiest way to find someone is to know where they're going to be," I said. "This is what we have here. We know exactly where the banker is going to be and when."

Connor returned to the table with his coffee. He pounded my shoulder with a loose fist. “Don’t get too big a boner over this,” he said. “This is showing us his past routine. If he were still traveling this route, this could help us, but if he’s swiped a shit-ton of cash from his clients, who are all probably eager to kill him, he’s not sticking around town. He’s long gone.”

“You’re right. He is long gone.” I studied the atlas. “But his identity is somewhere right here. On these highways. We ID him, and it gets a whole lot easier to find him. It doesn’t matter where he is now.”

“And how you going to do that? You got a time machine around here? Go back a few weeks, plant yourself in a lawn chair on the side of the I-465, and note every truck that laps you three times?”

“That’s exactly what I plan to do.” I smiled. “Minus the lawn chair.”

CHAPTER 24

THE TRIANGULATION REPORT WAS HELPFUL, but I still didn't have a name, and while I was one step closer to building my profile on the banker, I needed a lot more. If I could identify his vehicle and grab the plates, I could run him through the DMV database, and then I'd have him.

It used to be easy to use false information to obtain a sham vehicle registration, but since 9-11, those days are long done. Now, state DMVs cross-reference drivers' data with other federal databases to identify any fraudulent information. Try to get a license or registration using a social security number from a dead guy, and their system flags you. Chances are there would be something in the banker's registration that could lead me to him. An address, a name, a social security number, a VIN. There would be something in there. I just had to find it. But to get a vehicle registration, I needed his vehicle or his license plates, neither of which I had yet. But I'd thought of a way to get them, even if it was a long shot.

If the banker was traveling the same route every day, that meant he was passing the same traffic cameras every day. If I could get a look at that footage I might be able to match a vehicle to the banker's traffic patterns and times. Unfortunately, that information wasn't available on any database I had access to. It would require a contact at the Indianapolis Police Department, something I didn't have. I did, however, know of someone who knew someone at the Cincinnati Police Department who might be able to make an introduction.

I PULLED INTO THE PARKING LOT OF CINCINNATI Savings and Loan at 11:00 am. The security guard didn't give me a second look when I walked in, probably because I wasn't carrying a bulky duffle like before. I had only been in the lobby for a few seconds when Stephanie approached. This time she was wearing flats. They didn't look as good as the black high heels she wore last week, but they were probably much more comfortable.

"Mr.?"

"Finn," I said.

"Right. Back to see Mr. Cooper?"

"That's right."

"Do you have an appointment?"

"Probably not," I said.

"Let me see if he's in." She turned and headed toward his office. I didn't want to give Cooper the chance to tell her to turn me away, so I followed her down the hall. She had just poked her head into his office when I squeezed by her and sat down in the seat across from Cooper's desk. He exhaled, shook his head, and waved Stephanie away.

"What in the hell are you doing back here? I already talked to my wife and got your daughter on the squad." He lowered his voice. "She's on the squad."

"I know, and thanks for that. Becca is thrilled about it. She really wants to let her school spirit fly at the basketball game next Wednesday. Anyway, I'm here for another favor."

Cooper closed the office door and went back to his desk. "You can't just pop in here asking for favors."

"You have no idea how blackmail works, do you?"

He slumped his elbows forward on the desk and buried his face in his hands. "I don't have any money for you. I swear, I don't. If you're looking for money, I can't help you."

"I don't want your money, Cooper."

"Then what is it?" He lifted his head.

"Last week you said something about being friends with the Chief of Police. Is that true, or were you just blowing smoke up my ass?"

"He's my brother-in-law."

"I was hoping you'd say something like that."

"Why?"

"I need a favor. I need you to have the chief vouch for me with Indianapolis PD. And I need to get access to their traffic cameras. All the cameras for I-465."

"What in the hell does this have to do with cheerleading?"

"Nothing. We're well past that, Coop. Try to keep up. I need you to call him and make it happen."

"He can't do that."

"Sure, he can. It happens all the time. Just tell him you and I are good friends, and that I'm a PI, and I need access to the cameras for a case I'm working on." I smiled at Cooper. "Half of that statement is true."

"I'm going to need more than that."

"Tell him that I'm working an investigation into illegal drug activity in Indianapolis. Tell him it's big-time. Not street dealers, but a regional distributor. You tell your brother-in-law that if he gets me access to their traffic cameras, I'll turn over all the evidence I have to Indianapolis PD, and they can make the bust. They'll get all the credit, and your brother-in-law gets an assist. He'll love you for it."

I had no intention of turning Holbrook over to the Indianapolis PD, but I needed to give Cooper something to work with.

Cooper stroked his chin. "If I do this, you and I are square. You destroy all the photos you have, and you don't come back here again. I mean it."

I reached out and shook Cooper's hand. "I give you my word, Coop. You get me access to those cameras, and you'll never see me again."

I gave Cooper my encrypted email address and told him to send me the link and the log-in information for the I-465 cameras. Then I thanked him, stepped out of his office, waved to Stephanie, and walked out of the building.

CHAPTER 25

BROOKE HAD PUT on a brave face after her encounter with Adler, but she wouldn't be able to wear it forever. I wanted to talk to her to give her an update on the shitty situation her boyfriend had created for all of us, and to make sure she and Becca were okay.

"How's your sister's place?" I said.

"It's fine. Becca and I are staying in the guest bedroom."

"You still feeling all right? Any headaches?"

"No. I'm fine."

"How's Becca? Any nightmares? Does she talk about it? About Adler?"

Brooke was silent for a moment before she spoke. "She hasn't mentioned it. Probably still processing it."

"How's she taking to the new place?"

"I think she likes spending some time with Allison."

"Has Allison been asking any questions?"

"Nothing out of the ordinary," said Brooke.

"Did my name come up?"

"My sister never brings you up."

Allison never liked me. She hated me when Brooke and I dated and loathed me when we got married. To her, I'd always be an "I told you so." For as much as she crapped in my cereal, her husband Bill actually liked me. That probably made her hate me even more.

"Have you talked to Daryl?" I asked, recalling my earlier conversation with Becca.

"I'm not taking his calls. He stopped by a few times at the hospital to talk, but so far, I've been able to avoid him. I'm still too pissed to talk to him right now."

"You can't avoid him forever," I said. "Sooner or later, you're going to have to deal with the prick."

"We'll see." She paused. "What about you? Are you any closer to finding this person you're looking for?"

"Inching closer. This guy is a real ghost. No name, no location, no nothing."

"How are you going to find him then?"

"That's what I'm trying to figure out."

"What are they going to do with him if…" she caught herself, "when you find him?"

"If he's still alive, nothing good, I suppose."

"What did he do? Why are they looking for him?"

"He did what they always do. He took the money and ran."

There was a static snarl on the line, and it sounded like Brooke had covered the receiver with her hand as if she didn't want me to hear something. The sound of her breath returned a moment later. "Do you really think…" I could hear her tearing up through the receiver. "…

Think this guy is going to let Daryl out of this?"

I wasn't completely positive what Holbrook would do, but it wasn't something I wanted Brooke thinking about. "Yes, I do," I said. "We'll all get out of this, and then we can put it behind us."

I heard her swipe a tissue from its box. "Finn, thanks again for taking this on. You didn't have to do anything. Or you could have gone to the police. So thank you. And I… I'm sorry that I brought you into this."

I did think about going to the police, but that would have only made things worse. Holbrook didn't get to where he was by being stupid, and who knows how much police influence he had purchased.

"You didn't bring me into this," I said. "That's on Daryl. And don't worry about it, anyway. It's nothing I can't handle. Like I said, in a week, this will all be over." There was a long pause. "When Becca wakes up, tell her I love her. Now get some sleep yourself, and stop worrying about all this. It'll be over soon."

I clicked off the receiver and hoped I was right.

CHAPTER 26

I LOGGED into my email the next morning and found a note from Cooper.

FROM: MCOOPER@CINCISAVINGS.ORG

Sent: September 30, 10:13:34 PM EDT

To: finderskeepers@dbzmail.com

Subject: Traffic Cameras

I TALKED TO MY BROTHER-IN-LAW. I SHOULD HAVE had him arrest your sorry ass for blackmail. He got you limited access to the traffic camera system for 48 hours. That's it. He said if you find any-

thing to contact him and he can take any evidence to the Indianapolis PD.

Link: http://IndianaStateTrafficSystem/admin

Password: cooperTEMP1234

Don't come to my office again, asshole!

Michael Cooper

I wasn't sure that Cooper or his brother-in-law were going to come through, but apparently, the thought of a potential drug bust was enough for Indianapolis PD to give me temporary access to a few traffic cameras. Some law enforcement officers have a quid pro quo mentality, and that usually ended up in their favor. Over the years, I'd worked with detectives in several police departments. I could get information they couldn't get, and they had the tools and resources that would otherwise be off-limits to someone like me. Working together we did more good than harm, and it seemed Indianapolis PD was taking a chance on me. And it's not like they were giving me the keys to the armory. The traffic system only offered real-time and archival footage from the I-465 traffic cameras. What's the worst that could happen?

Connor hadn't arrived from his hotel yet, and forty-eight hours wasn't a lot of time, so I started without him. After logging into the system, a map of Indianapolis popped up on the left side of the screen. The map was speckled with what looked like a hundred green dots, which I assumed indicated the locations of the city's traffic cameras. The right side of the screen was divided into two quadrants. The upper section was blank, and the lower section displayed a dashboard with several drop-down menus. These menus allowed me to pull up real-time traffic feeds from any of the outer belt's traffic cameras or access the camera archives going back thirty days. I could also click on the green dots overlaying the city map and access the cameras that way.

Thanks to the cell phone triangulation report that Connor provided, I had the banker's approximate route along I-465, and thanks to the time stamp, I knew when he was in the general area. My plan was to pull up the archival footage from each of the traffic cameras near the banker's known locations along I-465. Normally that wouldn't amount to much because I assumed most drivers on I-465 pass the same cameras around the same time every day, especially as they travel to and from their home or jobs, but the banker's routine was different from everyone else's routine. The banker lapped I-465 three times before taking another highway. It reminded me of an old friend in the Army Reserve who was stationed near Cincinnati years ago. He told me that once a week, to maintain their driving skills, they'd caravan military trucks around I-275, the Cincinnati outer belt, for hours at a time, sometimes lapping it four or five times. The banker was doing the same thing, but he wasn't doing it to keep his skills sharp, he was doing it to protect his cargo.

If I could use the traffic cameras to identify a common vehicle, one that passed the same traffic cameras at the same time each day as the banker, I might be able to identify his vehicle. And if I could identify his vehicle, I might be able to pull a plate. And if I could pull a plate, I could run it through the DMV database, and that would identify our man. And even if I couldn't get a visual on his plate, I could at least search the DMV database for the make and model of the vehicle. The key was to get all the information on the banker that I could until I had something that provided a name and a face. You have to follow the breadcrumbs, and the only crumb I had was a burner cell number, which led me to the triangulation report, which led to me sitting on my ass, watching traffic camera footage.

Finding the banker this way was a long shot, but I've made long shots before, and I learned years ago that in this business you don't just believe in miracles, you rely on them. Time to start praying. But first, I headed back to the coffee pot.

WITH A CUP OF COFFEE IN ONE HAND AND MY notepad in the other, I dove headfirst into the Indiana State Traffic System. I knew that the banker was lapping the I-465 belt three times, and thanks to the Internet, I also knew that it was 52.79 miles around I-465. I also had a starting point, because according to the triangulation report, the first cell tower to pick up the banker's signal each day was near Exit 4 at 9:15 am. That didn't mean he entered the highway at the same time, but it was probably within a few-minute window.

I assumed if the banker was spending that much time on the highway, he'd probably set his cruise control around 65 mph. He'd keep his speed near the limit because he wouldn't risk a highway patrolman tagging him for going over the speed limit. And he was going nowhere in particular, which meant there was no reason to speed to get there.

I opened the calculator on my phone to figure the distance. If the banker was traveling at a constant sixty-five mph around a 52.79 mile track, it would take him forty-eight minutes to reach his starting point. Assuming he entered the highway on Exit 4 at sometime around 9:15 am, according to the triangulation report, he'd pass the Exit 4 camera again around 10:03 am. He'd pass it again on this third lap around 10:51 am.

Back on the traffic system dashboard, I clicked on the green icon for the Exit 4 camera. The live feed opened on the upper right-hand side of the screen, and I watched a flurry of vehicles pass by. The idea was to compare all the vehicles that passed by the Exit 4 camera around 9:15 am, with those that passed by it again around 10:03 am and again at 10:51 am and find vehicles that appeared on all three feeds. If I was looking for just any vehicle, the exercise would be impossible, given the sheer volume of traffic passing by the camera every second. Fortunately for me, I wasn't looking for just any vehicle.

The banker was moving at least five million dollars of Holbrook's money. That's a lot of physical cash. Hundred-dollar bills are still the largest bill a citizen can get their hands on, which meant if the banker had five million in cash, he was carting around at least fifty thousand bills. Since a single bill weighs about one gram, and the banker was carting around at least fifty thousand bills, he'd be moving about a hundred and ten pounds of cold, hard cash. And that's on the low end because it assumed the banker only hauled the cash in hundred-dollar bills. If Holbrook's balance was in fifties, twenties, or tens, the number of bills the banker was hauling around skyrocketed.

That's not the kind of money you throw in your trunk. Plus, that was just Holbrook's money. Holbrook said the banker also safeguarded cash for some of his associates, so there was no telling how much he actually moved at one time, but I knew it required something larger than the family station wagon or SUV. Something as large as a tractor-trailer and the banker would need a CDL, not to mention some real skills. And while he could have used an 18-wheeler to move the cash, that method seemed too cumbersome, so I ruled it out. Connor said he'd move the money in a box truck. I'd do the same. It was big but not too big. I decided to focus my search on those, and if nothing popped, then I'd widen the search to accommodate more vehicles.

I accessed the Exit 4 camera archive and entered the date from the triangulation report into the date field. Then I entered "9:10 am" in the time field. I figured I'd give the banker a five-minute window on each side of 9:15 am, knowing I wasn't dealing with exact times and to account for any inaccuracy on the triangulation report. There were other variables too. Maybe there was a traffic jam that day that slowed traffic below a constant speed. Perhaps the banker took an unscheduled exit to take a piss or get something to eat. The possibilities were endless, but I had to start with what I knew.

For what seemed like an hour, I watched a flurry of vehicles buzz past the traffic camera. I paused the feed and wrote down each box truck that passed the camera. After reviewing the footage, I had a list of 3thirty-one vehicles on my legal pad, complete with vehicle make, color, and time that it appeared on camera. Watching traffic footage is as exciting as watching someone conduct a tax audit using sign language, and I had a new-found respect for those troopers who parked along the highway aiming their radar gun down the line of oncoming traffic. At least they got to tear down the highway with light and sirens blazing after their target. I just sat there.

After a fifteen-minute break to rest my eyeballs and refill my coffee, I headed back to the table. I repeated the same process watching the Exit 4 camera footage from lap two, around 10:03 am. I identified twenty-two possible vehicles. Then I dialed up the footage for the same camera around 10:51 am. The camera captured only a handful of potential vehicles.

It took more than two hours to watch all of the video feeds and jot down the descriptions on my pad. I ended up with three columns, one for each camera feed. If my approach was correct, the banker's vehicle would appear in all three columns, since it should be the only common vehicle passing the camera at each interval. I compared the vehicles in each column and eliminated most as one-time appearances. What remained was a list of three vehicles that appeared on all three camera feeds—one yellow Penske truck and two white box trucks.

I rubbed my eyes, downed the last drop of lukewarm coffee in my mug, and hoped to God that I didn't have to expand the search beyond the vehicles I'd already captured.

A quick comparison of the Penske trucks in the three feeds showed different registration numbers on the side of the cabs, so those weren't the same vehicles. That left the two white box trucks as potential hits. I checked my notes on the legal pad and then pulled up the time when the camera captured each box truck. I zoomed in and checked the plates. I was able to rule out one of the box trucks right away because it had different plates. But I got lucky on the third one. The same plate—551EOD—meant this was the same vehicle that passed by the same camera in each feed. It was in the right place at the right times, and it had to be the banker, or one fuckload of a coincidence.

I leaned back in the wooden chair as a jolt of electricity fired up from my legs and radiated throughout my core. For once, it wasn't the coffee. If this was the banker, I was damn close to uncovering a big piece of the puzzle. A wide grin spread across on my face.

Then there was a knock on the door.

CHAPTER 27

CONNOR STEPPED into my living room, drinking a to-go cup of gas station coffee.

"Morning," he said looking around. "Where's Dad?"

"Still asleep. I'm the only early riser around here."

Connor looked at my laptop screen and saw the traffic camera footage still rolling.

"Is that what I think it is? Traffic cameras? How did…"

"You aren't the only one who can pull strings," I said.

He inched closer to the screen. "Did you find anything?"

"You're Goddamn right I did." I held up my legal pad. "I got the banker's license plate. At least, I think I did."

"Nice job, little brother. Tie it to a name yet?"

"I was just about to do that."

Some people think investigative work is intriguing and sexy. That's bullshit. It's not all car chases and shootouts. Ninety-five percent of what I do is sitting in front of a computer slumming search engines, diving into databases, or living at the library with my head buried in old records that aren't accessible online. It's about as sexy as syphilis, but that's where the information is.

The state of Ohio yanked my PI license three years ago, but I didn't need a PI license to maintain access to the usual information databases, like criminal records, motor vehicle registrations, driver's licenses, concealed weapon permits, professional licenses, voter registration records, and a slew of others. The people behind these databases don't care whether I'm running searches for some defense lawyer in Cincinnati or a mobster in Indianapolis.

I sat back down at the table. Connor stood behind me. I could smell his blueberry-flavored coffee over my right shoulder. I logged into the motor vehicle registration and licensing database and entered the license plate number from the white box truck. The screen went blank, and I felt chills as I waited for the record to load.

After a few seconds, the registration opened, and for the first time, we had a name—Thomas Coyne. The plate was registered to a business, Van Leunen Plumbing, located at 1053 Industrial Parkway in Indianapolis.

"Could it really be that easy?" said Connor.

"Easy? You didn't have to spend your morning watching traffic feeds." I heard Albert fumbling through drawers in his bedroom.

I wrote the address down on my legal pad and clicked on Thomas Coyne's name. A moment later, his driver's license record opened, and I was finally face-to-face with the banker, or at least his driver's license photo. According to his license, Thomas Coyne was sixty-six years old. He had short white hair that was neatly parted to the side. His face was narrow, and while it showed some age, he didn't look sixty-six. He might pass for late fifties. He wore thin eyeglasses that looked like designer frames. His license had him at five-foot-nine and 149 pounds. The address on file was the same from his registration, 1053 Industrial Parkway in Indianapolis.

Albert walked out of his bedroom and looked at the screen. "Who's that dapper gent?"

"The banker. It's the man we're looking for. Got him from his license plate."

Albert squinted and looked at the screen. "That's funny."

"What's funny?" I said.

"Thomas Coyne."

"What's funny about it?"

"You're looking for a banker, and his last name is coin."

"Shit," I said. "That's either one hell of a coincidence…"

"Or it's an alias," interrupted Connor.

"Maybe it's pronounced cone," I said. "Like ice cream."

"Nah, that's coin," said Albert. "Definitely a cover."

"One way to find out," I said.

I opened the IRB search database and dropped Thomas Coyne's name into the search field. Nothing.

"That's not good," said Connor.

I clicked open a new browser and went to www.usps.com. The postal service had an address finder tool on their website. I clicked open the tool and typed in "1053 Industrial Parkway, Indianapolis, IN." I clicked "Find" and groaned when the site indicated, in bold red letters, that "This address wasn't found" and prompted me to double-check it and try again.

"Can you go back to the traffic cameras," said Connor. "To his vehicle?"

I minimized the post office webpage and the motor vehicle database webpage and clicked open the Indiana State Traffic System site. I looked at my notepad, found the time I'd indicated when the banker's box truck passed the camera, and dialed it up on the screen.

"That's his truck," I said, as I zoomed in on the vehicle and studied the image. "Shit. I was so focused on the license plate I didn't see it before."

"See what before?" said Albert.

"There's no logo on the side of the truck. No phone number, no name, nothing."

The business name on the registration was a front because even a freshman business major knows if you run a service company, you put your name or logo on the side of your truck. The box truck on the screen didn't have any markings at all. That was either intentional or really bad business.

There was an easy way to confirm whether Van Leunen Plumbing was a real company that belonged to an inept businessman or whether it was a front to conceal the vehicle owner's identity. I steered my browser to the Business Services portal for the Indiana Secretary of State. All those records are public domain. I ran a business entity name search for "Van Leunen Plumbing" and nothing came up, which meant no such company existed now nor had existed in the past decade. Shit.

During the past ten minutes, I'd experienced what could only be described as a PI boner when I discovered the banker's name and address, only to lose the high after finding out everything was shit. But for all I didn't have, I knew this had to be the banker's vehicle and license plate. No one else would have gone to such lengths to hide their identity. Plus, I had the traffic footage.

Whoever owned the box truck had covered his tracks, but not as well as he could have. My vehicle plates are registered to a dummy corporation as well, but I was smart enough to take the extra step and establish an actual LLC. Run my plates or my apartment address, and you'll get the name of a business registered in Delaware. Look up the company name, and you'll find a physical address on Mayfield Road, as well as a list of corporate officers. Digitally, there's a solid paper trail, physically, there's an empty office at the end of the seventh floor of the Hollowell Building. Run my background, and you don't get a dead end. The banker didn't go that far. He figured the false business name and crap address would hide his footprints, and it would, for a while. There was one piece of information I hoped he'd overlooked. Right there on his registration record, tucked between the certificate title number and the purchase date was the vehicle serial number, otherwise known as a VIN.

VINs are good for more than running a vehicle accident history. They also provide a vehicle's ownership history. If I couldn't find the current owner, maybe I could find the previous one.

I went back to the motor vehicle database and plugged in the truck's VIN. Everything else on the banker had turned up cold, and it was possible the VIN would be a dead end too, but at the moment, it's all I had.

"Smart," said Albert.

Besides Van Leunen Plumbing, there was one previous owner. It was last registered to Miller Moving and Storage, which was also located in Indianapolis. But unlike Van Leunen Plumbing, Miller Moving and Storage had all the hallmarks of a real business. I ran a business search using the same Indiana Secretary of State database, and within seconds, I had a location, contact information, and an owner for Miller Moving and Storage. The company was located on Morse Road in Indianapolis.

Time to put on some miles on Connor's Escalade and a tie around my neck.

CHAPTER 28

CONNOR and I drove to the Miller Moving and Storage complex at 2280 Morse Road in Indianapolis. I slipped on my gray suit jacket, gabbed the yellow file folder from the passenger seat, and stepped out into the parking lot.

"It'll be less intimidating if I go in alone," I said. "Why don't you just sit here and look pretty?"

"Fine with me. I've got a few calls to return anyway." Connor was already dialing his cell before I finished readjusting my gray-and-blue striped tie in the driver's side mirror. I gave the tie one last tug and then started toward the front door.

The VIN search identified Dale Miller as the previous owner of the white box truck. According to online records, Dale was the founder and current owner of Miller Moving and Storage. It wasn't a huge operation. The lot in front of me consisted of a dozen moving vans and two rows of self-storage units, which sat behind a ten-foot razor-wire fence. The main office sat off to the side.

I walked into the office and found a young blonde woman, who looked no older than twenty, sitting at the front desk under the watchful eye of a large blue-and-white Miller Moving and Storage logo. Behind the woman were stacks of moving supplies, flat boxes, rolls of packing tape, and industrial-sized bubble wrap.

"Hi," she said. "Can I help you?"

"I'm looking for the owner. Is he available?" I flashed a smile, and she picked up the phone.

"Dad," she stopped herself. "Mr. Miller, there's someone here to see you."

A moment later, a man in his fifties, wearing a light blue button-up shirt tucked neatly into his department-store khakis, stepped out of a side office and extended his hand.

"Hello," he said. "Dale Miller."

"Agent Roger Mathers," I said, shaking his hand. "I'm with the Ohio Bureau of Workers' Compensation."

Most of the time when I'm looking for information from a business owner, I pretend that I'm with the Ohio Bureau of Workers' Compensation. That's because some people are leery of private investigators, and they clam up and won't share anything useful. But every business owner loves investigators from the Bureau of Workers' Compensation because they save businesses money by investigating false claims against them. A business owner might hate the press, the IRS, or even the police, but every business owner loves investigators from the Goddamn Bureau of Workers' Compensation.

"Did someone file a claim against me?" said Dale, his smile wilting like a newspaper in the rain.

"No, it's nothing like that. I'm investigating a potentially fraudulent claim, but it's not related to your company."

"Then how can I help you?"

"Is there a place we can sit down and talk?"

"Sure," he said. "Right this way."

Dale led me into his office, which had a small circular table and two chairs. I took a seat at the table and opened the folder I had tucked under my arm.

"I'm investigating an individual who might be perpetuating a fraud against the state of Ohio, but we have reason to believe he filed the claim using a fraudulent name. All I'm trying to do is determine the man's identify to ensure everything is on the up-and-up."

"I'm not sure I can help you," he said. "I don't do a lot of business in Ohio."

"Right," I said, slipping the copy of the vehicle registration and a title transfer form from the folder. "But I'm interested in this vehicle you sold a few years back. It was a white box truck." I pointed to the VIN on the form. "This VIN comes back as being previously owned by your company. You sold it three years ago."

"That's probably right. We're always updating our truck fleet. Once they get too beat up, get high in mileage, or become too expensive to maintain, we sell them off and replace them with something more reliable. But what does an old truck have to do with me?"

"I believe the man who bought the truck from you is the person I'm looking for. So I was hoping you could tell me anything that might help me confirm the buyer's identity."

Dale scooted his chair back and crossed his legs. "Can I see your paperwork?"

I slid the information I had across the table. He slipped his glasses from his shirt pocket, placed them on the bridge of his nose, and studied the documents.

"Okay. Let me see what I can pull up." Miller went to his desk and started typing on his keyboard. I watched as he nodded his head and typed more keys. "This VIN does match one of our previous vehicles. Let me see." He stood up and walked over to a six-drawer file cabinet and opened the second drawer from the bottom. His eyes shifted from the file tabs to the form in his hand, and back to the tabs. He yanked a folder from the drawer and slammed it closed.

"It's your lucky day, Agent Mathers," said Miller. "I thought this might be at our off-site storage facility, but it's still here. It was a while ago." He sat back down at the small table and opened the folder. He plucked a bill of sale from the folder and repositioned the glasses on his face. "2011 Ford E350 truck. 115,442 miles. Sold to Thomas Coyne for $11,250." He studied the form. "He paid in cash." Miller flipped through the folder. "This might help. I have a photocopy of his driver's license."

For a moment, I thought this could be the breadcrumb I needed, but the feeling quickly vanished. The photocopy Miller provided had the same name and address information as the documents I pulled from the DMV.

The banker was still a ghost.

I tapped my finger on the photocopy of the license and slid it back across the table. "This is the same contact information we have on file, but it's a dead end. Do you remember anything about him?"

"Not really. It was a few years ago." Miller studied the gray-and-white face from the photocopy. "I remember meeting him and showing him the inspection report on the vehicle, but I wouldn't even remember what he looked like if it wasn't for this picture."

"How did he contact you?"

Miller rifled through the folder. He grabbed a piece of paper and handed it to me. "Here's the online ad we ran on the truck. He might have emailed or called us. No way to tell." Miller looked at the paperwork again. "There's no record of an email address in here."

"What about your email system? Maybe you still have the correspondence on your computer?"

"Our email system automatically deletes anything older than 18 months, so I wouldn't have any emails from him."

"Do you have an IT guy I can talk to? Maybe the emails were archived somewhere."

"I'm the IT guy." He smiled apologetically. "Like I said, we're a small company. I'm also the head of HR and the facilities manager."

Miller must have recognized the disappointment on my face. "I'm sorry I couldn't be of more help," he said.

“Thanks for your time, Mr. Miller.” I slipped a crisp white business card for Roger Mathers from my suit pocket and handed it to Miller. “Please call me if you think of anything that might help. We’re very anxious to find Mr. Coyne.”

Miller ran his fingers over the embossed Ohio Bureau of Workers’ Compensation logo on the card. “I’ll do that.”

I stepped out of his office, thanked the young woman at the front desk, and walked back to the Escalade. My head hung a bit lower than when I walked in.

Connor abruptly ended his phone call as I climbed into the passenger side.

“What’d you find out?” he said.

“Nothing we didn’t already know. The banker bought the truck here, but he paid in cash and used his alias, so we’re still shitting goose eggs.”

I scanned the dashboard of the Escalade until my eyes fell on the glove box. “You keep your registration in here?”

“Yeah, why?”

I clicked open the glove box, and the leather door dropped toward the seat. On top of the vehicle's owner's manual was a white envelope.

"It's in there," Connor said.

Inside the envelope was the vehicle's title, registration, and a copy of Connor's insurance card. I skimmed each document. "This is all your real information?"

"Yeah. I'm not hiding from anyone. I'm just a normal guy in a normal SUV." He thought for a moment, probably trying to determine where I was going with my question. "What's on *your* registration?"

"My car is registered to a fake company, but my real name is on it. Anyone running the registration would get my name but a fake address." I jostled the envelope in my hand. "My apartment is under my company name too. An extra layer of misinformation."

The key to not being found is the ability to hide in plain sight. While I like to operate in the shadows, I have no reason to hide from the police. Take my license and registration, for example. With the exception of a fake LLC as the owner of my vehicle, everything else works out. If I get pulled over and a cop runs my plates and license, it's all going to come back as accurate. No reason for the officer to dig further. He writes a ticket and drives away.

Most criminals get nailed at routine traffic stops because they've done something stupid to manipulate their license or registration. Maybe they walk into a DMV with a fake birth certificate or a fake social security number and try to get a license under a false name. The system automatically cross-references the information and immediately alerts the DMV employee of any suspicious information or mismatched data.

Years ago, if you wanted a false identity, all you had to do was find some deceased person who was close to your age. It would take some time, but you could get their birth certificate and social security documentation, take it to the DMV and get a license in their name. As long as the sex and the age matched, and you weren't sweating bullets at the counter, chances are you'd walk away with a new license with someone else's name on it.

That's not the case today. Now, all the government agency computer systems talk to one another, and a lot of them do it in real-time. Try the same method to get a fake license today, and when the DMV clerk keys in your social security information, the Social Security Administration will flag you for being dead while you're still standing at the counter.

That's why, next to getting a fake passport, getting a fake driver's license is one of the hardest things for a criminal to acquire. It's not like in the movies, where someone pays a master forger to make the documents. That might work on the surface, but the first time a cop runs your license through their system or a TSA agent scans your passport at the airport, you're fucked. The information on the back end doesn't sync up with what's on the document. And while it's easy to change what's on the document, it's damn near impossible to change what's in the system.

"We're going about this all wrong," I said.

"How's that?" Connor tossed his phone onto the console.

"Let's take a step back." I turned in my seat to face Connor. "If you needed to get a fake identity through the DMV, how would you do it?"

Connor thought for a moment. "I wouldn't go through the DMV. That's pretty much impossible. I've got a guy who'll produce a document that's almost as good as the original, but I'd use an out-of-state license to throw anyone off."

"But if you got pulled over and a cop ran your info, they'd nail you."

Connor tapped the white envelope in my hand. "Which is why I have a real license."

"But the banker doesn't, and if he's driving around the interstate for hours every day, he's likely to get pulled over once in a while. It's just probability."

"Maybe he's sure to keep his speed down, so he doesn't get tagged."

"He's too cautious. Everything he's done until now tells us we're dealing with someone who takes his time to stay hidden. He's got a license and registration under a different name, but he'd be too cautious to risk getting caught at a traffic stop with bad paperwork. We're not talking about a couple of underage college kids buying beer with a fake ID. He'd need to have legit information to show a police officer if he was ever pulled over."

"So?"

"So how did he get it?" I said. "How would you get it?"

"Like I said, I wouldn't try. It's nearly impossible to con the DMV. They cross-reference everything. You'd need a workaround."

"Right. You'd need someone on the inside. I read an article a year or so ago about a DMV employee who was selling fake driver's licenses to people who flunked their driver's exam. He was making something like two hundred dollars a pop. It went on for years until they snagged him during an internal investigation."

"But that's different," said Connor. "All those people still had their info in the DMV system. They weren't fake licenses. The documentation was legit; the clerk was just circumventing the testing procedure, not the database. Run their license and registration, and all the right information comes up. Run the banker's information and the wrong information comes up. It's not the same."

"I know it's a different situation, but the fact is, these people had an inside man helping them, so it's plausible that the banker had an inside guy at the DMV who helped him."

"But, it still doesn't add up," said Connor. "Even if he had an inside man, the employee still couldn't enter the fraudulent information into the database. The system would still kick it out when the name, social, and DOB didn't sync up. Having someone on the inside really wouldn't help."

"What if the employee didn't enter the banker's fraudulent info at the DMV counter?"

"I don't follow," said Connor.

"What if the banker went into the DMV and got a license like usual, presented all the right information just like everyone else? Real name, real address, real everything. Nothing triggers in the system because it's all legit. All the info checks out. It's all accurate. But then, the inside man goes into the database to edit the information right there at the DMV. Maybe editing the information isn't subject to the same triggers and review as issuing a license from scratch."

"So the employee alters the accurate info, changing the identity, reprints the license, and hands it to the banker for a chunk of cash?"

"Just like your friend at the phone company. You said it yourself. Wouldn't be hard to find someone making 30K a year who's willing to fudge some figures for a nice quarterly bonus."

"It's a good workaround." Connor glanced down at the white envelope and back at me. "Strong theory, little brother. How in the hell are you going to test it? I've got zero contacts at the DMV. Do you?"

"No. We'll have to get creative."

CHAPTER 29

Connor and I returned from Indianapolis to my apartment to find Albert sitting on the couch watching an episode of *Longmire* and nursing a cup of coffee. He watched as we walked into the living room before propping his feet on top of the wheeled suitcase in front of him.

"I suppose we're going to talk about that?" I said, eyeballing the suitcase.

"I booked myself on a train to Meddybemps," said Albert.

"Trains don't go to Meddybemps."

He shook his head. "I meant I got a ticket to Portland. Mitch is going to pick me up there and take me the rest of the way."

"Mitch Skinner?" said Connor. "I'm surprised he's still alive."

I looked at the suitcase again. "What are you two bastards up to?"

"Not up to anything," he said. "Just got to go settle something."

"You're seventy-one years old," I said. "The only thing you should be settling are healthcare bills."

"You're an asshole."

Some people have a romantic fascination with train travel, but riding the rails to Meddybemps, Maine is about as fun as a colonoscopy with no sleepy juice. Meddybemps is in the Downeast region of Maine, about 25 miles from Eastport. My father bought the summer camp on Meddybemps Lake in the sixties and spent most of his summers there until he stopped going a few years ago.

I'd looked into that train route before when I was considering visiting my father there one summer. First, it's a 15-hour trek from Cincinnati to Washington, DC. Then you have to switch trains for a 10-hour ride to Boston. Then you switch trains again in Beantown, and you've still got another two hours to Portland, Maine. After stepping off the train in Portland, you've got another four-hour car ride to Meddybemps. High-speed-rail it isn't. Add in all the waiting around time and you're looking at a thirty-hour trip. And departure times are as inconvenient as shit. For the same price, it's much easier to hop a three-hour flight.

But my father wouldn't fly. What he wouldn't admit, and what I didn't have to ask, is that he was taking the train because there's less security, and he's got a piece stashed somewhere in that suitcase. To settle something in Maine.

I poured a cup of coffee and sat in the chair opposite the couch. "You're not going anywhere until you tell us what this is all about."

Albert shifted in his seat but kept his brown leather boots on the suitcase. "I ever mention the name Ollie Stoner to you?" he said.

"No, you haven't mentioned him," I said. I knew who Ollie Stoner was. His name was always on the tip of someone's tongue in Meddybemps. He was a fixture, like fish frys and mosquitoes. His name even came up when I was there on my last case.

Ollie ran a junkyard near Meddybemps and was rumored to be wrapped up in petty crime. Mostly, he'd steal cars, appliances, copper, or anything else he could resell at his junkyard. He had a bad temper, and two boys who could punch through an outhouse without breaking a sweat, but he kept his operation small so he wouldn't draw any attention from the authorities. "What about him?"

Albert paused as if choosing his words carefully. "About four years back, Mitch and I had a little run in with Ollie."

"Define run in," I said.

"Ollie used to break into homes around town and steal shit, but a while ago he upped his game. He started threatening locals to sign over the titles to their homes. He essentially put a gun to their head and threatened to kill 'em and their kin unless they signed over their property. Anyone who said anything got a beat-down courtesy of Ollie's boys. People were scared shitless. A lot of 'em just packed up and left town. And those that stood up to Ollie didn't last long."

"Why didn't they go to the police?"

"What police? Constable Hafner was the only law we had up there, and Ollie'd paid him off, so *he* wasn't gonna do shit."

"Couldn't you go higher up? The state police?"

"They don't give two shits about what happens in Meddybemps. And with no one willing to point a finger at Ollie, it wouldn't matter anyway."

"I didn't know Ollie was into anything that big," I said.

Albert smirked. "So you do know who he is?"

"I never said I didn't. I said you never mentioned him. So how did you and Mitch get involved?"

Connor laughed as if he'd heard the pending explanation before.

Albert went on to explain. "One day Ollie figures out the property around the lake is some of the most valuable around town, so he starts going after those deeds. Eventually he comes looking for me and Mitch. Wantin' our properties, so we figured we had to put a stop to it. Mitch comes to me looking for a solution because we knew Ollie wouldn't take no for an answer. So, together we came up with a plan to put Ollie and his boys out of business."

"I'm almost afraid to ask," I said. "What was the plan?"

Connor laughed again. "Oh, you're not going to believe what they cooked up."

"How do you know about this?"

"Never mind about that," said Albert. "Anyway, we knew Constable Hafner was as crooked as a piece of driftwood, but I knew the game warden in Meddybemps. Guy by the name of Neil Cutter, and we went to see him. We told him everything we knew about Ollie. What he'd been doing and how he was coming for our property. Well, Cutter lives on the lake too, and wasn't happy with what Ollie was up to, so we came up with a solution to our problem."

"What'd you do, Dad?"

"Turns out that someone ransacked the game warden's field office earlier that year. Made off with rifles, ammo, cameras, computers, and a bunch of other equipment."

"Ollie was dumb enough to hit a warden's outpost?" I said.

"Probably not," said Albert. "I'd wager it was some kids. Ollie might have brass balls, but he's not stupid enough to go after a game warden."

"So how'd you tie it back to Ollie?"

"Cutter was right pissed about the break in. It didn't look so good that his office got popped and he had to ask for all new equipment. Especially since they got off with several firearms. That looked real bad. Cutter wanted to nail whoever did it."

"I'm still not seeing the connection with Ollie," I said.

"I'm gettin' to that," said Albert, kicking over his suitcase. "We wanted Ollie, and Cutter wanted someone to pay for the break in. Turns out Cutter had a boat on a trailer sitting near the warden's dock. He amended the incident report and added the boat and trailer to the descriptions of items stolen from the field office. That night, someone made sure that boat and trailer ended up in the back of Ollie's junkyard. The next morning, someone called in an anonymous tip to Cutter's office. Cutter bypassed Constable Hafner, got a warrant to search the yard, found the boat, and popped Ollie and his boys for possession of stolen property. Stolen federal property. Ollie ended up getting three years in the clink. His boys each did one."

"Let me guess," I said. "Now they're all out and looking for you and Mitch."

"Sounds about right," said Connor.

"Something like that." Albert polished off his coffee and set his cup on the end table. "That's why I have to get back to Maine."

"Seems like a lot of trouble to me," I said. "Surprised you and Mitch didn't just shoot Ollie and toss him in the lake."

"Thought about it, but I didn't want blood on my hands. Honestly thought someone would shank the dickhead in prison. Everyone hated that prick. Or maybe he'd die of old age. He's in his sixties."

"Anything else to the story?" I said.

"That's mostly it. Might have left out the part about Mitch and I helping ourselves to the two duffle bags of money Ollie had stashed in the back of an old Buick on his lot. Figured Ollie owed us something for all the trouble he put us through."

"That was the $20,000 I fished out from under your boathouse a few weeks ago?"

"That's right," said Albert. "So, you can thank Ollie for this nice place here."

"That's some secret you're cartin' around there, Dad."

"We've all got secrets, kid. Some are just bigger than others."

"Ain't that right," said Connor.

I turned to Connor. "And you knew about all this?"

"He ran the plan with Cutter past me a while ago," said Connor. "Wanted to see what I thought."

"What did you tell him?"

"I told him it was the stupidest plan I'd ever heard and he'd probably get himself killed. But since when did he listen to either of us?" Connor picked up the suitcase and wheeled it out to the kitchen.

Part of me wanted to know what else my father had stashed up in that head of his, but the other part was okay not knowing.

"I'm still not clear on why it's so important that you go now," I said.

"Mitch is in Maine and he's in trouble. We got each other into this and now we have to get each other out. Plus, some day that property in Maine will be yours and Connor's. It's only a matter of time before Ollie figures out some other way to snake it out from under me. I got to put a stop to it, and I got to do it now."

The last thing I needed to worry about right now was my father running around the back woods of Maine trying to settle some vendetta, but I also knew there wasn't anything I could say or do to stop him.

"You want one of us to come with you?" I said. "I can't send you off to Maine by yourself."

"I won't be by myself. Mitch'll be with me. Besides, you got more important shit to handle here.

Take care of that. I'll let you know if we run into any trouble we can't manage." Albert checked his watch. "I do need you to take me to the train station, though."

I looked at the suitcase and then back to Albert. "What time does your train leave?"

"3:27 am."

"Well, that's inconvenient as shit, isn't it?"

CHAPTER 30

I CAUGHT a few hours of sleep after dropping Albert off at Cincinnati Union Terminal to catch his train to the backwoods of Maine. Two hours after I woke up, Connor arrived wearing his green baseball cap, a khaki jacket and holding two breakfast burritos and more blueberry coffee.

“Dad get off okay?” he asked, handing me a cup.

“As far as I know.” I checked my watch. “He should be well on his way by now.” I shook my head. “I feel like a shitty son letting him go off on his own like that. Who knows what he’s going to get into.”

“He’ll be fine.”

"How do you know? He's seventy-one."

"He's tougher than you think. If you're going to worry about anyone, worry about Ollie. Dad and Mitch can do some serious damage when they want to."

"How do you know what he can do?" I unwrapped my breakfast. "I feel like you and Albert have some strange partnership going on. You knew about Ollie, and he's obviously been feeding you intel on me if you knew about my Brooke situation. We haven't talked in five years, but I get the impression you two chat like old ladies at a book club."

"We chat on and off." Connor set his coffee and breakfast burrito on the table and sat down. "After all this shit went down in Maine, Dad was pretty shaken up. He knew Ollie was connected and he didn't really know how safe it would be to stay up there. He and I talked and decided it might be safer for him to be back in Cincinnati year round instead of spending the summers in Maine. He sold his apartment here and moved into that nursing home to stay under the radar."

“I thought he did it because he didn’t want to be a burden on me.”

“A burden?” said Connor. “I think he relishes being a burden. No, it was to lay low for a while. I think he was more concerned about Ollie’s boys than Ollie himself, considering Ollie was locked away in Machiasport.”

“And you think he’s capable of handling Ollie?”

“If I didn’t, I wouldn’t be standing here eating a shitty burrito.”

The more I learned about my father, the less I thought I knew. Connor jammed what was left of his breakfast into his mouth.

“Now stop worrying about it,” he said. “Dad and Mitch have it all covered. And I’ve got a feeling they might get some help once they’re up there.” He wiped his mouth and pushed his coffee aside. “Now, can we forget about Dad and get back to the banker?”

“No, we can't.”

“What?”

I slammed my breakfast onto the table and watched as the foil wrapper exploded, sending bits of tortilla, egg, cheese, and sauce across the kitchen. "This bullshit ends now," I said.

"What are you talking about?"

"You." I leaned in close. "You waltz into my living room after being MIA for five years. You interject yourself into my case, which I don't even know if I should trust you with. Who are you?"

"I'm not sure what…"

"Where the fuck have you been for the last five years and why are you here all of a sudden?"

"I thought you were happy to see me?"

"I'm waffling between happy, concerned, and suspicious as fuck."

"I can't come back to see my family?"

"No. You can't. Not after five years of nothing. No phone calls. No goddamn Christmas cards. No nothing. There's something you're not telling me, and I want to know what it is. Why did you disappear and why are you back?"

Connor took a breath and then sipped his coffee. He pulled a chair out from the dining room table and sat down.

"I've been in a military prison in Kansas."

"What?"

He cocked his head to the side. "You asked where I've been for the past five years. Well, I've been in Leavenworth."

"As in, you worked there?"

"Not exactly," said Connor.

"Go ahead. You can't end on that."

"I won't go into details, but we were conducting recon operations near Mosul and picked up two-high value targets. We were ordered to interrogate both men and uncover details of a possible ambush on our forces in the region."

"And?" I said.

"And, it didn't go well. What started as an interrogation ended in me being court martialed for violating Articles 128 and 134 of the Uniform Code. They tossed me in the brig for five years. Four months ago they let me out with full benefits and reassigned me to a base near Boston."

"What do Articles 128 and 134 refer to?"

"Assault mostly. There's some other shit in there too, but let's just go with assault. The government was getting pressured to crack down on detainee abuse. It was a shit charge, but they needed to do something to show they were taking the allegations seriously. They had to act."

"So you were a scapegoat?"

"No, I assaulted the piece of shit." He smiled. "Look, the world's a messy place. Sometimes you get dirty."

"What do you do in Boston?" I said.

"Civil affairs training mostly. On base. And my side business, but I already told you about that."

"Why did you pick now to come back?"

"You and dad are the only family I've got left. After the Bishop thing, I thought you might be in trouble, so I came back to make sure you didn't need any help." He slipped his baseball cap off and scratched his head. “And as it turns out, you did need my help.”

“Does Albert know about your prison stint?”

“He knows.” He paused. ”The Army contacted him. It’s protocol.”

“How did you talk to Albert about Ollie then? If you were off the grid?”

“We wrote to each other. No rules against that. But I didn’t really want to contact you. Being in prison isn’t easy to hide, and I wanted to keep it to myself as long as possible.” He looked at me and squinted. “You’re the PI. If you were curious, why didn’t you ever look into me?”

“Who says I didn’t?”

I did look into Connor a few times, with shitty results. Getting intel on someone in Indianapolis is one thing, but it gets a lot murkier when you step outside the country. And it gets even worse when the military is involved. I knew Connor joined the Rangers and was deployed to Iraq, but the trail ended there.

“So now you know,” he said. He slipped his cap back on. “So, we good?”

I studied his face. "Yeah," I said. "We're good. For now. Let's get back to work."

CONNOR FOLLOWED ME INTO THE DEN, AND I booted up my desktop computer.

"Since I told you what you wanted to know, can I ask you a question?"

"You mean there's something you don't know about me? From our conversations thus far, I got the impression you already knew everything there was to know."

"So is that a yes or a no?"

"Shoot," I said.

"What happened between you and Brooke?"

"Take your hat off," I said. He slipped it off, and I stood up and snapped Connor's photo with my mobile phone, then connected the phone to my computer. "Not sure we have enough time to get into that. It's a long story."

"How about the highlights?"

"Long story short is she was sick of me being a PI. She didn't like the idea of me getting shot and bleeding to death in an alley somewhere. And she hated the hours. You know how it is, nothing runs on a schedule. Sometimes you're in at 3:00 am and sometimes you have to disappear for days at a time to track someone down."

"So it wasn't about you losing your PI license?"

"Not really." I grabbed a sheet of thick stock from the printer stand and placed it in the printer tray. "It was more about her wanting me to have a safer, steadier 9 to 5. Why all the questions about Brooke?"

"Just wanted to know what happened. Dad mentioned you two were done, but he didn't elaborate on why."

I turned back to the computer and clicked and dragged Connor's photo into a template. Then I clicked open another file and pulled my own photo into the same template.

"There's probably more to it, but I can sleep better at night thinking it was all about the job. To be honest, the relationship just ran its course. Probably would have ended before it did had we not had Becca. She kept us together longer than we should have been."

"You still get along?"

"Have to, considering we're raising a daughter together. Well, not together-together, but you know what I mean." I went back to work on the template.

"And this Daryl guy?"

"She met him at the hospital where she works. I never asked her if she hooked up with him before we split or not. I really don't wanna know. I'll just assume she was committed to our marriage until it officially ended. I always was. The ironic thing is she told me she shacked up with Daryl because he was the safer alternative. Always came home at the same time every night. Mr. Dependable."

"And he's the reason you're neck-deep in this shit?"

"Like I said, ironic." I opened my browser and grabbed an image of the Indiana state seal.

"You seeing anyone else?"

"A few weeks ago I met a nurse at Becca's school."

Connor cracked a smile. "Really, a school nurse?"

"Her name is Jennifer." I dropped the image into the template.

"How does Becca feel about you nailing her nurse?"

I went back to typing. "You know, crazy thing, but Becca and I usually don't chat about my sex life. We tend to stick to lighter topics like cartoons, video games, and absentee uncles."

I opened up a box of thick plastic name-badge backs, and grabbed two metal clips. I wanted to change the subject as I fumbled with the name badges.

"What about you? You a swinging Bostonian bachelor?" I clicked 'print' on the screen and the printer surged to life.

"Married to my career, little brother," Connor raised his voice over the sound of the printer. "A few casual flings, but that's about it. You're asking for trouble getting too close to anyone in this business. Bad things tend to happen."

“Yes, they do.” The printer spat out a sheet of thick perforated paper. I grabbed the sheet and tore two sections apart. Then I peeled off the sticky front of the paper, carefully aligned it to the plastic backs, and applied the adhesive side.

“A Catholic school nurse?” “That probably says something about you on a physiological level.”

“Yeah, it means I like getting laid.” I ran the new badges through a lamination machine and attached the metal clasps.

“Here you go, Special Investigator Brian Tipton,” I said, handing one of the name badges to Connor.

Connor scrutinized the ID. “It looks just like me.”

CHAPTER 31

Brooke pulled to a stop in front of the Cincinnati Catholic Academy. A woman in her mid-twenties approached the passenger side of the car, the vibrant school logo patch on her white polo shirt gleaming in the morning sun like an angelic halo.

The attendant opened the rear passenger door, helped Becca out of her booster seat, and then waved to Brooke before closing the door and ushering Becca into a line with a few dozen other students all waiting to be released into the school.

Brooke polished off what was left of her coffee and wedged the large stainless steel tumbler into the Range Rover's cup holder. Twenty minutes after pulling away from Becca's school, she parked in a corner spot on the third floor of the Christ Hospital parking garage. She didn't see the red minivan pull in behind her.

Brooke looked on the passenger floor for her sneakers, but they weren't there. She turned and looked into the back seat but still didn't see them. Remembering she had tossed them into the rear of the SUV the night before, she stepped out of the car and opened the lift gate. Bingo.

She grabbed the sneakers, placed her right leg onto the rear bumper, slipped her stiletto heel from her foot, and replaced it with the sneaker. She was lacing up the shoe when someone behind her wrapped a thick leather-clad forearm over her mouth. His other hand grabbed her left arm and pinned it behind her back. She struggled to free herself, but the man behind her tightened his grip, halting her struggle.

"Hello again, sexy," said the man.

She didn't have to see him to know it was Adler. Brooke arched her head up away from his arm so she could speak. Her heart pounded in her chest.

"What do you want?"

"I want you to tell me what your boyfriend's got on our banker friend. We haven't heard from him in a while. Just want to make sure he's still on the case."

Brooke tried to pry Adler's forearm away with her free hand, but Adler jerked on her left arm, pinning it higher on her back. Pain shot through her shoulder, and she clenched her teeth and buried her mouth back into Adler's forearm, afraid of what he might do if she screamed.

After a moment, he relaxed his grip on her left arm. "One more time, Brooke. The banker? What does Mr. Finn know about him?"

She took a deep breath. "I don't know. He doesn't talk to me about what he's working on. I don't know anything about it."

A car turned onto the third floor of the parking garage. Its tires squealed as it made the turn onto the same row as Brooke's Range Rover.

Adler moved his forearm from around Brooke's throat, grabbed a clump of her red hair with his right hand and yanked her head back so her ear was next to his mouth. "Scream and I'll break your head open," he whispered. He released her hair and her left arm and rested his hand against the Range Rover's open lift gate.

A blue BMW slowly rolled past them and then turned onto the ramp to the upper level.

"I tell you what," said Adler. The next time you talk to him, you ask him what he's found." Adler tossed a Post-It note into the back of the SUV. "And then you call me at that number and tell me what you find out. Mr. Holbrook is a patient person, but he's getting agitated that he hasn't heard anything. We're starting to think Mr. Finn isn't taking this very seriously."

Brooke nodded.

"Okay, I'll ask him"

"You better hope he finds the banker, or I'm gonna have to step things up. Maybe come back and see you again. Or maybe go over to that nice big school where you dropped off your daughter."

"I said, I'll tell him."

"Good," said Adler. "Now, there's something else I came for." Adler slammed his fist into the back of Brooke's head, sending her tumbling into the back of the Range Rover. He grabbed her waist and pulled her out so her feet were on the ground. She put her hand under her body and struggled to raise up, but Adler hit her again, this time slamming her head into the carpeted floor in the back of the vehicle.

He kicked her legs apart with a leather boot and reached up under her dress. Her head spun as he yanked her panties down around her ankles. She was about to black out when she heard the loud chirp from the parking garage emergency alarm. She couldn't see it, but she knew the blue emergency light was flashing somewhere nearby. It must have been the driver in the BMW.

Brooke closed her eyes, and everything went dark.

WHEN BROOKE CAME TO, SHE WAS LYING ON THE concrete floor of the parking garage. She rubbed her head and then noticed the three men standing in front of her. Two were security officers, and the third was a man she recognized from her office.

"Are you all right, Ms. Harding?" said one of the security guards. He held her wallet in one hand and her driver's license in the other.

She sat up, blinked hard, and tried to stand when the other officer placed a hand on her shoulder. "Don't move, ma'am. Someone is bringing a gurney. We've also notified the police." He motioned to the man from Brooke's office. "Mr. Kendrick here gave the police a description of the man who was with you, and they're searching the hospital campus."

"Thank you," she said, trying again to stand.

"Ms. Harding, please stay still."

"I'm all right," she said. "Really. I just need some ice for my head. I'm okay."

The officer, realizing Brooke wasn't going to stay down, helped her stand. "Do you know who that man was? Mr. Kendrick said he assaulted you." He handed Brooke her wallet and license.

Brooke shook her head. "Never seen him before. He came up behind me while I was changing my shoes for work. I never even saw his face."

She turned around and saw the Post-It note lying in the trunk. She snatched it up with her right hand and stuffed it inside her wallet.

"Are you sure you're okay, Ms. Harding?" said the security officer.

"I'm fine. Really. Thank you." She turned to Kendrick. "And thank you for activating the alarm."

"Of course," said Kendrick.

"I think I just want to get to work. All I need is some ice for my head, and I'll be fine."

The officers looked at each other. "Ms. Harding, we can't let—"

"I said I'm fine. Really."

Brooke grabbed her remaining sneaker from the rear of the SUV and closed the liftgate.

"You should really be evaluated before—"

"I'm fine," she said as she closed the liftgate, ran across the parking lot, and disappeared into the hospital's elevator bank. They didn't see her start to cry.

CHAPTER 32

CONNOR and I left my apartment, walked to his Escalade, and picked up I-74 to Indianapolis. A quick search on my phone showed eleven DMV locations near Indianapolis. I knew the banker had been operating within a thirty-mile radius of Holbrook's farm in Greenwood, Indiana, so I decided to focus on the closest DMV to Greenwood, which was the South Meridian License Branch on South Meridian Street.

More than a hundred miles later, we pulled into the DMV parking lot.

One summer, when Connor and I were kids, we stayed up late to watch *David Letterman* and somehow ended up prank calling random phone numbers around 1:00 am. After getting bored messing with people we didn't know, Connor decided to prank 9-1-1 but hung up the phone before he thought the dispatcher had answered. Letterman was still on when two uniformed police officers knocked on the front door. Connor and I opened the door, and one of the officers asked if everything was okay. We told him everything was gravy. Then he instructed us to wake our parents. I'm not sure why, but we decided to take our chances with Albert.

A few minutes later, a groggy Albert stepped to the door in his underwear and demanded to know why he was talking to two police officers instead of sleeping in his bed. They explained they had received a 9-1-1 call from our address and assumed, correctly, that one of us had dialed and hung up. My father made Connor and me apologize for wasting the officers' time and explained that he'd think of an appropriate punishment for us in the morning. The officers, satisfied, went on their way, and Albert went back to sleep, saying he'd deal with us later. He never brought it up again, and to this day, I believed Albert thought he'd dreamed the entire episode.

Aside from learning not to fuck with the 9-1-1 system, I also learned something else that night. I learned that if you look the part, people will take you at your word. There's no doubt in my mind that the two men on our doorstep that night were police officers. Of course, they were. They wore blue uniforms and had badges pinned to their chests. They also wore thick shiny black belts with a holstered revolver on their right hip and a black baton and leather pouch for their handcuffs on their left hip. The leather belts and silver buckles sparkled in the wash from the front porch light.

There was never a doubt as to who these two men were. My father never asked for their badge numbers or called the Cincinnati Police Department to confirm their identities. He didn't need to. They looked the part.

There's an old adage that says if you walk briskly and carry a clipboard, you can gain access anywhere. That's oversimplified, of course, but the main idea holds true. If you appear confident and look the part, few will question you. I'd employed what those two officers had taught me many times, and I was about to do it again, this time at the South Meridian DMV.

CONNOR STRAIGHTENED HIS TIE AND RAN HIS hand through his hair. He tugged on the sleeves of the navy-blue suit jacket that had hung in my closet only a few hours earlier.

"When did you get so short?" he said.

"Sorry. You should have packed your own suit."

"Didn't know I'd need one."

I grabbed a leather portfolio that contained a yellow legal pad and pen, and we headed for the front door.

The young woman behind the counter stood up when we came in. Every other time I'd ever been to the DMV, it was packed. But apparently, everyone in town had some place better to be, because the place was empty except for three DMV employees and two men in navy-blue suits pretending to be government employees.

"How can I help you, gentlemen?" said the woman as she looked at the ID clipped to the front of my suit jacket.

"Hello…" I waited for her name.

"Barb."

"Hello, Barb. I'm Special Investigator Roger Mathers, and this is Special Investigator Brian Tipton." Connor nodded. "We're with the Inspector General's office."

Barb leaned in closer and folded her hands on top of the shoulder-high counter. Hearing our introductions, the two other women walked over and stood next to Barb.

"Inspector General? What can I do for you?"

"We're investigating a potential fraud." I opened the leather portfolio and clicked open the pen. "I'd like you to access a registration for me."

"For who?"

I read from the registration we printed out earlier. "Thomas Coyne. D.O.B is May 20, 1949."

"I've got it," said Barb. The two other women inched closer to her shoulder. According to her name tag, one was named Emma. The other one didn't wear a name tag. "Thomas Coyne, 1053 Industrial Parkway."

Emma leaned forward. "Is this your perp?"

Connor's face strained to hold back a laugh.

"Possibly." I leaned across the counter and rotated the monitor so I could see it. The green flickering computer screen looked like something from the '80s. "What can you tell me about this record?"

Barb studied the screen. "It's a standard license. No restrictions. No fines."

"Can you tell me if it's been edited? The information in the system?"

Barb slapped a few keys on the graying keyboard. Emma maneuvered closer. "Yes. It was edited."

Connor looked at me. "When?" he said.

Barb smacked more keys. "Let's see... Wait, that's odd."

"What's odd?" I said.

"Someone edited it two days after they created it."

"That *is* odd," said Emma peering over Barb's shoulder. "Who did it?"

Barb hit a few more keys. "Jeff Collins."

"I knew it," said the third woman, throwing her hands up into the air. "I'da bet my lunch it was Jeff Collins."

Part of me wanted to see where this side conversation went, but Connor must have been anxious.

"Can you look in the edits?" he said. "To see what information this Jeff Collins fella altered?"

"Uh-huh. I can revert it back to the original," said Barb, clicking more keys. A moment later the printer behind her spat out a sheet of paper. Barb swiped it from the tray and peered down at it.

"He changed the whole damn thing," she said.

"That boy was always messing up," said Emma, looking up at me. "He went and got hisself fired. Too many mistakes."

Barb waved the printout in the air. "Like this one. Nobody's perfect, but he messed up this whole record. Had to change it all."

I glanced up for a moment and noted the three cameras watching us from the wall. “May I see that, Barb?” I said.

Barb handed me the printout. I took a deep breath and watched as the banker materialized in front of me. Everything we’d been searching for was looking back at us from a grainy gray-and-white printout. Thomas Coyne was gone. The banker’s real name was William Burns. The photo on the printout matched the one we pulled from the DMV database yesterday, but the printout included all the real information the banker used to get his license. He must have paid Jeff Collins to alter the information later, but while Jeff could change the information in the system, he hadn’t erased the edit history.

William Burns, 4408 Ivy Way, Cope, Indiana. I wanted to believe this was the banker, but he’d duped us before. Everything we got from the DMV was based on the truck’s VIN from the registration, but why didn’t the banker swap the VIN to add another layer of misinformation on top of the steaming pile of shit he’d already left for us?

I turned back to the three women staring at us. I placed the printout on the counter.

"You said all the information had been corrected," I said. "What about the VIN? Does the history show any changes to that?"

Barb smiled wider than I thought was humanly possible. "You can't change the VIN, honey. It's a locked field. Once you create a record and enter a VIN, it's there to stay."

"Jeff Collins hasn't worked here for two years," said Emma. "Is he in trouble?"

I folded the printout and placed it inside my leather portfolio. "We'll see." I nodded to Connor. "Thank you, ladies. We appreciate your time. This is very helpful."

"You're welcome," said the three women in unison.

Connor and I walked out of the DMV and moved one step closer to finding Holbrook's five million.

THE BANKER HAD ALREADY LED ME TO ONE DEAD-end with Thomas Coyne, and I wondered if William Burns was the real deal or just another speed bump on the road to finding his real identity. One way to find out. When we returned to my apartment in Cincinnati, I pulled up the IRB search database and entered "William Burns" into the search field. Within seconds, I confirmed his identify and his address. According to the data in the system, William Burns was a real person living a real life, with a real past. William Burns was genuine, but was he the banker?

CHAPTER 33

My phone vibrated on my desk, and Brooke's photo appeared on the screen.

"Hey," I said.

"Adler attacked me!" Her voice was rushed like it had been the night she called to tell me Adler came to her home.

"What are you talking about? How did he find you at your sister's place?"

"Not there. He cornered me at work. In the parking garage at the hospital. He must have followed me there."

"What happened?"

“I’m calling the police,” she said.

“Wait. Tell me what happened.”

“What difference does it make? He attacked me, and that’s all that matters. This has gone too far. I’m not protecting Daryl anymore.”

“Brooke, you can't go to the police. Let me take care of this. Going to the police is only going to make it worse.”

“Goddamn you, Finn. He tried to rape me, and you want me to keep quiet? Fuck you, I’m calling the police.”

“If you go to the police, nothing is going to happen to Adler. He’ll walk. Holbrook will make sure of that. But I can hurt him. I can make him pay for it.”

“I don't want revenge, Finn. I want justice. I want him to rot in prison where he belongs.”

I thought back to the background report I ran on Adler before I met him at the coffee shop. He didn’t have a criminal record, probably because Holbrook had insulated him.

"He won't see a day of prison, Brooke. People like Holbrook own the police. Let me get him."

"You were the one who told me to go to the police in the first place, and now you're telling me not to? He attacked me, and if it weren't for some Good Samaritan, he might have killed me." She paused. "Adler came looking for information. Why haven't you called them? To give them an update? That's what he said he wanted. Why didn't you call them?"

"Because until today, I haven't had anything to update them on. We've been running around in circles looking for this guy, but I think I've finally found him."

I felt comfortable dealing with asshats like Adler. That's the environment I work in, but until now, Brooke and Becca were safe. My work and my family were never supposed to intersect, but now they were careening toward each other like an out-of-control eighteen-wheeler with no brakes.

My grip tightened on the phone. "I'm sorry this all happened." I paused. "This will all be over soon, and I promise you I'll make Adler pay for what he did. If we get the police involved now, Holbrook is going to come at us ten times as hard. I can take care of it, but in the meantime, I want you to stay here with me."

"We're fine at my sister's place. No one knows we're here, and I'm not going to disrupt Becca any more than I already have by moving her somewhere else."

"Adler tailed you from somewhere," I said.

"I think he followed me from Becca's school."

"I don't like it."

"You think I do? Just make this go away. If Adler shows his face around me again, I'm going to the cops, Finn."

When I hung up with Brooke, it took everything I had not to put the phone and my fist through the wall. Brooke was safer at Allison's place anyway. With Albert gone and Connor and me out searching for the banker, there wouldn't be anyone to watch out for them. At least she had Allison and Bill to keep an eye on her at their place, but that still didn't make it any easier.

Adler and Holbrook had stepped over the line. I'd have to put them back in their place.

I dialed the number Adler gave me.

"Hello?" said Adler.

"Give the phone to Holbrook," I said.

"Anything you got to say to him, you can say to me."

"I've only got one thing to say to you, and I'll tell you that after I speak with Holbrook. Now pass him the phone, or you don't get your update."

A moment later, Holbrook was on the line.

"You got news for me?"

When I first met Adler and Darby in the coffee shop, they had all the leverage. I was trying to get Daryl out of a shitty situation, and I had nothing to offer. Now I had something to offer that was worth more than Daryl continuing to supply Holbrook with fentanyl. I had the banker's identity. Leverage had shifted, and I had enough to start making threats.

"Before I give you a goddamn thing, I want to know if Adler went after my ex-wife on his own or if you sent him."

"You need to be more concerned with finding the banker…"

I cut him off. "Answer my fucking question. Did you send Adler, or did he go on his own?"

"What does it matter?"

"It's gonna determine who walks away after this is all over." Holbrook was silent. "Let me be clear about something, Holbrook. You send anyone after my family again, and I'll slice his throat open so wide you can use him as a PEZ dispenser."

"We'll see who walks away when this is over." He paused. "Now, what do you have?"

"I've got a name, but if you pull this shit again, you'll never hear it. And you won't get a goddamn cent of your money."

"This is on you. I told you I wanted updates, but perhaps you didn't take me seriously."

"I'll call you when I have a reason to call you. It wastes your time and mine if I have to explain every road I go down. All you need to know is I'm close to finding your guy. I've already got a name, and soon I'll have his location."

"Who is he?" said Holbrook.

"I'll hang onto that tidbit until later to ensure you or Adler don't do something stupid again. I'll call you when I have your money. Not before. Now put Adler back on the line."

"I think you've forgotten who you work for."

"I didn't forget shit. Put Adler on the phone, or I walk away, and I take the banker's name with me."

Holbrook was silent for a moment, then he passed the phone to Adler.

"You upset with me?" said Adler.

"Upset doesn't begin to cover it, asshole. Get this one thing through your head. When this is over, I'm going to burn you to the ground."

"I look forward to that," he said. "I'm also looking forward to fucking your lady friend. We got interrupted last time."

The line went dead.

I took a deep breath, scanned my cell phone's directory, and dialed again.

"Cricket, I've got a gig for you. I need you to keep eyeballs on someone."

"Who is it?"

"My ex-wife. She's staying at her sister's place." I gave him Allison's address. "It's an upscale neighborhood, so you'll need to rent a car. Something European. To blend in."

"How long you want me to sit on the house?"

"A few days. A week at the most."

"That's gonna cost you, Finn."

"I know."

"Your girl know I'm gonna be there?"

"No. Just between us."

"Okay, what exactly am I looking for?"

"Guy by the name of Adler. About six-foot-two. Looks Italian. Short black hair. Stocky build. Mid-thirties. Likes leather. He might be traveling with another guy. Bigger. Bald with a mustache and goatee. Drives a red minivan."

"A minivan?" Cricket paused. "You serious?"

"Yup."

"Okay," said Cricket. "What do you want me to do if he shows?"

"You still got that street sweeper?"

"I could dust it off."

"Good," I said. "You see him, take him down."

"You sure?"

"Sure as shit."

"All right. He won't reach the lawn."

CHAPTER 34

ALBERT STEPPED out of the Portland Transportation Center, a red brick building that looked more like a small bank than a train depot. He pulled his suitcase across the white crosswalk onto a concrete walkway and scanned the adjacent parking lot. From across the lot, an F-350 pickup roared to life and pulled to a stop in front of Albert.

Mitch Skinner rolled down the window. “I see you made the trip.”

“Pretty easy to do,” said Albert. “All I had to do was sit there. Even you could have done it.”

Mitch looked down at the suitcase. “What are you waiting for? Get in.”

"Thought you'd be a gentleman and grab my bag for me."

"If that's what you're waiting on, we're gonna be here awhile. Now get your elderly ass in here." Mitch pointed to the truck's bed with a hitchhiker's thumb. "Be glad you're not riding in the rumble seat."

Albert hefted his suitcase into the bed, making sure it bounced off the small window separating the bed and the cab. He smiled, walked behind the pickup, and slid into the passenger side of the vehicle. "Nice truck. You push this thing here?"

"Would a brought my '68 Shelby Mustang, but I didn't want you to stink it up."

"And how did you get a '68 Shelby?"

"Ask your boy," said Mitch. "You had a lot of time to think on that train. You come up with a plan, or we just gonna wing it?"

"Can't wing it with Ollie. Gotta be smart this time. Make sure this doesn't come back to bite us in the ass again. I think we should start with Cutter. He helped us out before. Might be up for helping us out again."

“What if he ain’t?”

“Then we figure something else out,” Albert looked out the window as Mitch pulled onto Route 1. “Where we going anyway?”

“Ollie probably has eyes on my place,” said Mitch. “Won’t be smart to hang around there. I got a room at Boley’s Motel.”

“What about Dottie?”

“Shipped her off to our daughter’s place in Kittery. She’ll be safe there until things blow over.”

“A motel, huh?”

“Yeah.” Mitch looked at Albert. “You can sleep on the floor tonight. We’ll go see Cutter first thing in the morning.”

CHAPTER 35

THE ADDRESS we pulled from William Burns' real driver's license led us to Ivy Fields, an upscale neighborhood near Cope, Indiana. Connor drove us through the neighborhood's entrance, which was flanked by two large brick walls, both adorned with ivy.

I pulled Burns' address up on my cell phone's map and studied the aerial view. It showed about thirty homes. According to the map, there were four cul-de-sacs and one entrance, the same one we'd just passed through. Burns lived two streets away from the entrance.

"Take this left, and then another left," I said. "He's the fourth house on the right."

From the street, each home looked larger than 4,500 square feet. Most of the homes had four-car garages, and a few had large RV-storage garages, a perfect place to shelter a box truck at night.

Connor slowed the SUV as we turned onto Ivy Way. Burns' house was a federal-style red brick. White trim popped against the dozen or so windows on the front. Two white columns flanked the black front door. A single black iron light fixture hung over the front door. There were four newspapers on the ground where the sidewalk intersected the driveway. Someone wasn't home. The cobblestone driveway gently curved toward two single garage doors attached to the house and two more garage doors on an outbuilding next to the house. No RV parking.

Connor pointed out the Escalade's front window. "Looks like we found our cover," he said.

Up ahead about ten cars, mostly European sedans, were parked in front of a large cedar home that sported several large windows, a green roof, and a "for sale" sign. The drivers were eagerly awaiting the open house, which, according to the sign in the home's front yard, was to begin in ten minutes.

Connor followed Ivy Way until it dead-ended into a cul-de-sac, and then he turned around and parked behind the row of vehicles waiting for the open house. Some of the couples had left their luxury cars and milled about the front lawn, probably explaining to one another how they would landscape the flower beds should they end up getting the place.

About five minutes after we parked, an attractive brunette wearing a bright red blazer and a brighter smile stepped onto the front porch of the cedar home and ushered everyone inside. Once everyone had disappeared, Connor and I stepped out of the Escalade and headed toward Burns' home across the street.

The four newspapers lying in their green wrappers hinted that Burns wasn't there. If this was the banker's home, I expected him to be long gone by now, which would mean more than four orphaned newspapers. It's possible, if the banker had skipped town with Holbrook's cash, that someone was looking in on the home for him and collecting the papers to keep up appearances. Or the realtor could be tossing them to keep the neighborhood tidy, but if that were the case, why didn't she swipe these four in advance of her open house? Of course, maybe the banker only received the newspaper a few days a week, in which case, four papers fit the timeline. I'd been looking for him for a week, and Holbrook mentioned he'd been MIA for a week before that.

Everything I knew about Burns told me he was a smart guy, and he'd have to be scrambled in the head to take that kind of money from someone like Holbrook and then stick around for someone like me to put a gun to his head and ask for it back. More than likely, he skipped town two weeks ago or longer and was relaxing on a beach somewhere far away from Holbrook's horse farm. Even with Burns gone though, I hoped there was something inside that brick house that could warm up the trail.

I'd learned a lot about criminal behavior since I started working as a PI. One of those nuggets is that criminals don't use moving vans. They're prepared to skip town at a moment's notice, and they don't pack up all their belongings to take with them. That means there was a high probability that something in that house could push us in the right direction. A file, a ticket stub, a receipt, something. There's always something. Now it was time to find out what.

Connor and I jogged up the driveway. Connor peered through the window of the detached garage.

"Nothing in here," he said. "Let's focus on the house."

A moment later, we stood on the back porch away from the prying eyes of any potential homebuyers across the street. The back yard was tidy. A cedar pergola stood on a flagstone patio, the remnants of the previous season's wisteria vines tangled around its top. Burns' back yard was surrounded by evergreen trees and shrubs, providing a blanket of privacy between his neighbors and us. Connor and I surveyed the inside of the home through a glass door on the back porch. Directly behind the door was a small table, and next to that an impressive kitchen with marble countertops and a large kidney-shaped island in the middle. Beyond the small table was the great room, which was also connected to the dining room. The floor plan was wide open, and I could see most of the main floor, with the exception of whatever waited behind the two closed French doors adjacent to the front door. On the wall directly next to the French doors was an alarm system keypad, but I couldn't see a light indicating that it was armed.

I hadn’t finished surveying the home’s layout when I heard a muffled cracking sound. I turned to find Connor slipping his jacket back on, a set of brass knuckles wrapped around his fingers.

“What?” he said. “No one’s home, and this is the quickest way in.” Connor pocketed the brass knuckles, reached his hand through the fractured glass panel, and unlocked the deadbolt on the other side. We held our breath as he turned the knob. If the alarm was active, we’d find out in a matter of seconds. Connor pushed the door open, and we exhaled. No piercing beep. That unnerved me. Why would the banker have an alarm on his home, but not activate it? Was he home? Was there someone else watching the house who forgot to set it? Maybe there was no reason to set it because the cash wasn't there. Or maybe the banker forgot. Another thing I’d learned over the years was that criminals made stupid mistakes. Even the smart ones.

We moved quickly once we stepped inside. We couldn’t see it from the patio, but there were six cardboard boxes on the kitchen floor, behind the marble-topped island. The boxes were filled with glassware and cooking utensils, mixing bowls, and cutting boards. Connor gave them a cursory glance as he passed through the kitchen, looking for an entrance into the garage and a potential delivery vehicle. I moved past the kitchen and slipped through the two French doors into the den, which doubled as an office.

Inside the den was a dark brown desk, a leather chair, and a storage cabinet that held a printer stand. A small stack of flat cardboard boxes leaned against the cabinet. Two large windows covered with white plantation shutters opened to Ivy Way. From my position inside the den, I could see if anyone pulled into the driveway. After checking the street, I turned my attention to the desk.

The desk was neat, and the rest of the room was as clean as a funeral home. Not a speck of dust, which wasn't surprising given the vacuum tracks on the carpet.

There were two photos on the desk. One of the photos was Burns and a middle-aged brunette. A stone wall, a black cannon, and a slim tree trunk, maybe a palm tree, stood behind them. Given the age difference, they didn't look like a couple, but I couldn't rule it out. The other photograph showed a much younger Burns, by thirty years or more, with a blonde woman and an awkward-looking teenage girl. A quick comparison revealed the girl to be the teenage version of the woman in the other picture. Maybe a daughter. I took a mental snapshot of the photos and moved on to the pile of mail that teetered on top of a black metal desktop organizer.

I flipped through the envelopes, all addressed to William Burns. There were several bills, some junk mail, and two envelopes from Prudential Insurance.

I piled the mail back on top of the organizer and tried the desk drawer. The two left drawers contained the usual office supplies; pens, paper clips, Post-It notes, thumbtacks, and binder clips. The bottom drawer held a stapler and two boxes of stationery, but nothing else of interest. The long center drawer revealed a tangle of charger cords, a key ring with four keys, more pens, address labels, and a few crinkled photographs. The drawer on the right was a double drawer that had a hanging file system built into its sides. There were six dark green hanging folders, each containing several more file folders. I thumbed through the folders, noting the labels on each. “Phone,” “Utilities,” “Electric,” “Taxes,” “Lawn Care.” Nothing seemed interesting until I hit “Condo” and “Storage Unit.” I yanked both folders and opened them on the desk.

The folder labeled Condo included a purchase agreement for a unit at the Cedar Woods condominiums on East Sycamore Street in Morgantown, Indiana. The folder labeled Storage Unit included monthly invoices for S&F Storage, an RV storage facility on South Centerline Road in Mt. Pleasant, Indiana. The invoice didn’t specify a unit number, but the condo purchase agreement did. Both documents indicated William Burns was the owner.

I was flipping through two years’ worth of storage rental invoices when Connor stepped into the den. I’d almost forgotten that he was with me.

“There’s an Audi in the garage, but no sign of the money,” he said. “I checked the basement, but nothing there. The bedroom is torn to shit. Moving boxes everywhere. Looks like someone’s packing the place up.”

"That explains the boxes in the kitchen," I said.

"Did you find anything in here?"

"Maybe." I tucked the invoices back into the folder. "I've got a purchase agreement for a condo and some rental information for a unit at an RV storage park."

"They local?"

I double-checked the addresses on the forms. "Looks like it."

"He could have stashed the money at either of those places. The vehicle too."

"Only one way to find out." I stacked the folders on top of each other and tucked them under my arm.

"There doesn't seem to be anything else here," said Connor. "If the banker needed a place to stash a large amount of cash or a truck, that storage unit looks pretty good."

"It fits," I said. "Let's follow up on the condo first. Burns might be using it as a safe house. Maybe we can ask him where the money is personally."

"It's your show, little brother."

"Let's go." We were already in the great room when I turned around, headed back to the den, swiped the keyring from the center drawer, and slipped it in my pocket.

A few minutes later, we were back in Connor's Escalade, heading to the entrance of Ivy Fields, and then later, back to Cincinnati for a date with my daughter.

CHAPTER 36

SOMETIME AFTER WE SPLIT, Brooke mentioned that I was a better part-time father than a full-time one. When she first said it, part of me wanted to put her through a wall, but after the pain of the divorce subsided, I realized she was right. I *was* a better part-time father. I loved Becca, but when I was around her all the time, I wasn't engaged. I was a player in the background, not on the main stage. There was always something else that needed to be done. Crap around the house, client work, errands. Becca got whatever time was left after I finished all the other shit. I knew that wasn't right, but I was too caught up in the inertia of daily life to change it.

When Brooke and I decided to go our separate ways, we discussed visitation, and I made a promise to myself that when I was with Becca, she got a hundred percent of me. Nothing else mattered. All that other shit that I used to prioritize over her went away. That was why I had no issues with setting aside Holbrook's investigation for Becca's weekend visit.

On Friday, we had our usual pepperoni pizza and a side of grapes at Dewey's on Montgomery Road. With Albert playing detective in Maine, I asked Connor to join us, but he went back to his hotel instead. He said he had other business to take care of. I was disappointed but also relieved, since I wasn't sure how to introduce him to Becca for the first time. She's a smart girl and would want to know why he'd waited so long to visit, and I wasn't eager to explain the concept of a black-site prison.

After pizza, we hit an arcade. Between us, we pocketed about a thousand prize tickets, which Becca redeemed for a lava lamp and a bag of Skittles. Back at my place, she picked out a Disney movie from the DVD vault under my flat-screen television. We both fell asleep on the couch before the movie wrapped, but I'm pretty sure she conked out before I did.

Becca and I spent Saturday at an indoor water park, then hit one of those industrial-sized Halloween stores that seemed to erupt from the parking lot asphalt eight weeks before Halloween. I had promised Brooke I'd help Becca with a Halloween costume, and I wasn't going to disappoint. I ushered her at fire-alarm speed past the aisles featuring the sexy nurse, sexy cheerleader, sexy nun, and sexy vampire costumes until we found the children's section. Thankfully, at six years old, she was still interested in the more innocent costumes. After waffling between the black cat and unicorn, she settled on the cat. I knew at some point those costumes were going to get shorter and shorter, and I'd have to medicate myself to get through future Halloweens, but for now I was happy envisioning my daughter hitting up the neighboring houses for candy, her only concern not tripping over her tail as she walked.

CHAPTER 37

Mitch's pickup rolled onto the unnamed dirt road and stopped next to the small pine building that served as Meddybemps' game warden office. The sign on the door indicated Neil Cutter, the only game warden in the area, was out.

"Probably checking fishing licenses or countin' life jackets," said Mitch.

Albert checked the door to confirm Cutter wasn't there. It was locked. "Guess we have to wait."

The two men returned to the pickup and watched out the windshield as the morning sun danced off the lake. Albert pulled the .45 from underneath the seat and placed it in his lap.

THE KNOCK ON THE DRIVER'S WINDOW WOKE BOTH men. Albert jumped in his seat, sending the handgun tumbling onto the floor mat.

Mitch rolled down the window.

"Howdy. Fellas," said Neil Cutter shifting the rifle in his arms. "On a stakeout?"

"Jesus Christ," said Albert. "Don't sneak up on someone like that. Could have shot you."

"You'd have to pick up your weapon first." Cutter leaned against Mitch's door. "Assume you're here to see me?"

"That's right," said Mitch. "Gotta talk about Ollie Stoner."

"Figured as much." Cutter stepped back from the pickup and opened Mitch's door. "Reckon we should get to talking then."

Cutter's office included a desk, four chairs, a few file cabinets, and two large storage cabinets, all pine, and all shellacked to a high gloss. There was a large map of the Downeast region tacked to the wall. It had sections cordoned off with large black rectangles.

Cutter placed his rifle against the wall behind his desk, took a seat, and motioned for Mitch and Albert to do the same.

"Now that we're all here, let's get to it," said Cutter.

"Ollie's out of prison," said Mitch. "He came to see me at Palmer's, him and those two inbred boys of his. Tried to drag me out of the place. Would have done it too, if Jack hadn't stepped in."

"You go to the police?" said Cutter.

"You mean Hafner?" said Mitch. "Everyone knows he's in Ollie's pocket. He ain't gonna do nothing 'cept lock me up until Ollie can come put a bullet in me."

"So, I guess you haven't heard about the constable?"

"What about him?" said Mitch. "I've been hidin' out in a motel. Haven't spoken to anyone."

“Someone beat him to death in his office. Blew his secretary’s head clean off too. Found her under his desk.”

“What was she doing under his desk?” said Albert.

Cutter shook his head. “What Constable Hafner does around or under his desk ain’t my business.”

“But what happens to a police officer in Meddybemps is your business,” said Albert.

“Not my jurisdiction,” said Cutter. “Calais police are handling it.”

“Not your jurisdiction?” said Mitch. “Someone murders a police officer in town and you don’t investigate. What kind of LEO are you?”

“It’s not a Fish and Wildlife issue. Local police need to handle that.”

“You nailed Ollie for the stolen boat,” said Albert. “How’s that any different?”

“The boat was IFW property. Totally within my authority.”

“That’s bullshit,” said Mitch.

“That’s how it works,” snapped Cutter. “If Calais police ask for my help, then I’ll give it to them. Otherwise, it’s not my problem.”

“Calais isn’t going to ask for help,” said Mitch. “They’re not going to do a Goddamn thing to Ollie.”

“Probably not,” said Cutter.

Albert shifted in his chair. “So, where does that leave us?”

“It leaves us up shit creek,” said Mitch standing.

“You got yourselves into this mess,” said Cutter. “You can get yourselves out.”

“You’re just as much in it as we are,” said Mitch. “You’re the one that popped him for that boat. Without you, he’d never been locked up.”

“And if he comes to settle anything with me, I’ll handle my shit.” Cutter leaned forward and placed his elbows on the desk. “I’d suggest you two handle yours.”

“So that’s it then?” said Albert.

"If the situation changes, I'll let you know." Cutter looked at Mitch. "What motel you staying at?"

Mitch eyed the rifle against the wall. "I prefer not to say."

"There's only one motel in town, Mitch. It won't be too hard to find you."

"Who said I was staying in town?"

"Suit yourself." Cutter stood. "If I hear anything out of Calais, I'll let you know. Otherwise, try to stay out of trouble. That'll be a stretch for you two."

"We'll figure something out," said Mitch.

"What are you going to do?"

Albert stood. "You said we should handle our shit. We're going to go handle it."

Cutter nodded. "Keep your head down. You two are a lot of things. Hard to find isn't one of them."

Mitch and Albert looked at each other, walked out the door, and climbed back into the pickup.

"What's our play?" said Mitch.

Albert grabbed for the .45 from the floor. “I’ve always been keen on the direct approach. We need to bait him out.”

“What did you have in mind?”

“Not sure,” said Albert. “Have to think about it over lunch. Maybe over some clams.”

“You heard Cutter. Not sure being out in public is the right thing to do.”

“We’ll get ‘em to go then.”

Mitch grabbed the steering wheel and drew in a deep breath. “Let’s go make some bad decisions, then.” He shifted the truck into drive and turned the wheel toward Palmer’s Restaurant.

Mitch’s first-floor room at the Boley’s Motel had enough pine paneling to give a lumberjack a permanent hard-on. The room had a twin bed, a small bathroom adorned with photos of wild birds, a twenty-two-inch television with a built-in VCR, a small pine desk, and little else.

Mitch lifted a flap of the orange and red curtain with a single finger and scanned the parking lot. "I've been thinking about how to get Ollie, but I need to know how serious you are."

"If you're asking me if I've got the nut sack to kill a man, you should already know the answer." Albert opened the to-go box from Palmer's and dug into the fried clams.

"I just want to make sure we're both ready to dole out a death sentence," said Mitch.

"We kicked that can down the road once before and look where that got us. What you have in mind?"

Mitch let the curtain fall back into place and walked over to the desk. He opened his own box, plucked a clam from the pile, dropped it in his mouth, and popped the top off the plastic container of blue cheese dip. "We can't go to the Calais police. Ollie's been in with them for a while. Talk to the wrong person, and we'll invite trouble."

"Trouble's already here," said Albert. "And she brought a date."

Mitch moved over to the bed and propped his feet up on the mattress. "So, what's our play?"

"We got to end this now before it gets out of hand." Albert ran a hand through his thinning white hair. "Ollie doesn't know I'm back, so let's use that to our advantage."

"What you got in mind?"

"You call him. Tell him you fucked up and you want to make it right. You draw him out, and I'll blow his fucking head clean off. Then we drag his dead ass up in the Moosehorn Refuge and leave him for the bears."

"That's your plan?"

"You got a better one?" said Albert dropping another clam into his mouth.

Mitch thought for a moment. "Where would we do it?"

"That junkyard of his seems like the best place. No houses around. No one would hear a thing."

"What about his boys? That whole family is as fucked up as they come."

"If they're at the junkyard when we do it, then they go too," said Albert. "We're not leaving any witnesses. This has to end now."

"Fine with me. How do you want to do it?"

"You call Ollie and tell him you're coming over there tomorrow to talk. Don't give him a chance to suggest another place. It's got to be at the junkyard. You'll drop me off first. I'll get into place, and then you show up. You get Ollie out in the open, and I'll pick him off as soon as I get a shot." Albert looked around the room. "You still got that old deer rifle?"

Mitch leaned over the side of the mattress, slid the rifle out from under the bed, and handed it to Albert.

"Does it still pull to the left?"

"A little," said Mitch.

Albert propped the rifle against the wall and pulled the .45 caliber Remington Rand out of his waistband and handed it to Mitch. "You tuck that behind you. Once I take Ollie out, you pull it and take care of his two boys. If somehow I miss Ollie with my shot, then you're going to have to drop him too. There's one in the chamber and eight in the clip. Use them all if you have to."

"Sounds like I'll be doing all the work."

"Not likely. I plan on drilling Ollie right through the eye socket. You just worry about the boys."

Mitch studied the weapon in his hand. "Been a while since I held one of these."

"You still know how to use it?"

"I think I can figure it out." Mitch tossed the pistol on the bed and went back to his clams. He popped the last few into his mouth and licked his fingers. Then he picked up his cell phone and dialed Ollie.

CHAPTER 38

I PULLED in front of Allison's and Bill's home on Sunday afternoon. I helped Becca out of the back seat and nodded toward the black BMW X5 parked across the street a few houses down. While I couldn't see him, I knew Cricket would be watching me through a set of high-powered binoculars. Brooke and a brown-and-white Jack Russell Terrier met us on the driveway.

"Good weekend?" said Brooke as she hugged Becca.

"Great weekend," I said.

Brooke looked at me. "You get a costume?"

"Black cat." I looked down at the dog. "Don't let the mutt chase her." I thought back to all the adult costumes we'd zipped past in the Halloween superstore. "Once she hits puberty, you're in charge of Halloween and bra shopping. I'm happy to handle everything else."

Becca dropped her penguin suitcase and ran to the dog.

Brooke smiled and sipped her coffee. "I'd invite you in, but we have to get over to Becca's school. We signed up as volunteers for the Fall Festival. Always something to volunteer for."

"I guess that's the problem with those Catholic schools. That expectation to participate and do good deeds." I checked the windows looking for a glimpse of Brooke's sister or brother-in-law. "How are the roommates? They pressuring you to leave yet?"

"Not yet. Bill is on the road a lot, and I think Allison actually likes having us around."

"You thinking about more permanent accommodations? Moving back in with Daryl?"

Brooke readjusted her grip on the cup. "Don't know. Trying not to think about it at the moment."

"You need something more stable, Brooke. We're carting Becca between three different places, and none of them are home."

"This coming from a guy who lived on a house-boat three weeks ago?"

I put my arms up in retreat. "Point taken. I just want her to have a stable environment, and at the moment, neither of us is all that stable."

"When things settle down, we'll discuss our next steps, but we're fine for now."

"All right," I said, hugging Brooke. "Tell your sister I said hello. And have fun at the festival."

The Jack Russell brushed past Brooke's billowy skirt, and Becca followed in pursuit. I was about to head back to my car when Brooke ran a hand through her long red hair, tucking part of it behind her ear.

"Want to come in for a cup of coffee?"

"What about the festival?"

She raked her hand through her hair again. “It can wait. Maybe if we go later, most of the work will already be done, and we won’t have to stay long.”

“Sounds like a good approach to me.”

Brooke whistled, and the dog turned and followed her into the house. Becca and I were a few steps behind.

Brooke refilled her mug and poured a fresh one for me, then she motioned me to the dining room table. Becca tugged her suitcase up the steps to unpack.

“That woman you’re seeing. Is it serious?” said Brooke taking a slow sip.

“I guess it’s as serious as it can be for a three-week relationship,” I said. I adjusted the silver watch on my wrist. “I’m in no rush to classify the relationship. We’re both having a good time, that’s all.”

“You’re pushing forty, Finn. Aren’t you too old to be just having a good time?”

I set the cup down on the table, leaned back, and crossed my legs. “It’s been two years. You’re with Daryl, although I’m not sure why, him being such a colossal fuck-up and all, but the reality is, you've moved on, and I have to do the same. I think at one point I held out hope that maybe we'd get back together. I know it's stupid, but something inside wouldn't let me admit it was officially over. That we'd failed at it." I took a drink. "I don't know what Jennifer and I will end up being, but for right now, I'm happy. At least, I'll be happy until she dumps me and moves in with some doctor who gets caught up in a drug-smuggling scheme with the Midwest mob."

Brooke cracked a smile.

"How's your investigation going, anyway?"

"I'm close. Connor and I have two addresses to check out. Hoping we find what we're looking for when we head back to Indianapolis tomorrow."

Brooke looked at me over her porcelain mug and tucked her hair behind her ear again. "I never got a chance to properly thank you for helping us with this."

"You thanked me." I downed what was left in my cup. "And besides, there's still more to be done. You can thank me again when it's all over." I stood up and set my cup on the sink.

“Where are you going?” she said.

“I’ve got to get back on the road, and you have a festival to prep.”

She looked at me with narrow eyes and an eager stare I hadn’t seen in two years. “You’re not leaving until you fuck me.”

She didn’t have to tell me twice. Before my brain had a chance to realize this was a bad decision, I’d already pushed her up against the kitchen counter and was reaching up her skirt. No panties.

I grabbed a clump of her long red hair in my hand and twisted, wrapping it around my wrist and pulling her head back. She braced herself on the counter with her right hand and reached around with her left, placing it on my hip. I grabbed her throat with my free hand and squeezed gently. I could feel the muscles in her neck tighten as she let out a low murmur.

It was over in less time than I’d later admit.

“That was quick,” said Brooke, smiling as she smoothed out her skirt.

"Figured Becca would be down any second," I said. "Didn't think she'd appreciate the show. Maybe we can pick it back up later?"

"Let's not make a habit of it," said Brooke. "I don't think your girlfriend would appreciate it." She smiled again and walked toward the stairs.

I zipped my pants, buckled my belt, and hobbled toward the door.

As I started back to my SUV, I noticed Cricket had turned his headlights on. He flashed them and kicked the BMW into gear. I instinctively turned to look down the street in the other direction and saw the red minivan slowly rolling toward the house. A moment later, the red minivan and the black BMW faced each other on the street in front of me.

I moved my right hand to the place where my waistband holster would have been, had I not been with my daughter. I didn't carry with Becca around. A moment later, I was staring at Adler's weathered face as he rolled down the window. Cricket opened his car door to get out, but I waved him off. I didn't need a shootout with me standing on the sidewalk.

"That looked like a tender moment you had with your daughter in the yard," said Adler.

My hand clenched. "I'm trying to convince myself not to pull you through that window and break your head open on the sidewalk."

"Violence never solves anything." He smiled. "I'm just here to pass along a message from Holbrook."

"What's that?"

"His patience has run out, and he wants his money. You're officially on the clock. You've got three days."

"Or what?" I said, not sure I wanted to hear the answer.

"Or this." Adler rolled down the tinted rear passenger window, and Daryl's face slowly came into view. Gray duct tape covered his mouth, and he was bleeding from the nose. "Deliver Holbrook's money in three days, or I skull fuck Dr. Daryl with a tire iron. Then I'll kill you and come back here for the redhead and the girl."

He rolled up the window and drove off before I could muster a response.

Cricket leaned out of the BMW. “You want me to follow him?”

“No. I know where he’s going. But stay here in case he comes back.”

CHAPTER 39

THE NEXT MORNING, Connor and I followed the Escalade's GPS toward Burns' condo in Morgantown, Indiana. We passed several strip malls and what appeared to be an abandoned industrial park before finding the Cedar Woods condos on East Sycamore Street. There was a stone arch at the entrance, but no gate or security guard. We rolled up to the main parking lot, which was half the size of a football field. Seven condo buildings stood in a crescent shape around the north side of the parking lot. The south side included a large swimming pool, which had been closed for the season, and two tennis courts. The top of two industrial-sized dumpsters poked out from behind wooden enclosures at the end of the lot.

Winding paved walkways led from the parking lot through neatly pruned landscaping beds to the front entrance of each building. Each of the buildings had four levels, with wrought-iron staircases that led up through a central breezeway to each floor. According to the purchase agreement, we were looking for building 7, unit F.

Building 7 was on the far left of the lot. Connor and I followed the paved walkway to the staircase and walked up to the third-floor breezeway, where we found unit F. The unit that Burns owned was at the front of the breezeway. There was another unit directly behind it, and two other units on the other side of the breezeway. After checking the area for any bystanders, we approached the door to unit F.

"I don't have my bump keys," said Connor looking at the brass deadbolt. "You wanna knock?"

"Might not have to," I said, reaching into my pocket to find the keys I'd taken from Burns' desk drawer. "That's a Baldwin deadbolt." I flipped through the keys. "And there's only one Baldwin key on this ring."

"It's never that easy."

Connor was right, it never was that easy, but I wasn't going to piss on good fortune when it reared its head.

"What's the plan?" he said.

"Draw your weapon, and let's try to not kill anyone."

I rubbed the brass key between my thumb and forefinger and slid it into the lock. I slowly turned the key, and the deadbolt slid with a clink that was louder than I expected. I removed the key from the lock, slipped the ring back into my pocket, and drew the .45 from the holster on the back of my belt. Connor already gripped his Glock in his hands. He kept his index finger on the slide away from the trigger. I turned the knob and gently nudged the door open with my shoulder. I could feel Connor's breath on the back of my neck.

We closed the gap between the front door and the living room in less than a second. A woman had just entered the living room from a side bedroom, folding a white bed sheet as she walked. I bent my knees slightly to lower my center of gravity, raised my weapon, and took aim at her midsection. Her eyes moved from me to Connor, who I could still feel right behind me. It took her a moment to realize what was happening.

Over the years, I've pointed weapons at a lot of people, and I've seen more reactions than I can count. When faced with a gun barrel, some people instinctively turn and run, others scream at the top of their lungs, and others dive for the first thing they can find to defend themselves. Some won't move at all. Others will plant their feet and slowly turn their body away from you, usually so their right side is away. Those are the ones you worry about. This motion is a dead giveaway that they're not backing down and instead are going for their own weapon.

I waited to see which way this woman was going to break. After a moment, she released the sheet, which fluttered to the ground, and covered her mouth with both hands, more in surprise than to stifle any sound, and dropped to her knees.

"Who are you?" I said.

She was silent, still processing what was happening in front of her.

"Who are you," I said louder this time.

"Jamie Burns." Her words were slow and steady like she'd been sedated.

I glanced around the condo. There was a hallway to our left that led to another room. Connor had already charged that way to sweep the place for anyone else who might be there.

"Are you going to kill me?" asked Jamie from between her fingers.

"I wasn't planning on it." I broke eye contact to check Connor's progress down the hallway. "Is there anyone else here?"

"No," she was shaking now. "Are you going to kill me?" she repeated.

"No, I'm not. But we have a lot to talk about." Connor returned from the back bedroom. He shook his head, indicating it was clean.

I nodded to the other side of the room. "What's over there?" I said.

"My bedroom and a sewing room," she said.

Connor crossed the living room with his Glock up and examined both rooms on the other side of the condo. He returned a moment later with the same headshake he'd given me earlier.

"Do you know why we're here?" I said, lowering my weapon and tucking it back behind me.

Jamie Burns looked about forty years old. She was maybe five-foot-three and one-hundred-ten pounds soaking wet. Her shoulder-length brown hair was stringy and frazzled as though she had something more important to focus on than her appearance. Her eyes looked tired, like she'd either been crying or fighting off sleep. She wore blue jeans and a faded gray long-sleeved t-shirt. She let a deep sigh escape, and for the first time, I noticed she looked relieved.

"You're looking for my father?"

"William Burns," I said, putting two and two together. "He's your father?"

"Yes," she said.

Connor extended a hand, helped Jamie off the ground, and led her to the couch in the living room. "Where is he?" he said.

"Why? So you can go kill him?"

"Nobody wants to hurt your father," I said. "But he's holding onto something that doesn't belong to him, and we're here to get it back."

"You're working for some criminal, then?"

"You must know about his business."

"I know enough to know that someday it was going to get him killed."

"Do you work for him?" said Connor.

A sneer crossed her lip. "No. I don't. I like to make my living legally. I run a small sewing business. I don't condone my father's work."

"Where can we find your father, Jamie?" I said. "It's important we find him before anyone else does."

"Who else is looking for him?"

"I'm not sure, but the man I work for hired me to retrieve his money because your father's been AWOL for a few weeks. I can only assume that your father's other clients are getting anxious as well. It's only a matter of time before they come looking for him."

She didn't say anything, but I could tell by the look on her face she was running through whatever options she thought she had.

"Where is he, Jamie?" said Connor.

She stood up and walked to the kitchen. Connor placed his hand on the Glock holstered under his jacket and followed her with his eyes.

She picked up a folder from the kitchen table and returned to the living room. Connor relaxed his hand and leaned against the doorway to the hallway that led to the bedroom and sewing room.

"You're two weeks too late," she said, handing me the folder.

I opened it to find a funeral handout. A copy of the photograph from the banker's desk, the one with him, the blonde, and the teenager was on the handout's cover. Behind the handout was a smudgy black-and-white photocopy of an obituary from a local newspaper. Behind that was William Burns' official death certificate.

"He's dead?" I said.

"Lung cancer. He complained of chest pains, and I took him to the hospital. He was dead in less than a week. Never even got a chance to go back home."

I looked at Connor, who stared back at me with a what-the-fuck look. Death was always a possibility, but I figured if the banker was dead it was because one of his clients popped him. Not cancer.

"I'm very sorry to hear that," I said.

"Really? Just makes your job easier." She snatched the folder from my hands. "Now you don't have to kill him."

"We were never going to kill him."

"I guess it doesn't matter anyway," she said.

"But we still need the money," said Connor. "That's what we're here for. Do you know where it is?"

"I know where it is," she said, walking back toward the kitchen. She opened a drawer in a small hutch next to the kitchen table. I watched as Connor placed his hand back on his weapon. Jamie pulled a thick black book from the drawer, walked across the living room, and handed it to me.

"It's all in there. Everything about his business. Who he worked for, withdrawals, and deposits."

I thumbed through the pages. Fine, sharp pencil lines told the banker's history. The ledger was divided into sections, and each section contained detailed information on the banker's clients, deposits, withdrawals, account balances, and the banker's commission. It was all there in gray and white. I found the tabbed section that contained Holbrook's information. The dates went back for years, and the current balance was $5,105,317.

"Where is the money now?" I said.

"It's in a storage facility. Before he died, my father told me I needed to contact his clients and give their money back. That they'd come looking for him and for me if I didn't." She looked up at me. "And here you are, just like he said."

"Why didn't you return it?" I said.

"What was I supposed to do? Call these guys and tell them I was driving up in a truck filled with millions of dollars, and please don't kill me? I never planned on keeping it, but I didn't know how to give it back and not get killed in the process."

"Maybe you were keen to keep it for yourself," said Connor.

"I don't want it. It's not my money, and I have no interest in continuing my father's business. I've got my own business to run. A legal business."

"Sewing?" I said.

"You're damn right, sewing." She studied my face. "Look, you can believe what you want. I wasn't going to keep the money, but I didn't really want to give it back to them either. I know the type of people my father dealt with. He might not have seen anything wrong with it, but I did. I'd just as soon stuff the money into a furnace than give it back to them."

"While I'd love to sit around and debate the ethics of all this, we really don't have the time," I said. "I need you to take us to the money."

"Are you going to kill me afterward?"

"I already told you, we're not here to kill anyone. My client hired me to find his money, and that's what we're here to do. You take us to it, we'll get his share, and you'll never see us again."

"What about the rest of it?"

"I don't care about that," I said. "Do whatever you want with it. It's not my problem."

"But I don't want it," she said. "Take it with you. You've got the names in that ledger, so you know who gets what. You can take my father's commission. I don't want anything to do with it. I just want it to go away."

The last thing I wanted to be was a delivery boy for the Indianapolis mob, but Jamie had a right to be scared. They'd eventually track her down. It would be easier to return the money, explain what happened, and let everyone go their separate ways. Of course, showing up unsolicited with a truck full of money, even if it was their money, was asking for trouble. It was a shitty position to be in, but then again, I was getting used to being in shitty positions.

"I'll consider it," I said. "Get your keys, and let's go."

She snatched her car keys from the kitchen table and took another keyring from the same drawer that contained the ledger.

"I'm Finn, by the way."

We arrived at S&F Storage, an RV storage complex on South Centerline Road in Mt. Pleasant, Indiana, about fifteen minutes after leaving Jamie's condo. A brown corrugated-metal building with a dozen garage-style storage units sat in the middle of the complex. About thirty more units arranged in a horseshoe configuration surrounded the center building. A black metal fence with a sliding gate wrapped completely around the property. The only structure outside the gate was the rental office, a small building that displayed a large red and white banner advertising that units were still available.

Jamie pulled her Subaru Outback to the front gate and dug out the key she'd taken from the drawer. She read the four-digit code written on the key-chain tag and punched it into the keypad. The pad beeped with every press of her finger, and after the fourth digit, the black gate slowly rolled to the right, allowing us to pass into the main area. Jamie drove to the back of the complex and stopped in front of unit 33.

"That's his," she said, handing me the key.

"Let's go," I said, pointing to the unit.

Connor stepped out of the back seat and surveyed the lot. He nodded toward a security camera attached to the building across from William Burns' rental unit. I kept my back toward the camera, inserted the key into the lock attached to the unit's doorframe, and turned. The garage door raised until it settled smoothly into the ceiling.

Jamie crossed her arms and shook her head at the white box truck parked in front of us.

At about thirty-five feet long, the box truck was larger than it appeared on the traffic footage I'd watched earlier. I walked toward the cab and noticed the faded Miller Moving logo on the truck's side. It hadn't been visible on the traffic camera footage. I checked the cab, but it was empty. Returning to the rear of the truck, I noticed the unlocked shrouded padlock on the truck's bumper. Connor stood in the open doorway with an eye on the parking lot and a hand on his holstered Glock.

I yanked the truck's locking lever up and pulled open the two rear doors.

The back of the truck was empty.

"Jesus Christ," said Jamie, her hands covering her mouth as they did back at her condo. "It was here, I swear. This is where it was."

I climbed into the empty truck and studied the inside. Blue painter's tape segmented the floor into seven sections. Each section contained several empty wooden pallets, which I assumed at one point housed the banker's stash.

"You saw the money in here?" I said.

"Yes. I checked it after my father gave me the key." She pointed into the back of the truck. "The money was stacked into piles. All along the walls. On those wooden things." She sensed my hesitation. "It was here. You have to believe me."

She ran her hands through her hair and gave me the same look, part surprise, and part terror, which she had worn when Connor and I burst through the front door of her condo. She was telling the truth.

“I believe you,” I said.

“Oh my God!” She drew her hand to her mouth again. “What are we going to do?”

I looked past her to Connor, who now had his hands on his hips. “The only thing we can do,” I said. “Find that money.”

CHAPTER 40

MOST PEOPLE ARE HELPFUL, especially when it comes to investigating a crime. It's in our nature to help others, as long as we don't put ourselves in danger to do it. Over the years, when I've interviewed someone to further a case, no one has ever refused to talk to me or told me to "go get a warrant." At least not anyone who didn't have something to lose as a result of my investigation. I've had plenty of people who didn't share anything useful because they didn't know the information I needed, and I had a few who told me to go fuck myself when I pushed them for information, but chances are they were trying to obstruct my investigation to protect themselves or someone close to them.

In reality, if they have nothing to hide, most people will bend over backward to help. Most never even ask to see a badge. Others might be skeptical of my intentions, but as long as I came off confident and non-threatening, they usually answered my questions. I think there's also a mystique about private investigators, and people get excited about the idea of helping catch a bad guy. Time to test my theories.

Connor stayed in the car with Jamie while I walked to the office on the other side of the black fence. A middle-aged balding man met me inside the office. As he stood up from his desk, an eager grin crossed his face. He probably saw dollar signs thinking he could sell me a storage unit for an RV I didn't own.

"Afternoon," he said. "Paul Boyle. How can I help you today?"

"Hi Paul, I'm Roger Mathers," I said. "I'm hoping you could help me with a criminal investigation."

"A criminal investigation? What happened?"

"My client rents a storage unit on the other side of the complex there. He recently had some items stolen from his unit, and I'm investigating who might have done it."

"When did this happen?"

"I'm not exactly sure, but I believe it was sometime in the past two weeks."

Paul Boyle sat back down at his desk, opened a black three-ringed binder, and flipped through the pages. "It doesn't look like anyone filed a loss claim with us recently." He looked up at me. "What unit was it?"

"Unit 33."

His eyes widened, and he shifted in his chair. "That's Mr. Coyne's unit."

"Yes, it is." I couldn't tell whether the look on his face was concern, surprise, or anxiety, but he knew the banker's public identity. "Do you know him?"

"Not really, but he's very peculiar."

"How so?"

He hesitated for a moment. "Look, most of these units store seasonal RVs, so we rarely see the owners. They pop in at the beginning of the summer to get them road-ready, and then they're gone. We see them again later in the year when they winterize the RVs and lock 'em up until next year. It's pretty much the same with the boaters, but Mr. Coyne was here every day." Boyle pointed to the black security gate. "He drives that truck out in the morning and rolls back in at 8:00 pm. Every day. You could set your watch by it. Been doing it ever since I've been here, and that's been five years. Nothing wrong with it, of course. Just odd behavior compared to everyone else." He scratched the back of his head. "Do you know what happened to him?"

"What do you mean?"

"I haven't seen him in a few weeks. Thought maybe something happened to him. When someone's that consistent, you notice when they're not around."

"Thomas Coyne passed away. Cancer."

"I'm so sorry to hear that."

"It was very sudden. His daughter hired me, which is why I'm here. She had an inventory of his unit, and I was going through his items to confirm we had everything when I noticed that several items were missing."

"Are you sure the items were in the storage unit? Maybe there was a mistake on the inventory?"

"No, they were accounted for only a few weeks ago."

"Okay," said Boyle. "How can I help?"

Paul Boyle was on the hook, but if I started asking too many questions, I could lose him. So, I decided to lay on the honesty to ensure that hook went as deep as it could go. It was a carefully orchestrated dance I'd used time and time again.

"Paul, first I have to tell you that since I'm a PI, not a law enforcement officer, you're not legally obligated to help me."

"If it protects our lessors, I'm happy to help."

"I noticed a security camera across the lot from unit 33. Do you have any archival footage that I could review?"

"We do, but it's on our internal system, so there's nothing to take with you. You'll have to review it here."

"That's fine."

Boyle waved me over to a second desk and took a seat in front of a desktop PC. "Let me pull it up." He clicked on the computer and opened a video player. "Do you have a specific time frame in mind?"

"It probably would have been sometime over the past week, but I'm sure that doesn't help you much."

"It's okay. Like I said earlier, we don't get a lot of traffic around here. I can run the footage to stop at any motion on the camera." After a few of Boyle's keystrokes, we watched the high-speed camera footage fly across the black-and-white screen. It looked like a Benny Hill chase scene but without the scantily-clad women or saxophone soundtrack. A minute or so later, the footage slowed to a real-time playback as a pickup rolled past the camera. A man stepped out of the cab, opened the door to unit 37, and stepped in.

Boyle clicked the mouse, and the footage sped up to almost comical speeds. The pickup was gone, and another three days of footage passed in a matter of minutes. The footage snapped back to real-time again as a dark Jeep Grand Cherokee pulling a U-Haul trailer stopped in front of the banker's unit. A man got out of the vehicle, opened the garage door, and then backed up the vehicle so the back of the trailer was inside unit 33. Whatever he did next was off-camera.

"What do you think?" said Boyle.

"That's not my client's vehicle. Can you speed this up a bit?"

Another click of the mouse and we watched the footage race by at sixty times the normal speed. Whoever was in the unit walked out, stepped back into the driver's seat, rolled forward a few feet, closed the unit's garage door and then left. I noted the timestamp as 1:13 pm on Friday, the same time Connor and I were rummaging through William Burns' home.

Boyle was about to click the mouse again when the SUV reappeared on the screen. At first, I thought I was watching the same footage over again, but ten minutes had passed on the timestamp.

"He's back," said Boyle. What Boyle didn't know was that whoever was in that SUV had piled the banker's money into the back of the trailer. He made several trips because there was a lot of cash to move. The driver probably took the payload to the parking lot and transferred it to a larger truck, and then came back for the rest of the cash. We continued to watch the high-speed footage and counted as the SUV made three return trips.

"Do you have a camera at the front gate?" I said.

"Yeah. Do you want me to pull up the footage from the same timeframe?" Boyle cracked a smile, and I knew he was getting the rush that came with finding a crucial piece of evidence. He was as deep on the hook as he could get.

"Yeah," I said. "I want to see who else is in the main lot."

A few more clicks and the screen showed the new angle of the main parking lot camera. The footage showed the dark SUV rolling to a stop, the driver poking out of the window to enter the code, the main gate opening, and then the vehicle pulling out of frame. If there was a larger truck beyond the gate, the camera hadn't caught it.

"Can you back up so we can see the vehicle at the gate again?"

More mouse clicking and the SUV returned to the screen. Boyle froze it, and I squinted to make out the license plate on the back of the trailer. It was too grainy to read all the digits, but it didn't matter. I saw enough to know who was behind the wheel.

I pointed to the screen. "That was last Friday. Were you here that afternoon?"

"No. I would have remembered seeing that SUV go by so many times. Peter was here."

"Does he work today?"

"No," said Boyle. "He's a part-timer. Only here on Wednesdays, Thursdays, and Fridays."

"What about keys? Do you have keys to the units?"

"We have keys for all the unit doors. In case there's an emergency."

Boyle returned to his desk again. "Peter, the part timer. I've got his phone number if you want to contact him."

"No, I've got everything I need." Boyle looked disappointed as if our now-concluded investigation might have been the high point of his day. "But you might want to check in with your part-timer."

"Why?"

"Because the man in that SUV didn't have a key to my client's unit. That means they got it from your employee. They either bribed him or put a gun to his head and took it. Either way, you might want to chat with him." I headed toward the door. "Thanks again for your help."

"Don't mention it," said Boyle, still putting the scenario together in his head.

On my way out the door, I grabbed a Post-It pad and a pen from Boyle's desk.

CONNOR AND JAMIE WAITED FOR **ME IN THE Outback.**

"Any luck?" said Connor.

"I know where the money is."

"You want to fill us in?" he said.

I scribbled a note and Holbrook's phone number on the yellow pad I swiped from Boyle's desk and handed it to Connor.

"If I'm not back in Indianapolis tonight, call this number and read this to whoever answers the phone."

Connor looked it over. "Why don't I just go with you?"

"I need you here. If what I do next falls through, I need you here to make that call."

Connor grimaced and nodded. I knew he didn't like the idea of staying behind, but he understood why he had to.

"Can I go home now?" said Jamie.

"I've got a deal for you," I said, climbing into the passenger seat.

"You can say no, and I'll leave you alone, but hear me out. We had to jump through a lot of hoops to find your father, which eventually led us to you. Your father worked with a lot of bad people who aren't happy that he's out of the picture—"

"He's dead," interrupted Jamie.

"They don't know that. From the looks of that ledger, they've got plenty of reasons to come looking for him, and they might find you. Just like we did."

"What am I supposed to do?"

"You ever hear the name Mason Holbrook?"

"No. Is he the person looking for my father? The person who hired you?"

"Yes. He's bad news, and I'm working on a plan that will ensure he never comes looking for your father or you again, but I'm going to need your help. You help us, and we can make this go away."

"What about the other people in that ledger? You can't stop everyone."

"I'm working on that too."

Jamie thought for a moment. "That doesn't do much to put me at ease. You found my father and then me. So could they."

"Truth is, we got lucky finding your father," I said. "There are only a few slivers of information tying him to the banker, and it's not a puzzle just anyone could put together."

I didn't know whether Jamie would ever be completely safe, but Connor and I could kick enough dirt over her footprints to make her hard to find. "Are you in or out?"

Jamie exhaled a deep breath. "What do you need me to do?"

I thought back to Jamie's condo. "You said you knew how to sew, right?"

CHAPTER 41

MITCH AND ALBERT climbed into the pickup and headed toward the junkyard. Ollie's junkyard was five miles outside of Meddybemps. Mitch pulled to the side of the road about a quarter-mile out.

"This'll do," said Albert. He stepped out of the pickup and grabbed the rifle from the truck bed. "Give me fifteen minutes, and I'll be in place."

"You sure you can move that quick?"

"I'll manage." Albert poked his head through the truck window. "I'll line up my shot with the front of his office, so you'll have to figure out how to get him out there. Keep him in one spot, and no walking around. I'll take the shot as soon as I can. We're in and out."

"I got it," said Mitch. "You're not going to cut his ears off, are you?"

"I think those days are behind us."

Albert tucked the rifle under his arm and disappeared into the woods adjacent to the highway.

"Hey," yelled Mitch into the trees. "Don't miss."

"I don't plan to."

Albert stayed close enough to the road to follow it to Ollie's junkyard, but far enough away to avoid any attention from the rig jockeys hauling lumber up to the North Mill. After navigating the branches and brambles for ten minutes, Albert came to the dilapidated slatted-fence perimeter of Ollie's junkyard. He made his way to the entrance to find the chain and padlock hanging over the side of the front gate, a sign that Ollie was inside. He scanned the yard from the gate and saw suitable cover about a hundred and fifty feet from the entrance to the office. Then he quickly maneuvered along the inside of the fenced perimeter until he settled behind a large pile of decaying automobile parts, tires, and hubcaps and the chassis of two unidentifiable vehicles intertwined with a tree that grew in defiance of the barren and rust-covered landscape.

Albert crouched behind the pile and slid the deer rifle between the spokes of a wheel and then repositioned himself on his knees so he had a direct line to the front door. The makeshift gun rest gave him enough leeway to track any target standing in front of the building. Albert was scanning the junkyard for any movement when Mitch's pickup coughed into the dirt pad that served as a parking lot.

Mitch stepped out of the pickup and untucked his shirt, letting it fall over the .45 that was tucked in his waistband. He approached the front door of Ollie's office and slammed his fist into the wooden frame five times before jogging backward ten feet from the door. He waited for Ollie to open it, but the door didn't budge. Mitch looked over his shoulder and then approached the door a second time to repeat his routine. Still no Ollie.

"Ollie, it's me," said Mitch. "Come on out so we can talk." Silence echoed back. Albert watched from the rusted pile as Mitch slipped his right hand behind his back and walked toward the side of the building. He poked his head around, keeping his body against the front wall. He stepped farther away from the office and surveyed the junkyard. No Ollie.

"Don't let him lead you in," said Albert to himself.

Mitch, as if sensing Albert's order, returned to the front of the building and again approached the front door. Albert watched as Mitch knocked. He watched the door open. And he watched a pair of hands grab Mitch by his shirt and yank him inside the office.

Then he watched the door slam shut.

"Shit," said Albert. He took a deep breath and slid the rifle's barrel from the wheel, careful not to rattle anything in the process. He slowly stepped away from the pile and then jogged, rifle in hand, toward the side of the office. He slid along the wall until he was next to the side window, and then standing as tall as he could, he peered inside. Ollie stood along the far wall behind a metal desk that looked like it came from the back room of an old post office. One of Ollie's boys drove a pointed finger into Mitch's chest, nudging him backward as he spoke. Albert ducked under the window, moved to the rear of the building, and found a back door. He gripped the rifle with his right hand, wrapped his left around the doorknob, and slowly turned. Locked. He placed his ear next to the door and listened.

"I don't know anything about the money," said Mitch. "I came here to make things right."

Albert exhaled, loosened his grip on the rifle, and rounded the corner heading to the front of the office. He made it to the front door, gripped the rifle again, and reached for the knob.

The blow hit Albert from behind, knocking him into the door hard enough to drive it open. The next thing Albert saw was two men looking down at him. Then he blacked out.

CHAPTER 42

Connor and I swapped the Outback for his Escalade and watched as Jamie walked up the wrought-iron steps and into her condo.

"You really think she's up for this?" said Connor.

"We're going to do the heavy lifting, but I'm working on a plan, and it involves her."

"Care to let me in on it, little brother?"

I tapped the side of my head. "It's still percolating up here. I'll let you know when it's ready. Course, it all depends on getting Holbrook's cash." I paused. "Speaking of that, it's time we found you a hotel."

Connor pulled into an Embassy Suites parking lot on the east side of Indianapolis and handed me the keys to his SUV.

"Be careful," he said.

"Always am." As I rolled away, I glanced at Connor in the rearview mirror. He waved with his right hand and clutched the note I'd given him in his left.

I picked up I-69 north, and four and a half hours later, I pulled into the DTC Woodworking parking lot. The shop's box truck sat in the same place it had been when I visited Dunbar two weeks ago. The dark gray Jeep Grand Cherokee sat in a different spot. I grabbed my leather messenger bag and walked through the front entrance.

Davy Bill stood behind the counter, the three fingers on his right hand holding up a folded magazine. When he saw me, he placed the magazine to the side and leaned forward against the counter, probably reaching for something that could turn me into a Detroit crime statistic. I'm not sure where Dunbar came from, but I felt his solid presence before I heard his voice.

"You reconsider that Shaker nightstand?" he said. "Or that blanket chest?"

"I'm here for Holbrook's money."

"I got nothin' to do with that."

"Bullshit. I reviewed the security footage at the storage yard. Saw Davy Bill and his Jeep. And the Michigan plates. Pretty easy to connect those dots." I turned toward Davy Bill, who shrugged, his palms up to the ceiling. "Holbrook hired me to find the money his banker stole from him. Took me a while to find it." I looked past Dunbar to the two large metal doors. "I assume it's here."

"It's here, but you ain't getting it," said Dunbar.

Davy Bill placed his left elbow on top of the counter. "Of course, you're welcome to try to take it," he said.

I'd been in trouble with Dunbar before, and while he usually had the upper hand, he had a weakness that was easy to exploit. He was intelligent. He was a businessman first, and a take-you-out-into-the-street-and-smash-your-skull-in thug second. Reasoning with him had saved my ass before, and it would save it again today.

"I don't need to take it," I said. "You're going to give it to me."

"Why's that?" asked Dunbar, cracking a smile.

"Because your operation is small, and I'm guessing you've got bigger aspirations than Detroit."

Dunbar didn't say anything.

"How much is Holbrook's operation worth to you?" I said. "I'd wager a lot more than five million. Consider it an investment in your future."

"What the fuck you talking about?" said Dunbar

"Mason Holbrook will be out of business in a few days," I said. "And then someone'll step up and take over his territory, maybe even his entire operation. If you want to be that person, you're going to give me Holbrook's five million dollars. You can keep whatever else you got from the banker, but I need Holbrook's cut."

"What if I'm not interested in being the next Holbrook? Maybe I just keep the cash and invest in my own operation."

I glanced at Davy Bill, who still had his right arm under the counter. "Then I drive back to Indianapolis and tell Holbrook I found his money, and I point him toward your address. And then it's between you and him. I think you'd rather keep it between you and me."

"Maybe we just kill you right now and stuff your body in a sawdust bin," said Davy Bill. "Problem solved."

Dunbar looked at me as if eager for my response.

"That would be a bad idea," I said. "I've made arrangements. If I'm not back in Indianapolis tonight, one of my associates calls Holbrook and tells him you've got his money. And you're still in the deepest part of the shit."

"He's fucking with us," said Davy Bill.

"You can't risk that," I said.

Dunbar glanced at Davy Bill and then back at me.

"All right, let's back up to the part about Holbrook's retirement party," said Dunbar.

He was on the hook. Time to yank. "Holbrook isn't going to be around much longer," I said. "He's punching out, and when he does, his entire operation will be up for grabs. I don't care who takes it over."

"Thought he just hired you to find his money. Why all this talk about pushing him out of business?"

I shifted the messenger bag on my shoulder. "I'm pretty certain that once Holbrook gets his money, he's going to put a bullet in the back of my head. He's got no reason to let me live. After everything he told me about his operation and the banker, I'm a loose end. And Adler, his right-hand man, doesn't like me very much." Dunbar's eyes told me he wasn't convinced. "And he fucked with my family, and that doesn't sit well with me."

"You're going to war with Holbrook over that?"

"You're goddamn right, I am."

Dunbar stared at the leather bag on my shoulder. "So, how are you going to do it?"

"I'm still working on the plan, but it includes getting that five million."

"If you're just going to kill him anyway, why return his money?" said Davy Bill.

"He's expecting me to find it. It's the only way I can get close enough to him."

I checked my watch. "Your time is ticking away. I need an answer."

Dunbar thought for a moment. He ground his teeth, and the muscles in his neck bulged. "I'm going to need more than two days to get something together," he said. "This type of transition takes time. I need to line up a few things. Learn who he has working for him."

"Look, I don't know how these things work," I said. "Maybe you drive to his farm, piss on Holbrook's corpse, stick a flag in his ass, and claim Indianapolis as your own. I don't know and I don't care, but I'm on the clock, and I've got to move quickly." I thought about Daryl in the back of Adler's minivan. "This is happening Wednesday morning, with or without you. You've got two days." I reached into my messenger bag and handed Dunbar the banker's ledger. "This names some of the people in Holbrook's network. You might get more info on his business."

Dunbar slowly riffled through the pages. "This'll help." He smiled. "So, what's next?"

"You give me his money, I head back to Indianapolis and make my plan. I'll call you when I'm ready, but you need to be ready to move when that phone rings."

Dunbar nodded to Davy Bill, who left the counter and walked through the double swinging doors. He returned a few minutes later, wheeling two large gray suitcases behind him. Dunbar scribbled something on the back of a business card and handed it to me.

"My number," he said. "I sure hope you know what you're doing."

"We'll find out soon enough," I said, pocketing the business card and grabbing the suitcase handles.

I was on my way out of the building when I turned around.

"How'd you find it?" I said.

“What?”

“The banker’s vault? How’d you find the money?”

“When you’ve been in this business as long as I have, you hear things,” said Dunbar. “Let’s just say that I know people who know people.”

“There was one thing I couldn't figure out. Holbrook said the banker used a courier to pick up the cash. That he didn’t do it himself. I never found the link to him. It was as if he never existed.”

“Like I said, you hear things,” said Dunbar.

I nodded, then turned and walked out the door. The suitcases thumped over jagged asphalt as I wheeled them across the parking lot and lifted them into the back of the Escalade. They weighed about fifty pounds each. I unzipped the first suitcase and checked inside. It contained twenty-five five-inch bricks of one-hundred-dollar bills. Each brick was wrapped in yellow and white bands marked as $100,000 per stack. I flipped through two random stacks to confirm they were real bills and everything looked legit. I opened the second suitcase to find a similar layout. Five million in cash. I’d never seen so much money in my life and doubted I'd ever see it again. I zipped up both cases, climbed into the driver's seat, and headed back south, the entire time trying to figure out a way to end this thing.

Halfway back to Indianapolis, I figured it out.

CHAPTER 43

When Albert came to, Peter, Ollie's son, was carrying him into Mitch's home on Lombard Lane. Peter dropped him on the sofa next to Mitch and then drove a heavy right hand into Albert's ribs, sending him over the couch's arm and onto the hardwood floor. Then Peter threw a left into Mitch's jaw, knocking him over the back of the sofa. Peter grabbed Albert's shirt, lifted him into the air, and then dropped him back onto the cushion. "Stay there," he said.

Ollie leveled his shotgun at Albert as Peter walked around the sofa, grabbed Mitch by the shoulders, and dropped him next to Albert. "Sit your ass down."

"Give me the phone," said Ollie.

Peter pulled a cell phone from his front pocket and traded the cell for the shotgun. Ollie dialed.

"It's me," he said into the receiver. "We're at Mitch Skinner's place. Bring the boat, and we'll meet you at his dock in fifteen minutes." Ollie looked at Albert and Mitch. "Bring two anchors."

Albert grabbed his side and leaned against the arm of the couch.

Ollie slipped the phone back into Peter's pocket. "If either one moves or says a word, crack 'em in the skull," he said. Then he turned and walked out the front door.

A FEW MINUTES LATER, OLLIE RETURNED WITH A file folder and two sets of handcuffs. He opened the folder and placed two documents on the coffee table in front of Albert and Mitch. Albert scanned the document. It was a warranty deed.

"What's this?" said Albert.

"This is the paper you're going to sign transferring the deed to your home over to me."

"The fuck I will."

"You're gonna sign it," said Ollie handing Albert a pen. "Or my boy here is gonna blow your skull right through that window into Mitch's backyard."

"You're going to kill us anyway," said Albert. "Why don't you take this pen and shove it down your dick hole?"

"I'm going to get those properties," said Ollie. "You can either sign them over to me now, or I can wait for your kin to take ownership after they pull your bloated corpses from that lake. And then I can go after them."

Albert shook his head. "This can't be legal."

Ollie tapped the document with his finger. "It's totally legal. Already notarized and everything." He smiled. "You sign it, I take it to the county recorder's office and then I own your island and everything on it."

"I'll contest it," said Albert. "No one'll believe you."

"You won't contest shit, 'cuz you'll be dead." Ollie motioned to Peter, who walked over and placed the shotgun an inch from Albert's forehead. Mitch scooted over to the far side of the couch.

"Fine, you piece of shit." Albert clicked open the pen and signed on the line where Ollie pointed. Ollie snatched the pen from Albert's hand and gave it to Mitch, who did the same on the other warranty deed.

"It's a pleasure doing business with you two." Ollie slammed his right elbow into Mitch's face, pushed him face-down into the couch cushion, and cuffed his hands behind him. He turned to Albert. "Hands behind you, or you get the same." Albert leaned forward and placed his hands behind him. Ollie intertwined the second set of cuffs with the first and then cinched them on Albert's wrists, securing both men back to back.

"You don't have to do this, Ollie," said Mitch. "I'll go to the police and admit what we did. Tell them it was me who planted that trailer."

"Too late for that." He pointed toward the back window. "You're both going to the bottom of that lake tonight."

The steady hum of a boat's motor rumbled through the pine trees and settled into Mitch's living room. Ollie looked out the large window at the back of the room and then turned to Peter, who still trained the shotgun on both men. "William's here. Let's go."

Peter handed the shotgun back to Ollie, grabbed Mitch by the shoulders, and yanked both men to their feet. "Move!"

Peter dragged the men through the back door and forced them down the steep backyard to the dock below. Fifty yards out, William angled the black and silver pontoon boat toward the dock. He guided it in until the side eased against the gray bumpers attached to Mitch's weathered dock. William grabbed the bowline and quickly tied it off on a cleat, then returned to the wheel.

"Let's go," said Ollie. Peter yanked both men forward and pushed them onto the idling boat. He moved them toward the rear of the boat, next to the two gurgling outboard engines and directly behind where William stood at the wheel. He kicked their legs out from under them, sending Mitch and Albert down onto the gray carpet.

"You don't have to do this," said Mitch.

"Shut up. You can't fuck with me and get away with it." Ollie propped a leg on one of the boat seats. "You shoulda run, Mitch. You shoulda run far away. And you." He turned to Albert. "You shoulda never come back."

Peter climbed out of the boat and had started to untie the bowline when a voice came from Mitch's backyard.

"THAT'S ENOUGH. NOW STEP AWAY FROM THAT line." Neil Cutter approached, his 9mm in one hand and a flashlight in the other. Peter looked up but kept untying the bowline. "I mean it," said Cutter. "Step away from that line, or I'll put you down." He looked past Peter and into the boat, where he saw William behind the wheel. Ollie stood next to him gripping a shotgun. "Ollie, you drop that shotgun. Then William, you kill that engine, and you both step off the boat onto the dock."

Ollie maneuvered behind the boat's windshield for cover. "This don't concern you, Cutter. Move along before something bad happens to you."

"Nothing bad is happening to me today," said Cutter, stopping about ten feet from the dock. "I said drop that shotgun, Ollie. I'm not going to ask you again."

After a moment of staring down Cutter's 9mm, Ollie bent over and laid the shotgun on the floor next to his feet.

Cutter shifted his aim to William, who still towered behind the wheel. "Mitch, you two okay back there?"

"Maybe a few broken ribs," said Mitch. "But we're still breathing."

Cutter took two more steps. "That's good." He glanced at Peter, who stood on the dock with his hands raised high and then focused back on William. "You've got five seconds to kill that engine, son, and I don't count."

Cutter saw Ollie's leg kick something to the right, and he tightened the grip on his 9mm. William bent down, grabbed the shotgun, raised it over the windshield, and braced it against his right shoulder. Cutter fired two quick rounds. Both shots found their way through the boat's windshield and into William's chest, knocking him into the steering column and then to the floor. Ollie dove below the windshield for cover.

Cutter checked Peter and then refocused on the top of Ollie's head, which was poking up just behind the windshield. "Your turn, Ollie," he said. "I won't miss from here."

Ollie hesitated. Then he slowly stood up, eyeing the shotgun on the floor. "You won't reach it before I get a round off," said Cutter. "But you can try if you want. I don't care either way."

Ollie looked at Cutter, then back to the shotgun. Then he raised both hands.

"That's probably the smartest thing you did today," said Cutter. "Now step out of the boat, and then you and your other boy walk toward me and lay face-down on the ground."

Ollie and Peter complied, and Cutter cuffed them together on the dock. Mitch and Albert struggled against each other's weight to stand. They moved together like partners in a three-legged race as they stepped off the boat, onto the dock, and toward Cutter.

"Now, there's a sight I won't forget anytime soon," said Cutter returning his sidearm to its holster.

"I thought you weren't going after Ollie," said Mitch. "That it was a state police matter. Not in your jurisdiction."

"It became my jurisdiction once they climbed aboard that boat." He pointed his flashlight toward the water. "On my lake."

"Sure took you long enough," said Albert, leading Mitch up toward the house. "How'd you know we'd be here?"

"Lucky guess, I suppose."

"Looks to me like you was using us as bait," said Mitch. "To draw these shitholes out."

Cutter crossed his arms. "Now that wouldn't be very professional of me, would it?"

"Professional?" said Albert. "Why start now?"

CHAPTER 44

BROOKE SAID something on the phone with me a few days ago that I couldn't get out of my head. She asked if I thought Holbrook would really let Daryl off the hook after I returned his money. The truth is, I didn't know, but I had a nagging suspicion that both Daryl and I would be dead weight once Holbrook had his cash.

To Holbrook, people like Daryl and me were a dime a dozen, and he's got more to lose by putting us back on the street than he did by putting two in the back of our heads. That horse farm was a big place, and I didn't like the idea of all that acreage hiding Holbrook's liabilities. I reviewed my options, and there weren't many. The most enticing option was to kill Holbrook to ensure I wouldn't be looking over my shoulder every day, but that wasn't going to be easy.

Holbrook was one man in a chain of people. Even if he was at the top, if I removed him, someone else would rise up and take his place, and I'd be in an even shittier position than I'm in now. Holbrook and his crew were like a hornet nest, and the thing about hornets is you have to kill them all at once, or you risk getting your ass stung and the survivors repopulating the colony.

Luckily, I had experience with hornets. When my brother and I were kids, we had a white aluminum shed in our backyard. It was about six feet square and was packed with lawnmower parts, rusted-out yard tools, old patio furniture, extension cords, and a few tiki torches we never used. One summer we found a hornets' nest stuck to the side of the shed. Connor and I ran to tell our father, who said he'd take care of it when he had more time.

My father explained how he'd do it. Said the best way to get rid of them was to park a grill under the nest, light it, and smoke them out. Then once they left the nest, you sealed up the hole. Then they left for good.

When you're a twelve-year-old kid, smoke is cool, but fire is cooler. That was why Connor and I decided to burn the fucker down instead. We doused that mud lump with lighter fluid and set it ablaze using one of the tiki torches from the shed. When the lighter fluid burned off, we'd add more and relight. It took a while, but eventually, the entire thing went up in flames like the Hindenburg. Some of the hornets came buzzing out of the nest, engulfed in flames. They'd circle around for a few seconds and then plummet to the ground like downed fighter planes.

My father must have seen the flames from inside the house because he ran out the back door screaming at us to get away from the nest. By then, it was burning on its own, and there wasn't anything to do but watch it sizzle. The nest finally fell to the ground and burned out in front of us.

My father wasn't happy. He smacked Connor in the head and threatened to kick both our asses up and down Linden Drive, but he didn't. I think it was because he was happy to see Connor and me working together to solve a problem, even if it wasn't our problem to solve. Nothing screams "teamwork" like a flaming mud ball and a few hundred hornet carcasses.

Killing Holbrook and his men was the only way to completely be sure Daryl and I were out. And to protect Brooke and Becca. But Holbrook wouldn't go down easy. He was the type of person who expected people to try to kill him. He dealt with that every day. That's why he had a bullet-proof vest under his white button-up shirt when I met him at his farm. He probably never left home without it.

I needed to be smart about our next step, and I needed to make sure Holbrook and his crew didn't see it coming. If he did, Daryl, Connor, and I would be as dead as those hornets.

CHAPTER 45

I CALLED Connor once I made it back onto the highway to tell him I'd survived my meeting with Dunbar and not to call Holbrook. After clicking off with him, I drove for three hours before pulling off at a truck stop an hour north of Indianapolis. I didn't like the idea of keeping Holbrook's cash out in the open, but I also didn't like the idea of falling asleep and careening through a guardrail somewhere on I-69.

For the next several hours, I slept with $5 million in my trunk and a .45 in my hand. The blast from an 18-wheeler's horn woke me around 6:30 am Tuesday morning. I fired up the engine, pulled back onto I-69, and arrived at Jamie's condo an hour and a half later. I hoped she was an early riser.

I jerked one of the suitcases out of the back of the Escalade and hoisted it up the iron steps to her unit. She must have seen me coming because she opened the door before I had a chance to knock.

"Is that what I think it is?" said Jamie.

"Probably."

"Why are you bringing it here? I told you I didn't want anything to do with it."

I grabbed the handle and stepped closer, nudging her backward. "Can we talk about this inside?"

She stepped to the side and waved me in. I wheeled the suitcase through her living room and maneuvered it into her sewing room. I kicked it over, and it hit the ground with a crash that sounded like it might break through the floor and end up in the unit below.

I unzipped the case, heaved it onto its side, and dumped two-and-a-half million in bundled cash onto the floor of Jamie's sewing room.

"Jesus Christ!" she said. "Is that all of Holbrook's money?"

"It's half of it."

Her eyes narrowed as she looked at me. "Why did you bring it here?"

"We're going to end this thing, but like I said earlier, I need your help."

"What do you need me to do?"

I looked at the row of fabric lining the back wall of her sewing room. Rolls of fabric, in every color imaginable, stood side by side in an orderly row like dominoes ready to fall. She'd organized them by color. Some had patterns on them, but most were plain.

"Is any of that fabric waterproof?"

"No, but I can get some," she said. "What's it for?"

I tapped the open suitcase with my foot. "I need to line the inside of this suitcase, but it has to be waterproof."

"Why are you lining the inside of a suitcase?"

"I'm not. You are. But it has to be watertight. Nothing can get through it."

She wiped her hand across her neck. "I can use Naugahyde. It's waterproof." She looked at the suitcase. "The whole inside?"

"Both sides, and then stitch a barrier in the middle to keep each side separate. Like one of those old McDLTs. Keep the hot side hot and the cool side cool."

"Okay."

I thought for a moment. "Can you stitch it in a way so the partition rips inside the suitcase when it's opened?"

"I'm not sure I follow you," she said.

"I want the partition to be stable and watertight, but I also want it to rip in two when the case is opened. Does that make sense?"

Jamie looked at me and then back down at the suitcase.

"It makes sense, but I'm not sure how to do it. I need the suitcase open to stitch in the partition, but …" She rubbed her mouth and squinted at the case. "That's like asking me to change a lightbulb inside a refrigerator without opening the door."

"Can you do it?"

She thought for a moment. "If it means those men never come looking for me, I'll find a way." Jamie shook her head, cocked her hip to the side, and scratched her neck. "But, you're not going to be able to open it. I can rig the inside partition to split once, but I'm going to have to stitch it as I close the suitcase inch by inch. You won't be able to open it without ripping it in two."

"That's fine. I'll make it work. Can you have it ready by tomorrow?"

"Yes, I think so."

"Remember, it has to be completely watertight."

"It will be." She rubbed her mouth again. "You want to tell me what you're going to do with it?"

"It's better if you don't know." I turned and walked toward the front door. "I'll be back first thing tomorrow. It's got to be finished."

"And watertight," she added.

THE TIME RIDING THE PAVEMENT BETWEEN Cincinnati, Indianapolis, and Detroit had begun to wear on me. I hate the road, and when possible, I'd rather work from the confines of my own home with my laptop on my thighs and a cup of hot coffee in my hand. Over the past several days, I'd spent more time on the road than I wanted to, but being in the field had yielded more progress than I would have gained otherwise. After two weeks and a few thousand miles, I'd discovered the banker's identity, found Holbrook's cash, and secured Dunbar's participation in my plan to bring the Indianapolis enterprise to its knees. All that was left to do was weave it all together, and Jamie Burns was doing just that, literally, with her Singer sewing machine.

I arrived at the Embassy Suites to find Connor polishing off a continental breakfast on a bench next to the front door. He jumped up from the bench and stuffed his paper plate into a nearby garbage can when he saw me.

Connor met me in the parking lot. I opened the liftgate and he eyeballed the gray suitcase. "You actually got it?" he said.

"I got it."

"All of it?"

"You're goddamn right, all of it."

He slapped me on the shoulder, nearly knocking me off balance. "I'll be honest with you, little brother. I thought you were full of shit. I half expected to have my nose buried in that dusty atlas again, starting from scratch."

"Part of me thought the same thing. But we got it."

"That all of it?"

"It's half. I left the rest with Jamie."

"Why?"

"It's technically her money, and she needed the other suitcase for what's going to happen next."

"What's happening next?" said Connor.

"I'll tell you in the room." I handed Connor the suitcase, shut the liftgate and started toward the lobby. Connor followed close behind. When we arrived in Connor's room, I slipped the Post-It pad from my pocket and scribbled down a materials list. When I finished, I plucked off the top sheet and handed it to Connor. "You know anything about these materials?"

He reviewed the list and then looked at me. "I know they don't play nice together."

"That's kinda the point."

He looked at the list again. "Binoculars?"

"To watch the show," I said.

"I don't see why we don't just walk in there and open fire on these asshats. Why all the MacGyver shit?"

"Because they'd expect us to walk in there and open fire. Holbrook was wearing a bullet-proof vest the first time I saw him. I imagine that's part of his daily wardrobe."

"Give me a few days, and I could get a rifle powerful enough to take his head off from a quarter-mile away. Won't matter what he's wearing."

"We don't have a few days. Plus, I'm not just after Holbrook." I thought back to that hornet's nest Connor and I had burned to the ground as kids. "We have to remove the whole colony, and we don't have that much time." I tapped the list in Connor's hand. "I need you to get all of these things today."

Connor looked at the note again. "I'll get them." He looked at me. "You gonna be able to get everyone together in one place to make this work?"

"I really hope so," I said. "But you might get to do some shooting after all." I tossed him the keys to the Escalade.

"What are you gonna do while I'm out shopping?"

"Take a long shower and get some rest."

CONNOR RETURNED WITH ALL THE MATERIALS ON the list by early evening. We stayed the night at the hotel to give Jamie enough time to knock out her part of the project. That night, I slept better than any night since I took on Holbrook's job.

The next morning, Connor loaded the materials he bought into the back of the Escalade. I loaded Holbrook's suitcase in the back, and we drove the twenty minutes to Jamie's condo. I had no reason to believe Adler wouldn't make good on his threat to kill Daryl if I didn't deliver Holbrook's money by Wednesday, and as long as Jamie delivered on her end, we'd be right on schedule.

A voice in my head urged me to call Holbrook now to tell him I had his money, but I still had some work to do before getting him face to face, and I didn't want to give him any more time to prepare for our meeting than I had to.

We arrived at Jamie's unit by nine o'clock in the morning. As soon as she opened her front door, she ushered us into the living room, as if eager to show us her handiwork.

"Is it all set?" I said.

"It's perfect," said Jamie pointing to the suitcase in the middle of the room. "But don't open it. You'll rip it in two."

Connor looked at me. “Am I missing something?” he said. “How are we supposed to fill…”

“I’ll explain it all later,” I interrupted. I turned back to Jamie. “It’s watertight?”

“I’d bet my life on it,” she said.

“It’s not your life I’m worried about.” I grabbed the suitcase and wheeled it to the door.

“So, we’re done then?”

“You’re done,” I said. “Connor and I’ve got a bit more work to do.”

“How will I know when it’s over? When I can stop worrying about who’s knocking on my door?”

“I’ll let you know.” Connor and I stepped out into the breezeway and headed to the Escalade.

“What’s next?” said Connor.

“There’s an abandoned industrial park a few miles up the road. We’ll take care of everything else there.”

We pulled into Zaleski Park, an industrial complex that, according to the empty parking lots and dilapidated factories, was long past its prime. Connor parked behind a fading gray building, and we went to work.

I yanked the suitcase from the back while Connor gathered the supplies.

“How much faith do you have in her?” said Connor. “How do we know she didn’t just zip this thing up and leave it in her living room?”

“This is her out too, so I’ve got a lot of faith in her. But keep your weapon close when we get there. If this plan goes to shit, you’re going to need to mop things up pretty quickly.”

I went to the bag of supplies and removed a drill with a 1/2-inch auger bit. I chucked the bit into the drill and cut two holes on opposite sides of the suitcase near the top. I poked a finger in and felt for the Naugahyde partition. It was there just like Jamie said it was.

I went back to the bag and pulled out two plastic funnels, which I stuck into the 1/2-inch holes in the suitcase.

"Which side you want?" I said.

Connor shook his head. "I'll take the powder, I guess." He went to the back of the Escalade, pulled out the first tub of pool chlorine, and started filling one side of the suitcase through the funnel.

I opened the large black plastic jugs and poured the liquid into the other side, holding my breath for the first fifteen seconds. "If this thing starts to sizzle, run," I said.

"Just try to catch up."

After ten minutes, Connor and I had used half the ingredients. We stepped back and surveyed the suitcase. It was stable.

"I'll be damned," said Connor. "That's twice you came through when I doubted you."

"Hope there isn't a third."

Breathing a little easier, we finished filling both sides of the suitcase. I removed the two plastic funnels and sealed the 1/2-inch holes with epoxy. Then I placed a patch of duct tape over both sealed holes. The tape wasn't a perfect match against the gray suitcase, but it came close.

“Sticks out a bit,” said Connor grinning.

“I’m hoping the promise of five million in cash inside might distract him. Plus, it’s better than seeing the epoxy.”

I stood up and inspected the suitcase. The mixture held, and I hoped the lining was as watertight as Jamie said it was. “Okay, moment of truth,” I said. I carefully tilted the suitcase on its wheels and rolled it to the back of Connor’s Escalade.

“I’m second-guessing our choice to bring my car,” said Connor as he gripped the other side of the suitcase and helped me lift it into the back of the SUV.

We both stepped back and watched as nothing happened. Then I grabbed my phone.

CHAPTER 46

I TOOK a deep breath and dialed Holbrook's cell phone. Adler answered it on the second ring.

"I've got Holbrook's money, and I'll be at the farm at 11:00 am." I hung up before he could offer an alternative plan.

The next call I made was to Micah Dunbar. I told him that I was heading to Holbrook's farm and that he'd be out of business by lunch, giving Dunbar the green light to do whatever he needed to do to move into Indianapolis.

CONNOR AND I PULLED ONTO IN-135 NORTH AND drove slower than normal on account of the suitcases in the back. We turned onto the two-lane road that led to Triple Bend Farm and pulled over next to the decaying gray barn that teetered a quarter-mile from our final destination. The rusted-out tractor and harvester that sat under the leaning planks looked like they hadn't moved in two decades. Connor stepped out of the passenger side and grabbed the silver suitcase from the back.

"You sure you got the right one?" I said.

"Of course." Connor closed the liftgate. "From where I'll be, I won't be able to see if things go south."

"You'll hear it before you see it."

Connor looked toward Holbrook's farm and then back at me.

"Good luck, little brother," he said, tapping the top of the suitcase.

"You too. If all goes well, I'll see you in about fifteen minutes."

Connor nodded and was off with the suitcase tight in his arms. I slapped the shifter into Drive and pulled back out onto the main road. A minute later, I turned onto the entrance to Holbrook's farm.

Nerves are a funny thing. They steal your appetite, fuck with your health, and even throw off your reflexes. I'd been in this business long enough to temper my anxiety to get the job done, but this time, it felt different. I imagined it was similar to what a military sniper felt when taking aim at the enemy from a few hundred yards out. One chance.

I was about to walk into a hornet's nest, and there was an absolute guarantee that something bad would happen. The only question was, who would it happen to?

I drove up the winding driveway to Holbrook's home, my hands coated in salty sweat. I swallowed hard and walked through the next ten minutes in my head. When I arrived at the colonial-style home, I found Holbrook, Adler, Darby, and two other men waiting for me near the front porch.

I rubbed my palms down my jeans and stepped out of the car.

“That’s far enough,” said Holbrook.

He motioned to Adler, who patted me down the same way he had when I first visited the ranch. He wouldn’t find my .45 unless he looked under the driver’s seat.

“Where’s my money?”

“Dr. Jennings first,” I said.

Holbrook looked up at me and didn’t speak. For a moment, I didn’t think he would say anything, but he finally motioned to one of the other men, who walked inside the home and returned with Daryl. The duct tape was gone from his mouth, but the dark bloodstains on his white button-up shirt revealed the ass-kicking he’d taken while in Holbrook’s custody.

For the first time, the irony came full circle. I’d spent the last two weeks trying to protect Daryl, and by association Brooke and Becca, from the repercussions of his own stupidity.

I motioned to Daryl to get into the Escalade.

"The money," said Holbrook.

I slipped my hand inside my pocket and pressed a button on Connor's key fob. The Escalade chirped, and the liftgate slowly opened into the air. Darby and Adler approached the back of the vehicle and yanked the suitcase onto the ground.

Holbrook stepped over to the case and hovered above it. "Open it."

Adler unzipped the suitcase and pulled it apart. Twenty-five bricks of one-hundred-dollar bills spilled out onto the driveway. I looked at Adler, who tapped his right index finger against the side of his holstered weapon. I couldn't tell what he was carrying, and I hoped I wouldn't get a closer look.

"How much is here?" said Holbrook.

"Two-and-a-half million," I said.

"You're light." Holbrook looked up at me. "Why is that?"

Adler slid his hand in place on his weapon's grip and looked like he was about to pull.

"Call me paranoid," I said. "But I thought it foolish to walk in here and hand you two suitcases of money when your man over there threatened to kill me just a few days ago."

"I only see one suitcase," said Holbrook.

"I'll tell you the location of the other one once Dr. Jennings and I are safely off this property. Figured that'd be a nice insurance policy against someone doing something stupid." The sneer disappeared from Adler's face. "I'll also tell you where you can find the banker. Then you can go do to him all the shitty things you were planning to do to us."

Adler smirked, still gripping his piece. "You think we can't get to you?"

"I know you can get to me. Counting on it, actually." I pointed to the two men standing next to Adler. "But the next time we see each other, it'll be a fair fight."

I turned to see Daryl watching from the passenger side window. Holbrook ran his hands over his chin and thought for a moment. He was a businessman, and he knew Daryl and I weren't worth two and a half million in cash. If he killed us, he'd never see the rest of his money. He turned to Adler and called him off. Adler slid his hand across his belt and tucked his thumb into his right front pocket. I exhaled for what seemed like the first time since I'd arrived.

"Okay," said Holbrook. "Off you go, then. You've got two minutes to make that call, or we come after you. And out here, there's no place to hide."

"And Dr. Jennings is out of the fentanyl business," I said. "Completely out."

Holbrook nodded. "I'm a man of my word. I'll stay away from him."

I walked to the driver's side and reached for the handle. It took two attempts to open the door, thanks to my numb fingertips and damp palms. It took another two attempts to slide the key into the ignition. Finally, I fired the engine and headed back down the driveway to the main road.

A minute later, I dialed Holbrook.

"Where is it?"

"The other suitcase is in your quarantine stable."

"In my own barn?" I sensed a smile on the other end of the line.

"That's right."

"And the banker?"

"His address is inside the second suitcase. Happy hunting." I hung up the phone.

A QUARTER-MILE LATER, I PULLED OFF THE ROAD and parked behind the old storage barn where I'd dropped Connor off. I grabbed my binoculars from the console, jumped out of the SUV, crouched in front of the decaying tractor, and aimed the binoculars at the quarantine stable. Through the lenses, I saw Connor standing behind the stable. Off in the distance, Holbrook and his men approached the front of the stable at a swift clip. Once they arrived, Holbrook unlocked the padlock hanging from the door, slipped it into his pocket, and walked into the stable, his men following close behind.

I watched as Connor waited. I couldn't see the inside of the stable, but I knew what was happening. Holbrook and his men approached the suitcase Connor had placed inside, eager to see the money and the banker's information. Holbrook opened the case or ordered one of his men to do it.

The next series of events unfolded in complete precision. Whoever opened the suitcase inadvertently tore the Naugahyde partition. As the partition ripped in two, it allowed the twenty pounds of calcium hypochlorite to mix with the three gallons of non-synthetic brake fluid. At first, the combination would produce a loud hiss and thick white smoke, which would send Holbrook and his men running for the stable entrance, but Connor would have already slammed the door shut and locked it with his own padlock. Within five seconds, the contents of the suitcase, now saturated, would ignite in a ball of fire that would reach the top of the stable. In small amounts, the reaction would only last a matter of seconds, but given the quantity of oxidizing agents and fuel we stuffed into the suitcase, this particular reaction could continue for several minutes. Generally, fire doubles in size every thirty to sixty seconds, but that's without an accelerant. Our suitcase of pool cleaner and brake fluid, combined with the hay on the barn's floor and the dozen hay bales lining the walls, would kick those statistics in the ass and engulf the stable in less than a minute.

I didn't need the binoculars to see what happened next. A bright orange plume danced out of the side of the stable. It looked playful at first, but then the flames turned more violent and clawed at the sky with orange tentacles. A wall of thick smoke billowed out of the barn, the wind carrying it off to the east, weaving a patchwork of black-and-gray smoke and blue-and-white sky.

A minute later, the first flames erupted from the roof. They burst through the wooden beams like an out-of-breath swimmer coming up for air.

I peered through the binoculars again to find Connor standing about a hundred feet from the barn, his Glock raised waiting for any survivors to slip out of the crumbling side wall, but no one came. After a few minutes, he turned, waved at me, and charged toward the main house. I stepped back into the SUV, threw it into gear, and kicked up enough gravel that I expected the storage barn to crumble behind us.

Daryl and I closed the quarter-mile and were up the winding driveway in thirty seconds, and I pulled to a stop in front of Connor, who slammed the handle down into the first suitcase, heaved it into the back seat, and climbed in after it.

"Let's go," he yelled, but I had already buried the accelerator. We stopped at the end of Holbrook's driveway and watched the stable's roof collapse into the structure, releasing violent plumes of smoke and flames high into the sky.

I pulled my phone out of my pocket and dialed. Dunbar answered. "It's done," I said. "Indianapolis is open for business." I hung up and slammed my right foot onto the accelerator.

CHAPTER 47

We tore away from Holbrook's farm with two-and-a-half million in cash and a hundred and ninety pounds of dead weight. Daryl didn't say much on the ride back. He stared out the passenger window and wore a look that said he was glad to leave Holbrook behind but wasn't sure what awaited him in Cincinnati.

I didn't know what Brooke would do with him, but I'd been the object of her wrath before, I felt bad for him.

Connor, on the other hand, wore a beaming smile that could be seen just as easily from Boston as from Cincinnati. I'd learned more about my brother in the last few weeks than I'd learned in the previous twenty years. We'd never had a strained relationship, just one built on unfamiliarity, a gap that maybe we'd begun to close.

I pulled off the interstate and drove to the Greyhound station in downtown Indianapolis. I turned to Daryl in the passenger seat. "You got your wallet with you?"

Daryl leaned forward and checked his back pocket. "I've got it, why?"

"Just want to make sure you can buy a bus ticket back home."

Daryl looked out the front window at the line of buses and grinned. "I'd rather rent a car."

"You can do that here too," I said. "I'm sure they can set you up with a nice ride. Maybe not as nice as your Mercedes, but something that'll get you home in one piece."

He waited for a moment to see if I was joking. I wasn't. He opened the passenger door and climbed out of the Escalade. He started toward the building's entrance, but stopped and walked back to the car. I rolled down the passenger window.

"Finn." He looked like a man who'd lost his job. "I'm really not as big a fuck-up as I might appear at the moment. Things kind of just snowballed. I had no idea any of this would happen." He reached through the open window. "Thanks for getting me out of this. For everything."

"Don't mention it," I said, shaking his hand. "We're all allowed one fuck-up per decade. Of course, you're going to have to work really hard to top this one." I smiled.

He looked down at the ground and then back up at me. He started to say something else, but he caught himself. "Take it easy, Finn. I'm sure we'll bump into each other again." At the moment, I didn't know if we'd ever see each other again, but fate is a fickle bitch, so I wouldn't discount it. I nodded and watched as Daryl walked into the bus terminal.

"He's kind of pathetic," I said to Connor.

"Isn't that pathetic guy sleeping with your wife?"

"Ex-wife," I said.

"You going to do something about that?"

"It's not my decision to make."

Connor nodded from the back seat. "Can I have the wheel back now?"

Connor found Jamie's address in the GPS history and drove us back to East Sycamore Street in Morgantown, Indiana.

"What are we going to do with that money?" he said, pulling into her parking lot.

"What do you think we should do with it? I feel like Jamie should get most of it. It's her money."

"She said she didn't want it."

"That was when it came with strings," I said. "Now that Holbrook is out of the picture, I don't see any reason for her not to want at least part of it."

"What about the banker's other clients? What if they come after her looking for their share? If we tracked her down, it's possible they could too."

"I've got an idea of how to plug that dike." I grabbed the Post-It pad and pen from the console. I scribbled a name on the note, plucked it from the pad, and stuck it inside my back pocket.

I got out of the car to find Jamie sitting on her balcony with a cup in her hand. When she saw me, she disappeared into her unit.

"You're cool with whatever comes out of this?" I said. "She might take it all."

"Not to sound like a corny piece of shit, Finn, but I really don't care about the money. It's hers, and she can do whatever she wants with it. Of course, if she wants to give it away, I won't turn it down."

"Is this where you tell me that the time we got to spend together was payment enough?"

"Fuck, no," said Connor. "You've worked up quite a debt. That pool chlorine alone cost me a few hundred bucks." He smiled. "But we'll call it even if you promise to keep Dad out of trouble."

I shook my head and laughed. "I'm not sure I'm comfortable with those terms."

Jamie emerged from her front door and walked down the breezeway stairs to the parking lot.

“Here goes nothing,” I said. I opened the liftgate, yanked the suitcase from the back and wheeled it over to where she stood.

“I assume, since you’re here, everything went well,” she said.

“All went according to plan.” I smiled.

“You sound surprised.”

“That’s because nothing ever goes according to plan.” I kicked the suitcase with my foot. “As far as I’m concerned, this is your money. Holbrook won’t be looking for it.”

“What about the others? What if they come looking for it?”

I pulled the note from my pocket and handed it to her. “If anyone comes looking for it, you just hand them this piece of paper, and they’ll be on their way.”

She opened it. “Who’s Micah Dunbar?”

“No one you need to worry about, but he’s got the rest of your father’s money. I doubt anyone will ever connect you and your father to the banker, but on the off-chance that they do, that’s your get-out-of-jail-free card. Give 'em that, and they'll go away."

"I've never heard of him."

"Anyone who finds you will know who he is, and by that time, they won't want to mess with him."

She looked at the suitcase. "How much is in there?"

"The other half of the five million. That'll buy a lot of sewing needles."

She glanced up at her unit. "The other half is still on my sewing room floor."

"That's probably not the safest place to keep it," I said.

"I don't know what else to do with it."

"I might be able to help you with that." I opened my wallet and handed Jamie a business card. "Here's someone who'd be willing to help you do whatever you want with it."

She read the card. "A savings and loan?"

I shrugged. "It beats storing it on the floor. Or in the back of your father's truck."

"That it does." She scratched her head. "It would help me start my business. And I'd give some of it away. That might scrub my conscience of all the shitty things the original owners did to make it."

I nodded.

"But I don't want it all." She pushed the suitcase back toward me. "Why don't you and your brother take this one? You deserve it. I'll sleep better knowing it won't be funding criminal activity."

"I can't promise that," I said. "Especially where Connor is concerned. But I won't turn it down."

"Take it, then. Consider it a thank-you gift for helping me put all this to rest."

"I feel like we caused more harm than good, bursting in and threatening you at gunpoint."

"That's probably going to give me nightmares for a while." She cracked a nervous smile. "But I guess it all worked out." She looked at the suitcase again. "And you're sure Holbrook is dead."

"I'd bet five million on it."

She looked past me at the Escalade and then reached out. "Thank you."

“You’re welcome.” I shook her hand and walked back to the Escalade, pulling the suitcase behind me. I turned back toward her condo. “Good luck with the sewing,” I said, but she was already gone.

I left Jamie’s condo with two and a half million more than I thought I would. From the look in Connor’s eyes, he was glad to see it.

CHAPTER 48

Connor and I were halfway back to Cincinnati when my cell phone buzzed.

"Where the hell are you?" said Albert. "I'm sitting in Union Terminal, and I need a ride."

I looked at my watch. "We can be there in about an hour."

"We? Your brother still with you?"

I clicked on the speakerphone. "How was Maine, Dad?" said Connor. "I thought you might be calling for some help."

"Wasn't nothing Mitch and I couldn't handle."

"So, you handled it?" I said. "No need to worry about Ollie Stoner anymore?"

"Not until he gets out of prison in another decade or two."

"I thought the whole reason for going up there was to get rid of him, not kick the can down the road again."

"Relax. Ollie's damn near as old as me. The only way he's rolling out of that prison is on a gurney inside a black zippered bag." Albert paused. "What about you two? Still chasing your tails?"

"No, we're just heading back from Indianapolis," said Connor.

"So, you found him?"

"We found him."

"Is it worth talking about?"

Connor smiled. "Probably not," he said. "Maybe we'll swap war stories over drinks sometime."

"All right, then. Get here as fast as you can. A train depot isn't anyplace for an old man. And try not to get lost." Albert hung up before I had a chance to respond.

"You have to put up with that every day?" said Connor.

"Every. Damn. Day."

"You're a better man than me. I would've had him committed a long time ago."

"I've thought about it, but he'd just escape and hunt us both down. Plus, I kinda like having him around. He's great with Becca."

"I'm sure he is." Connor motioned to the back seat. "You going to tell him about the money?"

"No way in hell."

CONNOR AND I STEPPED THROUGH THE FRONT doors of Union Terminal and walked into the large rotunda to find Albert sipping a coffee, his legs propped up on his suitcase. He looked at his watch as we sat down.

"Don't get comfortable," he said. "We're not staying."

My phone buzzed, and I pulled it from my pocket. Brooke had sent me a text reminding me about

Becca's basketball game that night at seven o'clock.

"Connor, you want to see your niece swing her pom-poms?" I said. "She's cheering at a second-grade basketball game tonight."

"Second-grade basketball? That's a thing?"

"They don't keep score," said Albert. "Waste of time."

Connor laughed. "I'd love to, but I can't. I've got to get back to Boston. Got my own problems, you know."

"I understand," I said. "Try not to go so long between visits."

"The highways run both ways, little brother."

"So they do."

He smiled and slammed a fist into my shoulder. "Maybe next time we can get together and not kill anyone."

"I don't want to break up such a nice moment," said Albert. "But I've got some Longmire episodes to catch up on, so if one of you girls would get my bag, we can be on our way." Albert tossed his coffee cup into a nearby trashcan and headed toward the front door, leaving his suitcase behind him.

"You sure you don't want to have him committed?" said Connor, grabbing the suitcase. "We could find a nice place on the way home."

"I'll consider it." Connor and I followed Albert as he kicked open one of Union Terminal's heavy art-deco doors and strolled into the parking lot.

CONNOR DROPPED US OFF AT OUR APARTMENT. Albert hugged him like he'd see him again soon and disappeared into the apartment, leaving Connor and me to say our piece.

I opened Holbrook's suitcase and divided the haul down the middle. One and a quarter million each. Not a bad payday, and a lot more than I expected when Brooke called me that Sunday night and asked me to get Daryl out of trouble. I'd planned on doing it for free, but the money was a nice bonus. Up until this point, I mostly broke even on the cases I took, usually generating enough cash to keep Albert and me going until the next gig. This should keep things moving for a long time.

The first order of business would be to get the hell out of our apartment for greener and more permanent pastures, but I had plenty of time to worry about that tomorrow. The only thing I worried about now was taking a shower, getting dressed, and making it to Becca's basketball game.

Neither of us was the sentimental type, so a goodbye and a handshake were all it took to get Connor back on the road. I watched him climb back into the Escalade, slip his green baseball cap on his head, and drive back into his own life. I was grateful to have shared the last ten days with him and hoped we'd cross paths again soon, but given what I knew about my brother, I had no idea when. Considering the last time I saw him was at my mother's funeral, I hoped he wouldn't wait for Albert to punch out before making it back home. Death had a funny way of bringing the Harding boys together.

I wheeled my half of Holbrook's cash into my bedroom closet before Albert had a chance to ask any questions. I stashed it in the back, next to a few suits that rarely saw the light of day, closed the closet door, and headed for the shower.

CHAPTER 49

FAT SAM PARKED the navy-blue Ford Expedition across from the home on Fort View Place in Mount Adams. A street lamp clicked on overhead as he climbed out of the vehicle and slammed the driver's door shut. He opened the liftgate and pulled two white cardboard file boxes from the back. Balancing one of the boxes on his enormous thigh, he stacked them one on top of the other and then smacked a button to close the liftgate before he stepped away from the SUV.

He checked for traffic and then crossed the street. He lumbered up the sidewalk to the front door, wedged the boxes between his thigh and the door-frame, and then fumbled to slide the key into the deadbolt. He turned the key, pushed the door open with a massive shoulder, and carried the boxes into the foyer. His size-sixteen Adidas sneaker searched for the door to kick it shut when someone pushed him from behind. His forehead plowed into the smooth foyer wall, the stacked file boxes buckled between the wall and his gut, and the business end of a handgun pressed against the back of his head.

"Hello, Sam."

"You again?" He recognized the voice.

The man behind him shut the door. "I'm not here to kill you this time either, but if you turn around, you'll be dead before those boxes hit the ground."

"You find Finn Harding?" said Sam.

"I found him."

"And?"

"Here's the deal. You're going to stop looking for him. As far as you're concerned, he's dead. You can keep your money."

"What about the Nolans? They're still looking for him."

"Not anymore."

Sam shifted the boxes in his arms. “You’re just going to let him off?”

“Here’s how this works. Finn Harding is no longer a threat to your Dark Brokerage business. He’s out, so you don’t have to worry about him.”

“Okay.”

“You don’t know who I am, but you do know that I’m on your distribution list. That means I’m going to receive any communications you send out. I know you can’t scrub your list or you’ll lose all your clients, which isn’t smart business, so I’ll continue to monitor your operation through your updates. If you send any communications that even remotely reference Finn Harding, I’ll come back, and next time, we won’t chat. We clear?”

“We’re clear.” Sam groaned and repositioned his grip on the boxes.

“Good. Sam, you’re still alive because I believed you when you said you didn’t authorize the hit on Finn. That Bishop set that up in advance.”

“That’s right, he did set it up.”

“Don’t make me regret that decision.”

"I won't." Sam shifted his grip on the boxes again.

"Plus, I'm still a client of the Dark Brokerage, so I have a vested interest in you getting that site back up and running."

"I'm trying. Lots to do."

"Okay, then, I think we're finished here. I want you to close your eyes and count down from sixty. I'm going to leave this door open, and if you turn around, I'll plug you."

"Okay." Fat Sam counted down from sixty, and when he was finished, he let the boxes fall to the ground. Then he closed the door without turning around.

CHAPTER 50

ALBERT and I parked in the Cincinnati Catholic Academy's lot and walked into the gilded lobby. We strolled down the hall and stepped into the gym. Becca stood on the side of the basketball court, dressed in her cheerleading outfit, a red-and-gold tank top with thick shoulder straps and a matching pleated skirt that went down to her knees. It looked too short to me. She saw us come through the double metal doors and waved, almost taking out a teammate with her scarlet pom-pom.

After waving back at Becca, I scanned the home-team bleachers for Brooke and Daryl, who were supposed to be saving our seats. Albert saw Brooke first and pointed. I followed his finger and saw Brooke standing with her arm over her head, waving to us. No Daryl.

Albert and I walked up the rickety wooden bleachers. Brooke and I hugged each other, and we sat down on the uncomfortable seats. A moment later I saw Jennifer walking toward us. Her blonde hair was pulled back in a ponytail, and it dangled down to the center of her back. She wore jeans and a long-sleeved t-shirt with the school logo, a maroon-and-white eagle. The shirt was tight enough to turn heads, but it didn't come off as though she was looking for attention. She'd get it anyway.

When Jennifer reached us, she leaned in and wrapped her arms around me, and I felt her breasts press against my chest. I would have hugged her tighter had Brooke not been standing a foot away.

Albert cleared his throat, and I could feel my ex-wife's stare burning a hole through the back of my head.

"Who's this?" said Brooke. She seemed much calmer than I expected, given the impromptu meeting.

"Brooke, this is Jennifer. Jennifer, this is my ex-wife, Brooke."

Jennifer extended a hand. "It's nice to meet you."

"You as well," said Brooke. She offered a smile that looked genuine on the surface, but like a volcano, bubbled with death and destruction underneath. "Why don't you join us?"

Jennifer looked at me with an expression that said, "Sorry," and turned back to Brooke. "I'd love to."

"Hello, Albert," said Jennifer. He winked toward her, elbowed me in the ribs, and leaned in. "You're fucked, son," he whispered.

"I have a feeling you're right about that."

I hesitated to make eye contact with Brooke, and once I did, I instantly regretted it. Her demeanor was calm, but her eyes looked like sharp, narrow cuts in a jack-o-lantern. I imagined that was how a pitcher looked before intentionally drilling a fastball into a batter's hip.

Brooke took her seat, Albert sat next to her, and I sat between Albert and Jennifer. I wrapped my arm around Jennifer's waist. "That went well," I said.

"Sorry about that. For some reason, I didn't think she'd be here." Jennifer turned and waved to someone sitting a few rows away. "I'll be right back," she said. "My boss is over there, and I should probably say hello." Jennifer slid down the wooden bench to talk to a middle-aged woman holding a maroon-and-white pennant.

Brooke leaned behind Albert and slapped me on the shoulder. "What sorority house did you find her in?"

Albert laughed. "Cut him some slack. She's a nice girl."

"How old is she?"

"She's twenty-five," I said.

"Jesus Christ, Finn. What are you doing with a twenty-five-year-old?"

"I know what I'd be doing with a twenty-five-year-old," said Albert.

Brooke smacked him on the shoulder harder than she had me. "Did you have to bring her here?"

"I had no idea she'd be here. Besides, you're the one who invited her to stay. Where's Daryl, anyway?"

"We're on a break," said Brooke. Her jack-o-lantern stare approached its flashpoint, so I turned away and scanned the crowd to find a distraction. The gymnasium was filling up quickly, and tip-off was only a few minutes away. Both basketball teams took practice shots on opposite sides of the court, and basketballs bounced off everything except the low backboards.

Becca stood next to seven other cheerleaders on the bright wooden floor. She said something to the cheerleader next to her and laughed. Her coach, a tall woman in tight black yoga pants and a school t-shirt, approached the girls and wrangled them into a small circle for final instructions.

I watched as the woman, who I assumed was Candy Cooper, backed away from the girls, tucked a clipboard under her arm, scanned the crowd, and then waved to someone a few rows away on my right. I followed her gaze and found Michael Cooper waving back. After he returned his hand to his lap, he turned and found me. I smiled and offered a short wave, but Cooper didn't reciprocate. Instead, he turned away and struck up a conversation with the man next to him.

"I never saw my granddaughter as a cheerleader," said Albert.

"Me neither," I said. "It took some finagling to get her on the squad."

"I'm sure she'll be a natural."

The referee approached center court with a basketball in his hand and blew a whistle. Both teams stopped their warm-up routines and returned to their sidelines, and then five boys from each team took the court.

Jennifer returned to the seat next to me. She squeezed my knee and then placed her hands behind her. Her hand slid down my back, and I felt her thumb tuck into the top of my jeans. A moment later, she leaned forward and cupped both hands on my right knee, but I could still feel a thumb on my waist. I glanced at Brooke. Her right arm wrapped around Albert and disappeared behind me. She winked as the referee blew his whistle again and tossed the ball into the air.

FINN HARDING WILL RETURN

Continue the Mr. Finn series with:

The Prison Guard's Son

A private investigator searches for two killers in witness protection while evading the US Marshals sworn to protect them and a hitman hired to kill them.

Finn Harding specializes in finding people who don't want to be found. Willie Baker is a grieving father hell-bent on revenge. Thirty years after his son's brutal slaying, Willie hires Finn to find the two men responsible. The only problem? They're in witness protection.

Finn begins his search in the small West Virginia town where the murders occurred and tracks the killers across the country. During his investigation, he crosses paths with a tenacious US Marshal determined to protect them at all costs.

After finding the murderers and learning details

about their new lives, Finn realizes they aren't who they seem and struggles with his conscience. That doesn't sit well with Willie Baker or the hitman he hired to enact his revenge.

Can Finn evade the US Marshals and the triggerman long enough to levy his own form of justice?

The Prison Guard's Son is the third novel by award-winning author Trace Conger. It is the third novel in the Mr. Finn P.I. series.

GET A FREE NOVEL

Sign up for my newsletter to receive a free novel and exclusive updates at www.traceconger.com/freebies.

Please leave a review:

Like this book? Please consider leaving a review at your favorite online bookstore. Reviews from readers like you can help other readers find their next favorite read. And it's a great way to support your favorite authors.

ACKNOWLEDGMENTS

THIS WORK WOULD NOT HAVE been possible without the generous support of several individuals. I'd like to personally thank the following people for their direct and indirect involvement in giving this project life:

Christine Grote, Scott High, and Denise Suttman for reading and providing feedback on early drafts; Ed Hackett for editing and making me look like a better writer; Doug Hunter for the PI perspective; Dr. Jonathan Bell and Jennifer Campbell for their medical expertise; Perry Gerome for fanning the flames; Micah Siegal for his legal and real estate knowledge; and Shannon Bibbee for the Army intel.

And a special thank you to Beth Conger for her continued love, support, and encouragement.

My sincere thanks to each of you.

ABOUT THE AUTHOR

Trace Conger is an award-winning author in the crime, thriller, and suspense genres. He writes the Connor Harding (Thriller) series and the Mr. Finn (PI) series, among others.

His Connor Harding series follows freelance "Mirage Man" Connor Harding as he solves problems for the world's most dangerous criminals. The Mr. Finn series follows private investigator Finn Harding as he straddles the fine line between right and wrong.

Conger won a Shamus Award for his debut novel, THE SHADOW BROKER. His suspense novella, THE WHITE BOY, won the Fresh Ink Award for Best Novella of 2020.

Trace lives in Cincinnati with his wonderfully supportive family.

ALSO BY TRACE CONGER

Mr. Finn Series:

The Shadow Broker

Scar Tissue

The Prison Guard's Son

Connor Harding Series:

Catch and Release

Mirage Man

Standalones:

The White Boy

Five Will Die

www.ingramcontent.com/pod-product-compliance
Lightning Source LLC
Chambersburg PA
CBHW030417310726
48979CB00002B/454

* 9 7 8 1 9 5 7 3 3 6 0 9 1 *